THE PÉREZ FAMILY

With best wishes to Mary Riggs

THE PÉREZ FAMILY

CHRISTINE BELL

Christie Bell
1991

W. W. NORTON & COMPANY
NEW YORK · LONDON

Lyrics on page 237 from "It's Now or Never," written by Wally
Gold and Aaron Shroeder. © 1988 Gladys Music. All rights
administered by Chappell & Co. All rights reserved. Used by
permission. Lyrics on page vii from "Bemba Colora" written
by J. Claro Fumero. Copyright 1947 by Peer International Cor-
poration. Used by permission.

The text of this book is composed in Aster, with display type
set in Albertus Titling and other typefaces. Composition and
manufacturing by The Haddon Craftsmen.
Book design by Charlotte Staub.

Library of Congress Cataloging-in-Publication Data

Bell, Christine
The Pérez family / Christine Bell.
    p. cm.
    I. Title.
PS3552.E489P47   1990
813'.54—dc20

89-25569
ISBN 0-393-02798-8

W.W. Norton & Company, Inc., 500 Fifth Avenue,
New York, N.Y. 10110
W.W. Norton & Company, Ltd., 37 Great Russell Street,
London WC1B 3NU
    2   3   4   5   6   7   8   9   0

With thanks to J. Alvarez, M. L. Bell, P. Bell, B. DePietro, M. DePietro, M. Hidalgo-Gato, A. Jacks, C. Jacks, I. Mendoza, M. Perez, L. Siniscalco, F. Thornton, S. Naranjo Webber, and R. Webber. With special thanks to Emelle.

Un pajarito—en su jaula
vuela—y vuela sin cesar
y siempre buscando—en vano
sitio por donde—escapar.

Pobrecito, cómo sufre
buscando su libertad
yo como—el pájaro quiero
yo como—el pájaro quiero
la libertad recobrar.

—"Bemba Colora," J. Claro Fumero

THE PÉREZ FAMILY

PART ONE

~~~~~~

FROM PRISON
JULY 1980

We are so jealous of their hatred. The new ones coming in, they are brimming with hatred. If you saw them you would understand our jealousy—they are so alive! Their eyes are clear and bright. Their cheeks are flushed. You can almost see the blood coursing in their veins. They are still alive. And we, we are already dead.

They are so faithful to their hatred. It has not yet turned inward in silent anger; nor has that anger had the chance to anesthetize them yet. And we as dead men, we love to see anything so alive. Blood so fresh. They are right and they are alive and we are dead. Their souls cry out against the injustice. The soul was meant to cry out so for justice.

Martí said, "To witness a crime in silence is to commit it." They are not silent. They cry out at the indignities. They cry out in hatred of what is defeatist and immoral. They cry out against their pain. Wasn't the soul meant to cry out against such pain? How jealous we are of their strong voices while we silently cry out with them. We are surprised that we are still able to remember pain. Are we jealous of that pain too, or only of having enough life to still feel pain? Until reality, like a dull knife already rusted in our hearts, remembers us, and we remember. They are no longer crying out. They are simply crying. They are in pain. And it is not the pain of a flesh wound which could carry them forward in battle. It is

3

the pain of the soul in defeat. But they are still alive and we are sorry they are so alive still; they do not yet have the numbness of prison that day by day will entomb them in the waking sleep of dead men until the resurrection.

Oh my Love, I am so numb sometimes, I barely know that I'm not dead yet.

CHAPTER 1

It was always Sunday in the dream. Always Sunday afternoon. Always bright. Always a long white beach, light breeze, and turquoise sea. The dream would start with a family gathering at the shore, an afternoon so like many he had spent twenty years before. In the distance, the guitar of the guajiros balanced high and clean. A voice sought refrain, "I am a simple man . . ."

Always a card table with old men playing dominoes. The old women sat under the palm trees on folding chairs. The younger women fixed the tables and watched the children. His father turned the meat on the open grill. His daughter played with her cousins and a red-and-white-striped beach ball. But in the dream, he turned his head for a moment and when he looked back, everyone, except for him, was in the shallow water. The old women sitting on the folding chairs in their black dresses, the old men with their table of dominoes, the children and the red-and-white-striped beach ball—all were in the water.

He would call to them to come back. He would tell them that it was silly, that they shouldn't all be in the water along with the picnic tables and the barbecue. But they always stayed there. And the beach where he stood would begin to move away. Come back here, he would say, you will all drown.

We will not drown, Juan, this water is shallow, it will not hurt your suit, his wife would call back. Why, he always wondered when his wife said that, why was he wearing his blue business suit at the beach on a Sunday afternoon?

Come here with us, she would continue. And the beach would continue to move away, leaving a dark hissing crack between the land and turquoise sea. He is afraid to look into the hole. Jump, they call to him, come here and be with us. And always he jumps, each time, and each time the change in momentum as he flies through the air is barely perceptible, a twitch in his muscles as he sleeps. Barely perceptible, but it is there. He will fall. He will not make it.

And always, at that moment when he starts to fall, the dream stops. If he cannot make it to the other side, he would prefer to fall, to tumble through the darkness and crack every bone in his being on the hard earth. But instead, the dream would stop and freeze the universe with a precision matched only in reality by the day they brought him to prison.

CHAPTER 2

He woke trembling with his heart beating fast and sweat dripping. As always, the wind of his dream lingered after he awoke, that light breeze that smelled of sea too far away to be real. As always, he had to take a deep gulp of that same breeze to catch his breath.

He swung his feet over the side of the bed and felt his pulse with his fingertips. One hundred and fifty, he thought. He had no watch to be certain of that number, nor did he need to hold his fingers to his wrist to find his heart's beat: its drum was everywhere—in the darkness pounding off unseen walls, echoing through unseen halls, waking Hernandez in the bunk above who mumbled eat shit and die and then rolled back over into sleep without missing a snore.

Juan Raúl Pérez began the litany he had devised to unfreeze the time—he counted. He counted, physically moving the time with his numbers. He counted everything and anything to thaw the frozen falling moment. He counted his pulse over and over again. He counted Hernández's snores. He counted the twenty years he had been in prison. He counted his daughter's age, the four years he was with her, the twenty more he hadn't seen her. He counted the three or four hours left until dawn. He counted the fifty-one years of his wife's life. He counted her teeth, her tits, her arms, and her legs. He counted the fourteen letters he had received from her in twenty years' time and counted the countless others undelivered. He counted the ninety miles from Cuba to the land he had sent his family to on the plane twenty years before. He counted the days after he had sent them on the plane, the days he had waited in the hospital room with his father, who was dying, and the hours in the day they had taken him to prison the week before his father died. He counted the first southwest street in Miami and the twenty-two more he would need to cross to arrive at the Southwest Twenty-third Street where his wife and daughter lived.

He counted his pulse, which had slowed to one hundred, and slowed his litany down to his pulse. With the slower count, he added images and ideas, now moving the time in strong large blocks rather than chipping away at the frozen universe.

He added pounds to his wife's body, age to her walk, gray streaks to her black block of hair which a letter of five years ago said had been cut to a short square surrounding her face. He added a starburst pattern around each of her dark eyes. He added height to his daughter, last seen at four years of age, until finally at seven feet he had to take off two feet to get her back into proportion. He added flowers to his father's grave, hoping it was next to his mother's on the outskirts of Havana.

He added sunlight to the Southwest Twenty-third Street in Miami, a milkman in the morning, a dog in the yard. He added anger; he didn't mean to, it crept out from his heart and bounded to his pulse. How absurd the charge of "enemy of the revolution" was on the day he was apprehended leaving the hospital where his father was dying. Yes, he had said at the trial which was nothing more than a sentencing. Yes, he had worked for a pro-Batista newspaper. But no, he had not aided imperialist powers, it was only that he was an advertising sales representative for that paper. Did he not receive payments from these imperialist powers for his covert operations against the revolution? No, he told them, only that the companies he sold advertising space to sometimes gave him gifts when he got them a good rate and a good page. And no, he didn't know if he would have worked as hard for a revolutionary newspaper, because he was a company man and couldn't imagine working for any other company. No, he hadn't been an enemy of the revolution at that time, but after twenty years as a political prisoner he had become one. Each year his hopeless anger deserved a hundred more life sentences.

He patted his pocket for his pencil and felt beneath the straw mattress for paper. Tomorrow, he decided, he would write his wife a beautiful letter: one filled with hope and life, one he could send her, not like the countless pages of despair he addressed to her but never sent. He only sent her pages he thought would not make her sad.

Maybe he fell asleep sitting on the edge of the bunk while great blocks of anger moved the time, unfroze the universe, dropped his pulse to a strong and steady seventy-six. He did not remember, only that he had never seen the man who shook his arm to wake him and asked if he was Juan Raúl Pérez. The man told him to come quickly. And he took a great last breath of air too ocean to be real in an airless cell in a prison too far inland. He had known all along the dream would have an ending.

CHAPTER 3

The shadows moved quickly through the halls under the unshaded light bulbs. "Rápido, rápido," one of the guards told him.

Juan Raúl Pérez remembered a man named Méndez years ago who had been taken from his bed like this and put up against the wall in the courtyard, the wall still wet from the previous execution. And they yelled fire, but they did not fire and carried Méndez back into his cell with Méndez screaming: "Fire, please fire." Méndez screamed fire for days afterwards, first in his cell and then in the infirmary, and then in isolation, and then he woke from death and stopped screaming because he had found immortality. And everyone, even the biggest of the guards, was afraid of Méndez after that because he walked around with a calm smile of immortality and followed the rules without caring what he was doing until he died in his sleep one night. It was a peaceful death, for Méndez's calm smile of immortality was still frozen on his face that next morning.

And now Juan Raúl Pérez prayed and vowed that he too would gladly scream fire, FIRE, like a prayer for the rest of his life if they also would not fire at him. If they would let him return to the safety of his nightmare.

"Move it, damn you," the guard said to him, and he moved. But they did not even pass the section of the wall used for executions but went through to the back, where he was loaded with other prisoners into an old bus. There, for the dark time of eternity before dawn, he did not know which wall he was being transferred to.

He watched in the darkness from the window of the hot bus. He found the strength to find his pulse and registered 106 beats of still-being. He thought 106 a calm and courageous number in the face of death but then felt ashamed to think 106 was all he could beat in these last hours. He thought that if he could make his pulse faster, he could move more time into his last remaining moments. His heart's beat had always said the same thing to him, had always said, "You are alive. You are a survivor." Now it raced in frenzied laughter faster faster, screaming, "Now you are dying. This is how many frantic beats you have left."

He dropped his wrist in disgust. He shifted his position and tried to imagine what his wife would be doing at this hour. Still in the same time zone, she would still be in bed sleeping. If he could slow his heart down to what hers would be at that hour before dawn. If he could get his rate down to sixty or fifty or wherever her heart was. He slipped his hand back down his wrist and with concentration, it seemed that his heart beat slower, becoming one with hers. It was just for a moment, just like the moment in the dream when eternity stopped, that he felt they were one. That he was with her in her sleep. That he had penetrated her dreams, slowly, unnoticed except for a warmth. In that bed where she was. Where they were. Asleep together in sheets that he had never seen before, not the linen ones with the hand-embroidered monograms that his mother-in-law had given them on their wedding, but soft white sheets with little yellow flowers on them. There was a soft chill, almost a breeze, that even tropical mornings offer for a moment or two before dawn. He heard the high undertone of crickets, a lazy distant car horn, a slight tremor in his wife's breathing as she pulled the sheet in closer to herself on that Twenty-third Street in Miami in the land ninety miles away.

CHAPTER 4

She felt her life like a sleepwalker. In the past few months all her movements, however ordinary, seemed to her acute, yet distant. She awoke from the sheets with the pale yellow flowers and sat by the phone. I think the phone is going to ring, she thought to herself, and the phone rang. I think it's going to be good news, she told herself, picking up the phone. I think they are going to tell me they've found him and he's on his way home.

"Carmela? Carmela, are you there?" her brother asked on the line.

"Yes, Angel, yes."

"They've closed off the lift."

But they had closed off the Mariel boatlift two months before and still boats were coming through. In the last four months, 116,000 had come. They had come since Castro, after so many years of refusal, had opened the doors, apparently in disgust, because several hundred people had stormed the Peruvian Embassy in Havana asking for political asylum and exit visas to the U.S.

Castro had not expected so many would want to go. The U.S. had not expected so many would be allowed to come. They arranged for two transit jets to bring them. And then pretended not to notice, as far as that was possible, the thousands of small boats coming after.

Go, Castro told them, if you want to leave here you are scum. If you are scum we don't need you here. He also quietly emptied prison cells and sent the prisoners also. "But it's really closed off this time," Angel told his sister. "Now there is a Coast Guard barricade up and the authorities are impounding the boats."

"Thank you for letting me know, Angel."

Her daughter, Teresa, had taken her to the doctor several times in the past few months. The doctor prescribed Valium, but Carmela ripped up the prescription as soon as Teresa left for school. Carmela could not sleep. The doctor prescribed Dalmane, but she ripped up that prescription too. She slept no better after not taking the Valium or the Dalmane but she felt stronger each time she ripped up the doctor's scripts.

She went to work each morning as if these days were no different from any others in her life. She sold perfume from a glass counter in Bal Harbour. Perfume to bring a man home.

One day when he was not down in Key West hiring boats to bring her man home, Angel bought Carmela a beeper. She wore it on the waistband of her suit. It looked very professional. But every time the phone rang at the perfume counter, the sculpted vials still shook in her trembling hand. Every time she came home, she still sat by the phone. I think the phone is going to ring, she would think, and the phone would ring a thousand times a day: customers asking for Joy and Opium, her daughter's friends asking if Teresa was at home, her brother to tell her there was no news, her brother's fiancé asking Carmela if she knew where Angel was.

One day when he was not down in Key West hiring boats to bring her man home, Angel bought Carmela a gun. Just a little one. Silver and pearl to keep in the glove compartment. Silver and pearl to keep in the night table. It's not like the last lift, her brother told her. That was the lift they had left Cuba on, twenty years before, she and her little daughter and Angel, who was only fourteen then. That was the lift in the sweet silver plane her husband had put them on, telling her not to worry. Kissed her on the cheek and told her not to worry, he wouldn't be long. He would come after his father got well.

Keep your doors locked, Angel told her, these people are different.

She started having nightmares with the silver gun in her night table. She would dream over and over again that her husband came to her at night and she did not recognize him. She waited in the darkness. She called out to him and he did not answer. She had the gun in her hand.

"My God!" Teresa said when she went into her mother's bedroom and turned on the light because she thought she heard her mother crying. "Mama, put that down, it's me," Teresa said.

In the morning, Carmela put the gun in a milk carton and covered it over with eggshells and coffee grounds. Then she put the milk carton in a paper bag and covered it over with more garbage. Then she put the paper bag into a green plastic trash bag and put it in a garbage heap on her way to work. Teresa made another appointment for her mother with the doctor. The doctor prescribed a stronger tranquilizer and Carmela felt stronger ripping up the prescription.

The Monday morning Angel told her the boatlift was really closed this time, she got dressed and went to work as if it were any other Monday morning. There they asked her: "Did he come? Did he come? You look so radiant, he must have come."

She had grown beautiful with her waiting. She hadn't meant to.

CHAPTER 5

They were led from the bus. Realization, like the dawn, came in erratic spurts across the tropical morning.

Juan Raúl Pérez asked if he could piss. The soldier with the gun told him to go ahead and piss and told him to shit too, asshole, because he didn't have to ask anymore, that is if he could still piss without having someone tell him to piss. So he pissed. So they all pissed in the shrubs by the side of the dark road. One last piss of cold fear, of a thousand days and a thousand nights in small gray cells. A thousand dreams that smelled of sea too far inland.

They were led over to the barracks where several hundred people were waiting for passage in the dozen small boats still left. Juan Raúl Pérez followed directions without caring, sniffing the sea air. The smell of salt in the air was edged like a razor, without sun yet to soften the edges, without any color in the dawn yet to distract the senses. A man asked for his name, checked it on a clipboard, and led him over to another line. In front of him, a young woman sang softly in a heavily accented voice, "Welcome to the Hotel California."

"Are we going to California?" Juan Raúl Pérez asked the man at the desk when his name was called. "No," the man said, "to Miami. Where they send you after that is up to them."

He was told to move to another line and he did, sniffing the razor air, watching the water in the distance, waiting for the water to start moving away from the shore. A palm tree cleared away a patch of blue, and the blue grew higher and wider across the sky. The sun began to play upon the water, changing it from blue to turquoise, dancing tiny diamond steps upon the surface.

He was led with some thirty others to a sleek fishing boat that smelled of diesel and oil even before the double engines roared to a start. The Penn-Yan was loaded beyond capacity and ebbed below the waterline; the bilge pump groaned to keep them afloat. Juan Raúl Pérez sat towards the back, as he was told to do, on the left side, and watched the changing colors of the Gulf Stream. He turned to an old man sitting next to him who had no hair and no teeth and told him that he had to piss. The old man flashed a toothless grin that wrinkled his face into a thousand crevices. "Go ahead and piss, you're a free man. Just don't piss on me."

Juan Raúl Pérez walked to the back of the boat and pissed into the royal blue ocean. It wasn't until that moment, his warm urine rainbowing across the sea-sky, that he knew he was not going to be shot at dawn. Not that the time of day had ever stopped a bullet before, but the dawn had come and gone and he was pissing over the side of a fishing boat as if he were alive.

Juan Raúl Pérez sat quietly in his place. It was a long ride. He thought he should be happy but he did not want to think of anything that might break the fragile spell of reality. There was cool water to drink which came around regularly. It was hot and he was nauseous but he did not want to move to vomit. The old man sitting beside him gave him half of a dark slender cigar and held a match for him.

"To freedom," the old man said, and smiled his toothless grin.

"To freedom," Juan Raúl Pérez replied.

He thought he would vomit from the cigar but he didn't. It tasted far away and lovely and somehow his nausea passed as he smoked it.

In the afternoon, as he walked back to his place from pissing over the side of the boat as if he were still alive, a woman they called Dottie, with big mother-Cuba hips and black madonna Cuban hair, put her hips against him and began to dance. There was little room to move without stepping on the others, which only directed more energy into Dottie's violent hips. Her dress, blue, Havana circa 1960 and crammed with white polka dots, swayed in the sea breeze. There was music from a radio, which no one could hear because they were clapping and keeping their own time. Juan Raúl Pérez had barely to move, only to let her move him with her mother-Cuba hips covered in so many swaying polka dots. Her dance was samba and salsa. Her dance was freedom and violence. It became more frenzied as the others clapped louder and laughed and shouted. "Rock-n-roll!" she called to them. "Li-ber-ty!" they chanted back to her. And he must have been laughing too when she sat back down beside him.

"What's your name?" Dottie asked. And he did not answer because the face of his still-being did not want to open its mouth to show her that he had no teeth, did not want to smile and crack the surface of his still-being into a thousand tiny crevices. "My name is Dottie," she said when he didn't answer, "not Dorita ever again." He nodded his head in agreement. She said, "I've been watching you piss all day, whatever your name is."

CHAPTER 6

Time and tide had waited for Dottie, née Dorita. She had been through too much for too long to be held in check by anything as common as time, as predictable as tide. There wasn't a government yet devised which could have stopped her dream of freedom and men like John Wayne, even if there wasn't a government yet devised which hadn't screwed her in some way. She had been screwed by basic patriarchy by being born a bastard child. She had been screwed by aristocracy by being born to a maid. She had been screwed by military dictatorship by having her common-law husband die fighting for Batista, and her next lover—on Castro's side, she wasn't taking any chances—died in the Bay of Pigs invasion. She had been screwed by capitalism because the U.S. had skimmed the fat off Cuba before the revolution. She had been screwed by communism the most skillfully because it had promised. And promised. And promised. And promised.

And she had been screwed. She had been screwed without her permission and fought. She had been screwed without her permission when she was too tired to fight. And she had screwed when she was too tired of being screwed. She screwed for favors and position. She screwed to be left alone. She screwed her bus fare to the Peruvian embassy when she heard rumors of the boatlift. She had screwed so she wouldn't be screwed again.

She found the door of the embassy already shut and no one left to screw. The authorities read a note on her papers from twenty years earlier stating "suspicion of prostitution." The charges had never moved beyond "suspicion" but that hadn't prevented her from being rounded up to work the sugar plantation—a loosely woven resettlement camp from which she had at first left many times before she realized there was no place, at least in Cuba, to go. However, her record since then noted that she was neither dissident nor malefactor but an exemplary worker and a good screw. She had no money for passage nor relatives in the United States. The authorities told her no, she could not obtain an exit visa either for the boatlift or for any other emigration. They asked what could make her request such a thing after the revolution had reformed her from suspect prostitute to exemplary citizen worker?

And she told them, almost without hope, almost without dreams, almost without time or tide: "John Wayne, Elvis Presley, rock and roll, blue jeans, nail polish. I want everything you say I cannot have." Then she told them she hated their fucking uniforms and that she hated men in uniforms. The authorities labeled her "unfit" and sent her out of Mariel Harbor on one of the last boats.

She could see Key West from the boat. She had arrived, along with a laundry bag containing all her important possessions: a towel she had taken from the Havana Hilton in 1959; a pair of black patent-leather high heels she had bought the same year; a can of hair spray she had bought in 1974 on the black market; a picture of her mother and herself taken in 1958 at the same Havana Hilton, both of them wearing their maid uniforms and caps; one very used Revlon lipstick (a bright red mislabeled Mystic Mauve), also black-market; a bobby pin she used to dig for what little color was left of the lipstick; a lace slip (a present from a recent lover); a one-piece Esther Williams bathing suit her mother had pilfered from the hotel they had both worked in before the Hilton opened. She had left her exemplary work clothes in Cuba, where she felt they belonged.

She dug for her lipstick, changed the brown sandals on her feet to her patent-leather pumps, and straightened her dress. The little money Dottie had saved from her work she had given to a beggar on the street before she left. Cuban pesos were worthless outside Cuba.

She searched for some boat chrome to apply lipstick and hair spray, wobbling on her stiletto heels. The boat wobbled in the water. "I wish I had a mirror," she said to Juan Raúl Pérez. "I'm going to have a mirror soon and a little compact with gold on the bottom and shells on the top." And lotion, she thought. She was going to buy lotion that would change her state-run-sugar-plantation hands into silk. And she was going to have a second chance to live the way she dreamed life should be and not the way it had turned out.

In bursts of sunburned mouths and sun-chapped hands, the exiles cheered the new shore and cried the forgotten land. As they left the open sea and passed through the wide entrance of the Truman Annex Harbor, Juan Raúl Pérez forgot the blue and white of Dottie's dress, forgot her lovely gestures that he had been watching—woman combing dark hair, woman applying lipstick in silver reflection—and remembered his still-being. He put his hand to his left wrist to find his pulse. After he steadied his fingers, he could not count with all the others cheering. When Dottie turned to him, he was still sitting, groping for his pulse and crying. Dottie was crying too because her new life was so close at hand. Because she was never going to harvest sugar cane again with her Cuban-madonna hands and because she was never again going to spread her Cuban-madonna thighs except for love and men like John Wayne.

"Mira, señor," she said to Juan Raúl Pérez, "Get up and look. It is very beautiful. Why won't you stand up and look!"

But how could he explain to her that he would not make it to the other side, that surely the sea would now begin to pull away from the shore. He tried to get up but only made it to his knees before he stopped to grope for his pulse again.

"I don't think I'll make it, señora," he said. "I didn't think I'd be so old."

Dottie couldn't hear his words but seeing him on his knees with his hands clutched tightly before him, she again implored him to get up. "There will be enough time later to pray, señor," she shouted.

But Juan Raúl Pérez wasn't praying. The god he had prayed to growing up no longer existed for him. And the only prayer he could still offer after twenty years in prison was to the carefully tended image of his wife. He had molded her. He had adored her. He had tended her like a well-loved shrine in the cemetery of his dreams. He did not feel strong enough to test the only prayer he had left. He only wanted to find his pulse to be sure he wasn't dead.

"Get up, señor! We're almost here," Dottie said. She had to bend over towards him to be heard, a difficult balance in her spike heels.

"I don't even have any teeth to kiss my wife," he said.

It must have been the heat of the moment, the dock was now only fifty feet away, for Dottie knelt beside the crying man and kissed him, feeling with her Cuban-madonna tongue the two rotting teeth still left in the back of his mouth.

"You don't need teeth to kiss your wife," she said. "But I feel a stub or two in the back. You'll probably need to get them pulled to get dentures in the United States. Is your wife in the U.S.? Will she be here to meet you?"

"I don't know," he mumbled, dropping his wrist to feel his mouth with his hand. It was the first time in twenty years that someone had kissed him and the sensation was so forgotten that it didn't even feel like his own mouth. "I'm not sure I understand what is going on," he said. "I was taken from prison on a bus this morning but I have not seen any of those I was released with here on this boat."

But Dottie was no longer paying attention to Juan Raúl Pérez. The boat was idling in the water and freedom was taking too long to arrive. She tugged off her patent-leather pumps and shoved them at Juan Raúl Pérez along with her laundry bag of possessions. Then she hoisted herself over the side of the boat with a smile and a splash.

Juan Raúl Pérez stared in disbelief at the empty space in the universe which Dottie had occupied a moment before. It could only be a dream, he thought; she had not fallen into the dark hissing crack between the sea and the land, she had jumped!

CHAPTER 7

Dottie's sunset entrance at the Truman Annex Harbor surprised her; she hadn't planned on doing anything except walking into freedom. But as soon as she landed in the clear sweet water, she knew it was better to swim to freedom: to arrive, at least symbolically, on her own. She dog-paddled the twenty feet to the inclined boat ramp, triumphantly emerged from the water, knelt down on the concrete, and kissed the ground.

The few officials left at the dock had seen this routine several times before and pointed her gently over to the line at the processing desk. Dottie, however, wasn't quite ready to move. She stood, hands on hips, and faced the grand expanse of sky, the new sky of her new land. Then she closed her eyes and breathed deeply. Each breath was as sweet as she had imagined it would be. "Hello, Elvis Presley," she whispered softly, "even though you are dead, hello."

"Lady," said a guard, tapping her on the shoulder, "you were told to wait in line. Are you here with anyone?"

"Yes," she said when she spotted Juan Raúl Pérez in the line. "He's got my bag." She smoothed the polka dots over her hips and hoped her swim had not damaged the dress she had saved for twenty years for just this occasion.

"Well, go on then," the guard told her, and she walked over to the line.

On an Anglo scale, Dottie was a good fifty pounds over-weight. On a Latin scale, she was perfect. Dottie didn't ex-actly walk, she flowed from one place to another, and not all in one direction at the same time: the flesh of her thighs wasn't on the tempo of either of her tits and her swinging arms did not quite match her bouncy step. Her body was short and not compact, and the effect, especially in a drip-ping-wet and clinging cotton dress, was awkward and beau-tiful at the same time. Her body moved in so many musical directions at once. Her smiling face, her dark blue dress and dripping black madonna hair were cool and breezy in the late-afternoon heat.

Juan Raúl Pérez was probably the only man on the dock not following Dottie's bouncy flow. He held her bag and shoes in one hand and shielded his eyes from the glow of sunset and his growing panic with the other. Where am I? he repeated over and over again in his head. The only rea-son he was able to stay calm was that everyone else around him appeared to be calm. Dottie had to yank the shoes from his hand before he realized she was standing next to him.

She put her hand on his shoulder to balance herself as she struggled her wet feet back into her heels.

"You don't mind, señor," she said, "if I slip in line here with you?"

"My pleasure, señora," he said. "I'm glad you are still alive. I didn't think you'd made it."

"I just swam a few feet, señor, not from Cuba."

There were no longer any film crews or reporters at the harbor, not even a stray tourist with an Instamatic peering through the fence. The boatlift was four months old now; curiosity and, for the most part, welcome had been used up months before. Only two refugee boats had docked that af-ternoon. Less than eighty refugees stood in line to be pro-cessed by immigration, a far cry from the thousands that had arrived daily during the previous months. Families were no longer able to pick up arriving relatives until pro-cessing was completed in Miami.

"Your wife, señor, have you seen your wife yet?" Dottie asked Juan Raúl Pérez.

"No, señora, but I didn't expect my wife to be here." And it was true—wherever here was was not where he could imagine his wife, standing beside him smelling of salt water and sweat like Dottie. The moment he stepped off the boat, he was sure his wife was waiting for him somewhere else, somewhere cool and shaded.

"I need to sit down," he told Dottie, and sat where he stood.

"I wish I could spit," Dottie said and coughed. "I think I swallowed some salt water. But I've never been a good spitter."

The line did not move quickly, nor was Dottie able to spit. She sat on her laundry bag next to Juan Raúl Pérez while the Key West sunset beat down on his sunburned head. Those who know sunsets say Key West stands without rival. Oranges and fuchsias spread like fires burning in suspended eternity. The blues twisted and turned with ribbons of purple and clouds of white.

He was between exhaustion and sleep, his head in his hands, when Dottie shook him. "Look, señor," she said. "Look up! It's our first sunset in the United States." But when he lifted his head he was blinded by the colors. The colors were no longer dreamlike as in that morning's dawn. The colors were no longer between sleeping and waking as they had been in the ten-hour passage from Mariel Harbor. The colors of his first sunset in the United States were aching and real, like the two rotting teeth left in his mouth. He was used to life in shadows. He put his head down to shield his aching eyes. Dottie had to take his hand and pull him forward when the man at the desk finally waved them ahead.

"Dorita Evita Pérez, age forty-four," senior official Orlando Rivera said as he took Dottie's papers and checked her name on the list.

"No," Dottie said.

"No what?" Rivera said.

"No Dorita, not ever again. Dottie."

"Are these your papers, ma'am?"

"Yes, but not my name. My name is Dottie Pérez. I don't like Evita either." Dottie had left the past behind. She wasn't going to carry her old names, "Little-Dora" or "Little-Eva," with her into her new life.

"Ma'am, I'm not talking like or dislike. Are you Dorita Evita Pérez?" Rivera was tired. It was Monday. He hadn't had a day off in a month and he had had a long day. True, it had been a lot more hectic at the beginning of the boatlift four months before, but it had also been more exciting. He had been interviewed by television crews. He had been quoted by reporters from New York and North Dakota. And he had been very much aware that he was part of a historic moment. The moment had lasted four months and now all that were left were the stragglers shepherded through the harbor by the Coast Guard. Rivera was tired of refugees. He was tired of each one of their faces, sunken cheeks and hollowed-out eyes, faces not knowing where they were, faces already homesick and regretting their voyage. When Dottie had first stepped up to his desk, he had liked her face, a little too old for him, a little too chubby for him, but likable. She had a nice face, but now he was tired of her face too. The man whose hand she was holding looked tired and confused. Rivera felt a sudden and deep sympathy towards Juan Raúl Pérez even though he didn't like his face either.

Oh Christ, Rivera thought, regarding Juan Raúl Pérez's prison fatigues, the poor old man gets out of prison and gets to deal with his batty wife.

"Well, yes, that was my name," Dottie said, dropping Juan Raúl Pérez's hand to better emphasize her point by waving both her hands. "But the second I stepped into the United States, I am a new woman." Not the woman born bastard to patriarchy, not the woman hips raped by convenience, madonna hands raped by sugar cane.

"Ma'am, please keep your voice down. This is a government agency. You are here for political asylum, you can change your name some other time."

"I am not here for political asylum. That's why I left Cuba, to get away from political asylum. And this has nothing to do with government," Dottie said. "I came here to get away from government, for nail polish and rock and roll"—Dottie wondered if this man knew exactly how much a bottle of nail polish cost on the Cuban black market when they did have it—"and for men like John Wayne." Her explanation had worked with the Cuban officials, she saw no reason why it wouldn't work with these officials. She was still explaining when Rivera asked for Juan Raúl Pérez's papers.

John Wayne? Rivera thought, looking at the scrawny old man. Rivera noted that his papers said he was fifty-seven years old, but he looked much older. He asked Juan Raúl Pérez about his former prison status and then asked him his standard list of political-prisoner questions. Juan Raúl Pérez's answers were satisfactory. If there were any discrepancies Rivera missed they would be dealt with by immigration at Krome Avenue. "You will be questioned further in Miami," Rivera told him. "Do you have any other relatives in the U.S.?"

"Yes, of course," Juan Raúl Pérez answered. "The Pérezes. If you ever need anything done in this life, ask a Pérez, there are so many of us."

Rivera chuckled at the worn old Cuban pleasantry, his mother's maiden name also being Pérez. Rivera marveled that a man just out of prison, with a wife like that, still had the time and inclination to pass along a little joke. He sent them on their way. They were detained for the night at the government holding area in the Junior League ballpark only because it was so late and there would be no seats available on the Greyhound bus until the next day.

CHAPTER 8

The bulletproof floodlights at the Junior League ballpark cast long shadows into the night. The floodlights droned like mosquitoes. The mosquitoes droned like the lights.

"Just a delay," a guard with a rifle assured Dottie at the fence the third time she tried to leave the park. "You'll be free soon enough."

She cursed him under her smile and turned back away. Dottie had been certain she would spend her first night in freedom in a nightclub or one of the discos she heard advertised on Miami radio back in Cuba. And even if freedom delayed wasn't new to her, she was having a hard time keeping still. The ballpark was too quiet for her. Ten hours on open seas had drained everyone. The only life stirring was a self-appointed welcoming committee of one guajiro with one guitar.

"Ah, Cuba," he sang, "land of my heart. Land of white doves flying and green mountains setting in sunlight. Was it so easy to forget me, when I remember so well, Cuba. . . ." The man had been in the U.S. for twenty years, but he was still guajiro, "country," and he had not forgotten. Dottie asked him if he knew "Hound Dog," but he shook his head no without stopping his song. The mosquitoes savored their high-pitched acoustic camouflage. Dottie turned her long shadow perched on stiletto heels and walked away. She sang softly to herself, "You ain nutin but a houn dog." She hadn't a clue to its meaning.

Juan Raúl Pérez sat on his cot beneath the bulletproof floodlights and patted his body to reassure his still-being. He was still alive! And he was going to be freed—maybe. The official at the dock had told them all that they weren't free yet, that they needed to pass immigration in Miami first. The man hadn't said what would become of them if they didn't pass immigration. Perhaps he had not missed his execution yet. But he had already passed immigration in Key West as husband of the woman who had been so kind to dance with him and talk to him on the boat. A natural enough mistake, he thought, as they both had the same last name and they had been holding hands. His "marriage" to Dottie Dorita Evita Pérez had gained them two adjoining cots in a choice corner of left field. Officials by then were suspicious of singles, especially men, who formed the majority on the boatlift exodus, as suspect criminals, homosexuals, and madmen emptied from Castro's jails. Families and couples were given preferential treatment. Not that Juan Raúl Pérez knew that. He knew that Dottie had been kind enough to lead him over to a cot before she wandered off.

What he couldn't understand was that his real wife seemed to have nothing to do with his release from prison. Every letter he had ever received from her had spoken of how hard she and her brother were working to obtain his release. If his wife had had a hand in his release, surely one of the officials at immigration would have mentioned her. "Your wife is waiting for you in a cool shady spot in Miami," they would say.

Or maybe she no longer waited.

Maybe she had died.

A cold shudder passed through his still-being. He felt for his pulse. As if his own heartbeat could confirm his wife's existence. He hadn't received a letter from her in sixteen months. That in itself was not unusual. Mail was often intercepted and always censored. He could not bear to think that his reason for existence could be dead when he was finally alive. Fear spread like ice through his body.

Juan Raúl Pérez shuddered again. If they really were in the United States, then why did everyone speak Spanish so well and all with Cuban accents? Even their faces looked Cuban to him. And why all the guards in uniforms with guns? And why, if he was finally alive, did he have moments when he felt so old and tired?

He got up from the cot and started pacing through the field. He found an empty paper bag and went back to his cot. When he felt more composed he would write his wife a letter, a cheerful one.

When Dottie came back to their cots, Juan Raúl Pérez was scribbling furiously on the paper bag. She gave him one of the box dinners she had gotten from a Red Cross volunteer: arroz con pollo and a sweet roll.

"Why are you writing on that piece of paper bag, señor?" she asked.

"I am writing to my wife, señora."

"Good. But you don't have to do that. I've been talking to some people to get information. The officials will try to contact your wife for you when we get to Miami."

This was reassuring to him. If she was still alive then she would know he was here.

"And you don't have to write on a piece of paper bag. They have paper here. I can go get you some."

"That would be fine, señora."

Dottie got a dozen sheets of yellow legal pad from the Red Cross volunteer and a Bic pen to replace his stub of pencil. Juan Raúl Pérez thanked her and smoothed the paper beside him on the cot.

"Aren't you going to eat your dinner, señor?"

"Yes, señora, of course. Thank you." But he didn't take a bite. The thought suddenly occurred to him that the food could be poisoned. He had felt so close to death that morning that he couldn't understand its being so far away now.

"I know this is a delicate question, señor, excuse me," Dottie said, "but when was the last time you saw your wife?"

"Twenty years ago."

"Have you heard from her since? Twenty years is a long time. Perhaps she has remarried."

"I get letters from her, señora. But of course it's still possible." Except that the possibility hadn't occurred to him, not recently at least. He shuddered again. The thought of her remarried made him feel colder than the thought of her dead.

"Señor, if you don't mind, I think we should stay married, so to speak, for now. It would be easier to pass through immigration that way. Unless, of course . . . Excuse me. I have another delicate question for you, if you don't mind."

"Go ahead, señora."

"Well, what were you in prison for?"

"I am a political prisoner."

"Are you some sort of hero?"

"No, surely not."

"Ah, too bad. But it will still make it easier for us. I mean, for you. They will let a man pass easier to this country when he has already shown himself against the communist policies of Cuba. And if your wife does come, will you take me with you? I have no relatives in this country. You can say I am your long-lost cousin or something."

"I don't understand, señora."

"Señor, I have been talking to some people, and we aren't exactly free yet. Even after we pass through immigration, unless you have relatives or a sponsor they won't just let us out on the streets. I hope this is only a temporary rule, but I do not know how long it will last."

The thought of being out on the streets after twenty years of prison sent another cold wave of fear through Juan Raúl Pérez. He had not thought of these possibilities while dreaming of freedom for twenty years.

"I would repay you both for the favor, señor, if you would take me with you," Dottie continued. She was eating her chicken and rice and talking between bites. "And if she doesn't come, it will still be easier to stay married, so to speak. One needs a sponsor out to the community, and it is easier to get one if you're married, I heard."

"You seem to know a lot, señora."

"I ask a lot of questions."

Dottie picked over a chicken bone and licked her fingers. "What does your wife look like, señor?"

The ground slipped below his icy feet. If his wife had remarried, if she was dead, then how would he stay alive? It was her face that had kept him alive for twenty years. He took a deep breath and bravely called up her image, the image he had carefully tended each day in prison. He tried to recall her not from twenty years before, when time had frozen, but as he had aged her, tenderly and carefully, each day.

"She cut her hair five years ago," he said. "It is mostly gray now, almost white. And she has gained some weight. Food is plentiful in the United States, no? She walks more slowly now. She has had a hard life. She wears a dress with flowers on it, a wide skirt. She works in a store. A small store by a harbor."

"Do they sell nail polish there?"

"I'm sorry, I don't know," he said.

"How long have you been in prison, señor?"

"Twenty years."

"You have seen her photo then?"

If there had been a photo sent, it would be one of the things censored from a letter. No good would come of showing pictures of U.S. propaganda of capitalist affluence to political prisoners. "No, señora. I have not seen a photo."

His still-being trembled. Dottie saw him then not as the man she had watched so boldly pissing over the side of the boat like a free man all afternoon but as an old and tired man. Perhaps it is better, she thought; he would leave her alone at night. But it would be better to make things clear from the start.

"We would be married in name only, señor. And only for immigration."

Please don't leave me, he wanted to beg her. Please don't let them send me back. Please don't leave me alone on the streets if my wife doesn't come. "Yes, señora," he said.

"Good. But please understand that it is in name only, that I am a free woman here. I need to make that clear. I don't have to fuck you or anybody else if I don't want to."

Juan Raúl Pérez stared at her in disbelief. The farthest thing from his mind was fucking. His reason for existence could be dead or remarried. Or maybe she wouldn't even recognize him as the toothless old man he had become. He wanted to laugh aloud at Dottie's supposition, to break his face into a thousand tiny crevices. But he composed himself and told her that she could rest assured.

"Thank you," she said and left.

He ate his boxed dinner and still didn't die. From the distance he heard the sad refrain of the guajiro stretching across the darkness.

Oh my Love, I am alive. I run my hands over my body. I watch my feet as I walk. I am conscious of my every movement, my every breath. This is how I breathe. This is how I move my hand to write to you. I can no longer remember how it is to dream. There is no need.

Everything around me spins with vivid color.

Oh my Love, I am alive! I say it over and over again. I long for you as I have longed for you for twenty years, only now I long as the living, and not as the dead long for life.

CHAPTER 9

He dreamed he was dead and heard the terrible gnashing of teeth in hell. He tried to comfort himself even in his dream, even in his death. You are not in hell, he told himself. That gnashing is only the sound of mosquitoes droning, the sound of lights buzzing.

When he awoke, he found himself alive, patting his body like a mother consoling a child, confirming his flesh. But the sound persisted, and, turning, he saw he was in his prison cell and his wife was in the cell with him standing by the bars. Her hair was long and dark. Her wide skirt was flowered. He thought she was dancing, the way her skirt rhythmically swept from side to side. It was lovely to watch her. But then he saw that she was holding a wide-toothed file and sawing through the bars of his cell.

"You had better stop," he told her. "That sound is very loud and it will bring the guards."

"No," she said. "Can't you hear that I am humming to disguise the noise? They will not hear it. You worry too much." She was intent on her task and smiling.

"I think you should not do that. You had better stop."

She was almost through the bar.

"Stop!" he shouted to her. "Stop! I have already done this yesterday. It would be better if you let me rest here a little while longer. Stop."

"All right, I've stopped!" Dottie said. "Do you always wake up so cranky?" She was sitting on her adjoining cot, filing her soon-to-be talons with an emery board she had gotten from a church volunteer.

"Who are you?" Juan Raúl Pérez asked.

She handed him a styrofoam cup half filled with dark sweet Cuban coffee and laughed. "I was just about to ask you the same question, señor. If we are to stay married until your wife comes, I'll need to know your given name. It was lucky enough that we've got the same last names."

"Juan Raúl Pérez," he said.

"You don't look like a Juan," she said. "But then I don't look like a Dorita. I am Dottie, remember? Not Dorita ever again."

The salt water from Dottie's plunge the day before had stiffened her dress, molded it to her every curve. It was not yet seven o'clock and the guard had told her their transportation wouldn't arrive till after eight, yet she had been ready for hours for her trip on the Greyhound bus to freedom. Carefully laid out on her cot beside her were clothes for her gentleman husband, who had been kind enough to sleep through the night without disturbing her, although he woke up cranky, like every other man she knew. She had acquired an oversized Hawaiian shirt for Juan Raúl Pérez, bell-bottomed blue jeans, and a pair of simulated-leather oxfords. The sooner he was out of his fatigues, the sooner he'd stop advertising his prisoner status.

"You need to hurry up," Dottie said. "And here are your clothes for the trip. I have forgotten a razor. You look terrible. I'll see if I can get one."

Juan Raúl Pérez did look terrible. The two-day beard on his chin was a patchwork of gray-and-white stubble. The previous day's sun had burned the top of his head into a red toupee of itchy blisters. He sipped his coffee slowly. It was the first cup of strong coffee, real Cuban coffee, that he had had in many years. Each taste brought a memory, and each memory was pleasant and warm. It was like drinking morning after twenty years of night. He took a final gulp and lay back on the cot content with his distance. Overhead the sky was blue. It seemed right that he should awaken out of doors on his first day out of prison, and yet he could not remember if he had ever slept out of doors in all his life before prison. But he could recall windows, many windows where the sun had once poured on his waking. There was a large bay window in his bedroom with tufted beige curtains. His wife would rise before him to make the coffee.

"Señor, you need to get moving," his wife called to him. No, his wife never called him señor. "The buses will be here soon," Dottie said. "Here's a razor. It's plastic, and you throw it away when you're done. I've never seen this kind before, but it's the best I could do."

Inside the aluminum cubicle labeled "Peterson's Porta-pottie," Juan Raúl Pérez stood facing the empty wall above the tiny sink and shaved his blank reflection by feel.

Freedom is a relative term, and Juan Raúl Pérez was as free as he could be a little over twenty-four hours since his release. He peeled off his prison fatigues slowly, and hesitantly replaced them with the clothes Dottie had given him. His first look in the wall where there was no mirror reflected a smiling young man in a suit, off to a full day of possibilities. But as he squinted his eyes to focus more clearly, he saw an old man, a stranger.

The bell-bottom jeans flapped above his ankles. The Hawaiian shirt hung almost to his knees, and the sleeves were well past his elbows. A large parrot motif shrieked across the shirt in orange and lime green. He left his fatigues in a heap in the corner. He rubbed his hand across his gums. Like a disguise, he thought, this is almost like a disguise.

Nor was it a Greyhound which transported them the 160 miles northward from the Keys but a solid yellow rectangle of old school bus which wove its way through the great ribbons of turquoise and light, mangrove and road.

Dottie was furious that they had missed the Greyhound

because Juan Raúl Pérez had taken so long getting dressed and ready.

The school bus had no air conditioning, and the last week of July 1980 was setting record high temperatures throughout the South. The bus driver listened to country music from a small transistor stuck in the sun-visor flap. Dottie thought it the worst music she had ever heard, even worse than guajiro music. She asked him twice to change the station before it dawned on her that the driver didn't speak Spanish. This irritated her more than the whiny music, since she had planned on sitting right down to a friendly chat with the driver to add to the information she had gathered the night before. Instead she had to sit next to Juan Raúl Pérez, who watched out the window as if he were in a foreign universe instead of a foreign country. "It's because of you we ended up on this old bus," she said. "How long does it take you to get dressed? It's not like you have hair to comb or makeup to put on."

If Dottie had known the bus's destination, she wouldn't have been so annoyed. Dottie wanted to go to Miami, which is where the bus she was on was headed. Because of overcrowding at the Miami processing center, the Greyhound they had missed was off to a military base camp in Arkansas.

"You should have left without me, señora," he said, ever so grateful that she hadn't left him. He didn't know where he was. He didn't know where they were going.

But she wouldn't have left him. She had her plans for the day already figured out, and they included Juan Raúl Pérez.

"When they interview you," she told him, "just tell them that your wife is a relative—don't tell them which one, in case she doesn't come and we need to stay married."

Dottie was certain that when Juan Raúl Pérez's wife did come they would take her with them, grateful that she had helped the old man through the journey. She was certain Juan Raúl Pérez's wife would be rich, just from the high-class accent and manners of her husband. She would take a bubble bath at their house, have a wonderful dinner, and then go to a nightclub.

"Make sure you stress that you were a political prisoner and not a thief or murderer."

"Yes, señora, I will be sure to do that."

At the nightclub, she would dance and drink champagne. She would also meet several rich handsome men who would love her. And since she was now truly free, *she* would decide exactly which one she loved helplessly, passionately.

"And if your wife is remarried or something, señor, and won't come for us, you don't have to worry. You only told them she was a relative. We'll just stay married and get a sponsor."

Dottie wasn't exactly sure what a sponsor was. Someone rich, kind, and influential to take them into his home. It didn't matter as long as she could still go to a nightclub tonight.

"And don't forget to tell them how much you hate communism when they interview you, even if you don't know anything about it since you were in prison so long, OK?"

"Yes, señora."

And if they had ended up at the Krome Avenue Processing Center, where they should have gone, they would have been interviewed. But the bus driver was headed over to the Orange Bowl, which hadn't been a refugee-processing center for months now. He only worked part-time for the bus company, and no one had told him that the Orange Bowl was now a shelter for homeless refugees who had long since been cleared by immigration. Or if they had told him, it wasn't in English.

CHAPTER 10

Miami in the afternoon sun is crayola and bright. Like a child's drawing, the city is imaginatively colored and unimaginatively out of proportion. Slender palms stand in disbelief against giant silver lego constructions. Soft clouds float by garish concrete. Rows of aqua and pink houses insult the shimmering sea and sky they frame. The streets themselves parallel and intersect with the simple logic of a children's board game.

Miami fit Dottie's idea of freedom perfectly—it was simple, gaudy, and close at hand. To Juan Raúl Pérez, it was not at all like the twenty-three streets to his wife's house that he had envisioned in twenty prison years.

"I didn't imagine these streets to look like this," he said to Dottie.

"You don't have to imagine anymore," Dottie said. "We're already here."

CHAPTER 11

Angel Díaz had a square body, a square jaw. His fiancée, Flavia Unzueta, dressed him in French-cut fashion, which rather than tapering his physique, made him appear strained at the seams. A gold Rolex encircled his muscular wrist. Angel Díaz liked to think of himself as a man who didn't waste time. Money, yes, sometimes he wasted a little of that and didn't mind that people knew he had enough to spend on the gold Rolex, the white French-cut shirt. But time was to be used wisely, which for Angel meant barreling through each minute as if it were a sticky ether that sometimes trapped him at a red light or in slow-moving traffic. He had alternate routes mapped around town which might not have gotten him anywhere faster but at least he kept moving. An indecisive customer at his store was enough to set his teeth on edge. If they didn't want the furniture he sold, fine, but why did they stand there smiling and nodding, looking this way and that, wasting his time? Angel would wave a hand in front of his face to brush away those sticky time particles of people who talked too slowly, drove like turtles, and got in his way with their inability to make up their goddam minds.

Angel Díaz was not a man who, confronted by a red light, took a moment for a deep breath, a hum along with the radio.

"Why are you beeping at a red light?" Flavia once asked him. "You think it hears you?"

"Your sarcasm is not appreciated," he answered, waving away the wasted red-light time.

This time Angel thought he had gotten a green light. When the boatlift started, Angel had been sure this time he could get his brother-in-law out of prison in Cuba and safely delivered to his sister's doorstep. Castro was letting prisoners out. And it had seemed so easy at first; if you had a relative in Cuba who wanted to get out, you sent a boat to Mariel Harbor to pick him up. But that wasn't how it worked. Boats sent for Grandma returned overloaded with strangers. Boats sent for political prisoners returned with shipments of thieves. That's what happened when you hired people to do work you could better do yourself, Angel decided after he had paid a lot of money and hired a wide variety of yachts, racers, and fishing boats to bring his brother-in-law home to his sister. In the next boat he had hired, Angel rode in the front seat himself. It was a sleek cigarette racer with an Anglo captain in a Miami Hurricanes baseball cap who drank Coors beer while slamming the boat across the waves as if it were the Indy 500. Oh, the speed was exhilarating.

Angel had expected Cuba to look different, to be encased in barbed wire with blood still on the strands. But instead it had looked brighter than he had remembered from his childhood and calmer than he had projected. There were bands of changing turquoise water meeting pale emerald by the shore. There was green grass and palm trees, a dock, buildings, civilization not far away. It looked like a Caribbean island in a travel brochure and not like a damp gray Moscow. There had been no news of his brother-in-law. The narrow racing boat had been built for speed, not waiting. For two days, they waited in the Mariel Harbor, sunburned and seasick, sitting and sweating, Angel swatting the flies and the wasted time that swam before his eyes. Then a family of eight strangers had been loaded into the boat and they headed back to Key West. Who the fuck did Fidel Castro think he was?

It was late afternoon when Angel woke in the pastel room at the Key West Pier House. The waiting made him sleepy. He was not a man who knew what to do when he had nothing to do. He was sorry he was no longer tired. He turned the TV on. He turned the TV off. He watched the room. Who the hell was Fidel Castro to waste his time? And why hadn't the U.S. just dropped a goddam bomb on Fidel's house?

Angel waved his hand in front of his face and flicked on the all-news Spanish radio channel from Miami. It announced the boatlift as permanently closed and denounced Fidel Castro as an agent of the devil. It also announced that Castro was dying—the same exclusive report it had run for twenty years now. "Goddamn dreamers," Angel said aloud. But the same dream passed before his eyes that always did whenever he thought of Castro dead. Angel would return to Cuba. No, he wouldn't be a furniture-store owner in Cuba. Somehow he'd have the years back that would have made him an educated man. He'd be a doctor, a lawyer, or at the least own the newspaper where his brother-in-law had worked so long ago. He'd buy Carmela and Juan the house they lived in twenty years ago. He'd send Teresa to an exclusive university. He and Flavia would marry and live in a mansion overlooking the water. Poor dreamers. He turned off the radio.

Angel got an outside line and dialed Flavia in Miami. Seventeen, count them, seventeen rings before she picked up.

"This phone rang seventeen times," he said. "Where were you?"

"In the shower," Flavia said. "I'm standing here dripping wet. Any news? I have to get ready for work."

The thought of Flavia naked on the other end of the line, dripping wet next to her phone in the bedroom, held Angel's attention for a moment. "The boatlift is closed," he finally said. "I'll be back tonight."

"Good, Angel, but you told me that yesterday too."

"But I mean it this time. Anything new?"

"No, Angel. I've got to rinse the soap out of my hair. I can't talk now. Bye."

His own goodbye was barely past his lips when he heard her hang up.

Soap in her hair. Water on her skin. But he demoted her anyway in his dream of a liberated Cuba. No, when he went back to Cuba and lived in that beautiful villa overlooking the water, he wouldn't marry Flavia. She'd be his dripping-wet mistress. He'd marry someone dryer, with clothes on, sitting in a formal living room. He'd marry someone more Cuban, not second-generation born in New Jersey like Flavia. Someone who didn't let the phone ring seventeen times before she picked it up.

Angel checked out of his room and headed his beige Eldorado towards the harbor. It wouldn't hurt to check one more time before he left Key West for good. The boatlift really was over this time, and Angel had failed to find his brother-in-law.

A pink sky lingered in the aftermath of sunset. The harbor was almost empty.

"Anybody arrive named Pérez?" Angel asked the immigration officer.

"Everybody named Pérez."

"Anybody named Juan Pérez?"

"About half of them named Juan Pérez."

Angel gritted his teeth. The same immigration officer had been giving him the same lines for the past four months. But now Angel didn't have to be nice anymore, wasn't ever going to have to ask him again. "Look," Angel said. "I ask you nice every day, and every day you try to make it into your little joke. This isn't funny to me. This is my sister's husband I'm asking about, a man who was a political prisoner for twenty years. He's not a joke. And I don't appreciate you making him into a joke. Now, anybody named Juan Pérez?"

"Relax, OK? I've already told you about the sixteen-year-old Juan Pérez who came at dawn and the eighty-year-old one yesterday and that fat woman named Pérez yesterday with her husband named Juan."

"Thank you. That's all I wanted to know. I gave you my number in Miami?"

"I've had it memorized for weeks."

Angel drove over to the Junior League ballpark one last time. He hated it over there with the buzzing hordes of mosquitoes and the glaring floodlights. There were so few refugees there now compared to the thousands the months before. A guard politely answered Angel's inquiries for the thousandth time. Three guajiros began to sing to a high-pitched guitar. The twang grated Angel's teeth. "I am a simple man," sang the toothless mouth in an emaciated face, "using simple words from a simple land. But these words come from my heart and fly like a dove where my heart cannot go."

Angel offered the man twenty dollars to stop singing. The man did not understand Angel's request. "Thank you, but I do not do this for money," he said and handed Angel back the folded bill.

Angel clipped back to Miami at a steady seventy-five. Ridiculous the waste, time.

CHAPTER 12

Carmela Pérez poured herself a glass of iced tea, turned on Channel 6, and settled down to the late show. Teresa was asleep, having spent the evening studying for her courses at Florida International University. In two more semesters, Teresa would have her master's in business administration. She had her father's gift for numbers and worked part-time for an accounting firm.

The boatlift was over. There was a straggler here, a small boat there, but for all practical purposes, the boatlift was really over this time. Carmela had heard the announcement confirmed on the eleven-o'clock news and again on the midnight newsbrief. The boatlift was over and her husband hadn't come. But the news hadn't taken hold in her heart yet. It had tried to, yesterday morning, when Angel had called her and told her the news with that exasperated calm in his voice. She felt his voice shove against her reality and she soothed it away. She would not let it take hold until she was ready. Until she no longer jumped when the telephone rang. Until Teresa stopped treating her like an invalid, hanging around on weekends when she should have been out with her friends, making doctor's appointments for her at the first sign of a frown. Until her friends at work didn't jump on her with questions when she made the mistake of arriving at the perfume counter with a smile on her face.

Until Angel dropped by casually in the evenings on his way home from work for dinner or a cup of coffee the way he used to. Until she weaned herself from the beeper Angel had given her. She even wore it around the house, attached to the sash of her robe while she watched TV, though the phone was only inches from her chair.

The boatlift was over and her husband hadn't come. She just needed to hold herself together a little while longer till life eased back to normal. Since Angel had told her the boatlift was really over this time, she had guided herself through her grief like a second person holding her own hand. The daily routine became more sacred, entered the realm of ritual. You must go to work, she told herself. Put on your shoes. Check your hair in the mirror.

But the beeper had gone off at work and she had dropped a thirty-dollar bottle of Crimes of Passion while showing it to a customer. It was all over her shoes, the tile. The glass crunched under her footsteps, and the counter reeked of passion all afternoon. That's OK, her co-workers told her. That's OK, we know you're upset about your husband.

Drive home. Eat quickly. Go to night school tonight just like every Wednesday night. Do everything normally done, normally.

She had gone after work to her adult ed class, a custom she had continued from taking night courses in English so many years ago. She had since taken U.S. History, Oriental Cooking, Astronomy. This was her second semester of Bridge for Beginners. She liked the game and played well when she didn't underbid. But it only mattered now that she made it through the routine, did not collapse in a corner of disappointment. There was a welcome distance just to be a student among others who didn't know she had a husband. Didn't know she had waited twenty years. All she had to do was play the cards. But her mind started drifting. Why so many hearts? she wondered, picking up the cards she had been dealt, which appeared before her eyes like tarots to be interpreted. And why the queen of hearts so far from the king? She moved them close, sorted the suits. The ace of diamonds—Angel, of course. And the jack of diamonds? Flavia. No jacks were men. Hard to tell with the long curly hair and the elaborate outfits. It didn't have a mustache like the king. Are jacks male or female? she mused, and then went pale with embarrassment when she realized she had spoken aloud.

"Male," her partner answered. "You're not sorting your cards by sex?"

They laughed. She tried to. The hand was halfway played when she realized she had passed when she should have bid a small slam in hearts. Her partner groaned as the cards fell. The teacher, who went from table to table, whispered in her ear, "You seem distracted tonight. Are you OK?"

Yes, she was fine. Wasn't she making it through the day? Hadn't she gotten out of bed, gone to work, come to class? Lucky she hadn't taken Scuba Diving as her friend Ileana was this semester. If her mind drifted off while she was deep underwater, would her body wash ashore in Cuba? She had to shake her thoughts away. Better not to think of anything as daring as scuba. Angel would find out about it somehow and lecture her on her age, her family, her safety. Maybe she'd take Film Appreciation next semester, she thought as she sat sipping her iced tea. It was Audrey Hepburn week on Channel 6; the moonlight of *Breakfast at Tiffany's* filled her living room. In Film Appreciation, she wouldn't have to bid, play, pay attention. She'd just have to sit there quietly, like now, and wait for the end of the film.

She had waited for twenty years.

Twenty years ago, the waiting had ached in her bed each night. She rose in the morning with tears in her eyes and longing by her side. She had dressed her little daughter in the prettiest embroidered dresses (just in case this was the day he would come) even though she could barely afford the rent on the small apartment with her cashier's job at a supermarket. She was thirty-one then, with a four-year-old daughter to feed and a fourteen-year-old orphaned brother who worked as a bag boy in the same supermarket. She had come from a well-off family, had married a well-off man, and had never had to fend for herself before.

Then the waiting became hazy, like a film out of focus. She'd wake from a sound sleep frightened that she could no longer recall her husband's features, frightened that her love for him was only illusion: a memory of love in love with a memory. She'd get up in the middle of the night and pull old photos from the drawer. At breakfast, she'd inspect her growing daughter's face, searching for a clue to her husband's features and seeing only her own: the delicately carved nose, the large doe eyes. Had he really existed?

And then the waiting had settled in like an old friend: spoken to for comfort, consulted for counsel, given daily occurrences with dinner, kissed gently on the cheek before bedtime.

Until the boatlift had opened four months ago.

She cleaned out half her closet in April. She emptied half her dresser drawers in May. In June she practiced sleeping on one side of the bed. To make room. How could she have let herself be so certain he would come? It was the end of July. The boatlift was closed. Fidel Castro was no longer the enemy. Time was no longer the enemy. Hope had become the enemy. Hope had carried her on strong sure wings high up over the middle of the ocean halfway between the past and Miami. She had flown too close to her dream and now she was falling.

There was no moon river between Cuba and Miami. The water was dark below her.

There was an ad for Bennie's Steakhouse on Miami Beach. Carmela had the feeling Angel was on his way. She got up and put water on for coffee. She got her slippers from the bedroom and unbolted the locks on the front door when she heard his car turning into the driveway. Then she sat back down in her chair. She knew there wasn't good news. She knew there wasn't any news at all, but she was glad

Angel was dropping by, just for a late cup of coffee, even with no news at all. What did they used to talk about before the boatlift? Something mundane perhaps, something tensionless and easy. She pulled the folds of her robe around her and hoped that there was still the possibility that life could return to normal.

Angel came through the door into the living room. Carmela saw that his face was red and wondered if he'd gotten sunburned in Key West. Or was he angry?

"Hello," she said and smiled.

Angel didn't answer. Instead he turned and put his right fist through the wall. Plasterboard and bone split. Carmela's hand flew to her mouth. The kettle whistled from the kitchen. Teresa ran from her bedroom through the hallway.

"What's going on?" Teresa asked.

Between his anger and his pain, it took a moment for Angel to find words. He tried to point his limp broken hand toward Carmela. "You didn't even have the door locked!"

"I heard you coming. I unlocked the door when I heard you coming."

"How did you know it was me? You should have been sitting there with the gun I gave you aimed at the door, Carmela. And you shouldn't have unlocked it without being sure. I spent an afternoon putting extra bolts on the door, and not one of them was on."

The kettle still screeched from the kitchen.

"Look at your hand. It's bleeding," Teresa said.

"Where's the gun, Carmela?" Angel shouted. "Where is the gun?"

"I threw it out," Carmela admitted.

"I threw it out," Teresa lied. "She had it pointed at me one night thinking I was a burglar and I threw it out. Now let me drive you to the hospital."

"Don't you understand? Don't you read the newspapers? How many times have I fucking warned you about the sleazy Mariel criminals wandering around out there? Don't you understand? Castro flushed his toilets on us—he emptied his prisons here."

"Guess he forgot to flush one toilet." Teresa said. "Guess he forgot to send my father."

"I didn't mean it that way, and you know it," Angel said to Teresa. And then to Carmela: "As if I hadn't done everything possible to get her father out. As if I hadn't gone to Cuba myself. As if I hadn't spent enough money and wasted all my time in the past four months."

Carmela got up and went to the kitchen. She took the kettle from the burner and sat at the kitchen table in the dark while Teresa and Angel shouted on in the living room. Carmela remembered when Teresa had been about seven or eight and had refused to address Angel as Tío anymore. Angel had come to her and complained. Carmela had told him to leave it alone, he and Teresa had grown up like brother and sister, she shouldn't have to call him uncle if she didn't want to. Carmela debated whether to put the kettle back on so she couldn't hear them so clearly. She hadn't heard them argue like this since they were children.

She went back out to the living room. "Don't you have school tomorrow, Teresa?" Carmela said. "And Angel, it won't take me a minute to throw something on and drive you right up the street to Coral Gables Hospital."

"I can take care of it myself," Angel said. Carmela looked so tired. He wanted to tell her he was sorry but wanted more to impress upon her that she was wrong. That her doors should be bolted at all times. That there were maniacs out there she needed to protect herself from. So he said nothing, moved his hand in front of his face to wave away the wasted time he spent trying to reason with her. The pain shot through to his shoulder. He had to carry his limp hand with his other arm out to his car.

The police, minus siren but with flashing lights, pulled up on the front lawn. Carmela and Teresa hadn't had time to sweep up the plaster yet, but at least Angel was gone.

"I'm sorry, Mama," Teresa said as she saw the police lights and put down the broom. "I'm sorry. I didn't realize we were arguing so loudly."

"Don't worry," Carmela said. "I'm only sorry that you never knew your father."

A western, without Audrey Hepburn, followed. No one thought to turn the TV off. Officer González diligently wrote down each of Carmela's lies concerning such a dreadful mistake that could have prompted one of her neighbors to call the police. He even wrote down her statement that the hole in the living-room wall had been there since she bought the house twelve years before despite the plaster fragments at their feet and the broom and dustpan on the floor. González was glad to sit down with the cup of coffee Carmela gave him. He never argued a "domestic"; they were always tricky calls to get through. He was surprised this one was moving along so smoothly. González had had good luck all week: no guns, deaths, or traffic accidents. He had even pulled a partner for the last two days. The Miami Police Department had been depleted beyond providing partners for routine patrol months before. But the federal government had provided an agent, John Pirelli, who was compiling statistics and on-the-scene crime reports.

Crime statistician Pirelli thought Carmela was the most beautiful liar he had ever met. She maintained her poise throughout the most ludicrous explanations, barely blinking her large dark eyes.

Carmela felt herself drifting away as they fired their questions. She wished she had taken scuba diving this semester. She could imagine herself at this very moment far out to sea. The water was calm. She drifted in moonlight. It was so peaceful there with the sound of the waves and the breathing of stars.

"Excuse me," Pirelli said.

Why was this man staring into her eyes with such intensity? Carmela wondered if he had seen her drifting in the moonlight so far from their questions.

"Excuse me," Pirelli said again. "If you don't mind my asking, why are you wearing a beeper on your robe?"

Carmela took a deep breath, returned from the sea. "Oh,

we thought my husband would come on the boatlift," she said. "So my brother gave this to me in case my husband arrived and I wasn't near a phone."

It was the first truthful answer she had given to their questions, and now they were staring at her as if she were lying. Even Teresa.

"The boatlift is over," Pirelli said.

"I know," Carmela said. The phone was on the table next to her. She felt for the beeper but didn't take it off. Perhaps tomorrow she would be strong enough to live without the beeper.

"He didn't come," Teresa said.

"I'm sorry," Pirelli said.

"We'll be going now," Officer González said. "Thank you for your cooperation, and please call us if you have any more trouble."

"There was no trouble, officers," Carmela answered. "But thank you for checking. Good night."

"I don't think I've ever heard you lie before," Teresa said to her. She was sweeping up the plaster.

"What did you want me to do?" Carmela said. "Turn my own brother in to the police? It's not as if he's done something like this before."

"But he had no right to walk in here and act like that."

"He tried very hard to bring your father here, Teresa. Even before the boatlift. You know that."

"I know," she said. "Good night."

The western was followed by a rerun of *I Spy*. Carmela wasn't going to work tomorrow; she could watch TV till "The Star Spangled Banner" if she wanted. She hadn't taken one day off from work since the boatlift had started. She had had the feeling that if she missed just one day of her routine she'd fall apart into more pieces than she could ever put back together. Now she didn't care. She needed some time to herself. Time away from questions. Time to be alone, to rest, to heal.

CHAPTER 13

Flavia Unzueta was a nightclub singer at the prestigious Club Macumba on Eighth Street. She wore her stage costumes with flair, and was now, at three in the morning, back home in her apartment, still attired in her heavy sequined dress and silver feathered headdress. She had presence on stage, and she danced well. The best thing that could be said about Flavia's voice, however, was that it was sincere. Sometimes when she sang "Happy Birthday" to a celebrant at the club, tears sprang to her eyes. She truly wished them happiness. And when she sang her disco version of "Born Free," everyone in the club knew why he had come to the United States. There were times when she would have liked to sing rock and roll, and sometimes salsa, but her thin soprano was more suited to the light pop her manager arranged for her. And the middle-aged Cuban professionals who frequented Club Macumba thought salsa too primitive and rock too modern. Flavia had been the star act at the club for three years. The only reason she ever got gigs outside the club was her manager's insistence that she play for "exposure," usually for free. She was scheduled to play at the upcoming Varadero Festival, and the anticipation of singing at such a large concert, headlined by the famous salsa singer Celia Cruz, was the only thing that had gotten her through her lonely weeks without Angel. She and her eight-piece backup band, known collectively as Flavia, practiced diligently. She had already conveniently forgotten that she wasn't being paid and that she was one of eleven warm-up acts for Cruz. Instead she and Cruz were onstage together, almost passing the mike between them.

But now she sat smoking a cigarette beneath her flammable feathers, humming "Yesterday." She missed Angel. She had much preferred Angel when getting his brother-in-law out of jail had been a hobby and not an obsession. Flavia had been his obsession then. They had been engaged for five years and renewed their betrothal each Christmas with champagne and a lavish exchange of jewelry. Before the boatlift, Angel spent most of his nights at Flavia's, returning to his condo in Kendall only for clean clothes and mail. He liked to keep the expensive condo pristine and found that the best way to do that was not to live there. Now he spent most of his nights in Key West. She missed him most at night, when she came home from work to the empty apartment.

Angel was her rock. Not at all like the American drummer she had been married to for eleven months when she was nineteen. Angel was hardworking, generous, and honest. Sometimes she didn't like the honest part: he cheated on her every few years and always told her about it. But at least, following Angel's line of reasoning, it was better than being made a fool of behind her back as she had been by her ex-husband.

She crushed the cigarette and headed for the shower. He had told her he'd be back tonight but if he hadn't come by three in the morning, she doubted he'd make it. She didn't really believe the boatlift was closed down for good this time. It had opened and closed so many times in the past four months. She hoped it was. It would be nice to have Angel home again. Besides, she couldn't imagine Carmela with one of those scrawny Marielitos she saw selling fruit and flowers on street corners. She left her stage clothes in a heap on the bathroom floor. Angel loved to watch her strip her gown off. She could do with some romance. Some roses too. There hadn't been flowers in her apartment since the boatlift began.

Her rock was sitting in the living room when she came out of the shower. His arm was in a cast to the elbow and his mind was fixed in a zone bordered by pain on one side and too many Tylenol with codeine on the other. The nurse in the emergency room had told him to take one pill every four hours. He was on his third and it hadn't been an hour and a half. The canvas sling which supported his broken hand covered his entire chest.

"You're hurt. My God. What happened?" Flavia said rushing to him.

"Why are you all wet again?" he answered.

"What?"

"When I called you this afternoon you were soaking wet on the phone, and look at you now." There was no doubt in his foggy mind—when Cuba was liberated and he went back there to the formal living room of his dreams he'd need someone much drier than Flavia. Someone who didn't walk around the house dripping wet, wrapped in a towel.

I need a map. I will ask them for a map. Do you remember the glove compartment, how many maps I had? Every time he goes around the corner in that new car, you said to your aunt, teasing me, he has his route all marked out on a map. That was so long ago, when I could only imagine getting lost within the perimeter of what I knew. I am outside those perimeters now. A map would tell me, of course. Everything would be marked clearly. Yellow for Cuba, bananas, and sunlight. Pink for the United States, I don't know why. Except when the U.S. map was delineated in states, then Florida was yellow like Cuba. I've never been here before. The light is like Cuba. They speak Spanish with a Cuban accent. It could also be another prison I've never been to before. We came by boat, but they could have brought us around to the other side of the island. Yes, I think it could be another prison but unlike any I know. It's round. Since you are not here, it could be prison too.

I don't know where I am. I can't tell anyone because they all know where they are, even to the point that they are weary of where they are. They are so certain of where they are that they are bored with their knowledge. I am so jealous of their knowledge. I can't even tell you, my Love, that I don't know where I am. It was I who knew the routes. You packed lunch. It is almost dawn. It looks as if it's going to be a lovely day for a ride. A map would clear this all up.

CHAPTER 14

Behind seat 18, upper bleachers, Luz Paz slammed the laundry bag down on the concrete. She heard a little crack, peered into the bag, put her handkerchief over her hand, and took the unmoving rat from the bag. With her hand still in the handkerchief, she twisted the rat's head off and poured the blood into a small silver bowl. She arranged the bowl and the rat's head next to three rose blossoms, a cup of café cubano, four pennies, and a cigar. She lit a candle and prayed before the small plastic statue of San Lázaro. She would have preferred chicken blood. But one made do. Her gods understood.

It was not yet morning. The sun began its ascent as Luz Paz began prayers for the soul of her daughter. She began formally as she always did, imploring San Lázaro's intercession with Christ and his Holy Mother to look kindly upon her daughter and to welcome her into the afterlife. But her formal prayers disintegrated as her grief poured forth. How could God have taken one so sweet, so young? How could he have let her die so far away from home? Please, San Lázaro, she begged, you walk back and forth between the dead and the living, bring word, tell me she didn't suffer.

She knelt until the pain in her legs refused to let her concentrate. The sun was already high. She heard no reply from San Lázaro. She packed her belongings into the laundry bag and started down the concrete steps.

She was dressed in white, swollen ankles stuffed into white nurse's shoes, white hair stuffed into white scarf, white blouse freshly stained with rat's blood. Around her wrinkled neck were beads of purple and white glass, San Lázaro's colors.

Luz Paz was tired. She was eighty-nine years old and suffered from high blood pressure and arthritis. She had made her journey from Cuba three months before to see her only daughter. But her daughter had already died. A kind nephew had shown her her daughter's grave and invited her into his house. But Luz Paz's grief could not be contained in the guest bedroom of her nephew's home. She took to wandering through the streets, screaming and crying. She wandered into the Orange Bowl one morning and was better able to deal with her grief in the large expanse of the football stadium. Her screams abated. Her tears dried to a palpable sadness. Her nephew came to see her on Sunday mornings but she would not leave with him.

The heat rose with the sun. She felt dizzy and slowed her gait on the four-yard line. The heat, she thought, as a man approached her. He looked like Lazarus frantic in daylight. Not the Lazarus she knew at all.

So many of them! San Lázaro thought as he watched Juan Raúl Pérez running towards Luz Paz. Who would have thought so many of them would come undone? Their resurrections burdened them more surely than the grave. San Lázaro barely had time to hear all their petitions, let alone answer so many prayers. Yet he had spent all morning telling Luz Paz that her daughter had not suffered. Her grief made her deaf to his words. Perhaps he needed to get someone else to tell her. He liked her very much. Everyone else brought San Lázaro water, it was traditional, but she brought him café cubano, and in times like these, with so many of them to take care of, he needed the caffeine.

CHAPTER 15

Dottie looked over the clothes in the donation box from Kinloch Park High. She found a red jumpsuit for herself and a T-shirt for Juan Raúl Pérez. There was no food there. She was hungry. There was food from the vendors in the parking lot, but it wasn't free like the dinner the night before and she had no money. Over by the tents she found a young man selling sundries from a supermarket shopping cart. There was gum, granola bars, flip-flops. She would have liked a pair of the flip-flops. They had thick cushion soles, and her feet hurt from her black patent-leather spikes. She refused to wear her brown sandals. Not in Miami.

"Do you have any samples?" she asked the young man.

"No," he said.

"Any compacts?"

No, he didn't and he didn't know what compacts were.

"I can probably get you some," he said. "I go downtown for supplies several times a week."

There was nail polish, a dozen or so bottles beneath a box of sanitary napkins. She examined the bottles one by one: A Dream of Cerise, Cherries in the Snow, Flamingo Pink, and a sparkling gold labeled Brass Band. She didn't know what the English words meant.

"How much is the nail polish?" she asked.

"A dollar," he said.

"I don't know what that means."

"Four quarters, ten dimes. A regular dollar."

"How much compared to Cuban money?"

"Well, comparing inflation rates—"

"No. I don't know inflation rates. What does a dollar buy?"

"About a loaf of bread."

"A loaf of bread. One dollar," Dottie said.

"OK, OK, I'll give you two bottles for a dollar."

Two bottles of nail polish for a loaf of bread. She tried to keep her composure. "I'll be back," she said.

Her hunger left just as surely as if she had eaten that loaf of bread. Two bottles of the most beautiful nail polish for the price of a loaf of bread. Dottie knew exactly where she was—in the land of plenty. Sparkling golden plenty. She had already held it in her hands.

Dottie was a lucky person. There hadn't yet been a disaster, in her life of disasters, to convince her otherwise. At the moment she was one of 374 applicants standing in line for one job as a dishwasher at a downtown Steak & Egg Kitchen.

At the moment, she was one of nine hundred homeless refugees living at the Orange Bowl in a section of town where the other refugees had already warned her it was dangerous to be out on the street.

She had arrived the afternoon before, leading Juan Raúl Pérez by the hand. She spent the afternoon and the better part of the evening waiting in long lines, only to find out that government assistance had been cut off weeks before for newly arriving refugees. The social services people who would try to find Juan Raúl Pérez's relatives had a waiting list of over two weeks before they could even speak with him to obtain the information needed to begin the search. Over at the desk where she entered their names on the waiting list for sponsors, Señor and Señora Pérez were number

287 in line. Not bad, Dottie decided. If she hadn't had the good luck to get married the day before she would have been a lot farther down the list than that and Juan Raúl Pérez would have been close to the last. Families were sponsored first, then couples, then singles.

By the time she had finished with the lines, including the line for the one free meal distributed each day at the Orange Bowl, it had been too late to get cots for the night. They had slept in the bleachers.

There had been lines like this in Cuba. She hoped there wouldn't be a line at the nightclub of her dreams whenever she got there. But as she stood on line for the dishwashing job at Steak & Egg, there was only one thought on her mind: she could buy two bottles of nail polish for the price of a loaf of bread. All she needed was one dollar.

Dottie didn't get the job.

CHAPTER 16

Juan Raúl Pérez had always assumed that people who were disoriented didn't know they were disoriented. He, on the other hand, was very aware that he was disoriented, and it increased his anxiety. He had stealthily watched an elderly woman in a print housedress for over an hour that morning. He had seen her sitting on a lawn chair under a banyan tree in the west lot. She was reading a book. He wondered if she was his wife. Hadn't his wife loved to read? Wouldn't she be waiting for him someplace cool? But after strolling by her several times and receiving no hint of recognition from her, he decided to wait before introducing himself as her long-lost husband. He waited until he found Dottie and then casually, very casually, said to Dottie, "You know, that woman reading over there reminds me a little of my wife."

"How old is your wife?" Dottie said.

"Fifty-one," he said.

"Well, I don't mean to insult your wife," Dottie said, "but that woman looks old enough to be your grandmother."

"I only meant that my wife likes to read," he said. Yes, he saw clearly now that the woman was too old to be his wife. It was only that she was reading and he was losing his mind.

Dottie gave him two assignments before she went to apply for the dishwasher job. The first was to get them cots and a tent and a place to put them so they wouldn't have to spend another uncomfortable night in the bleachers. Juan Raúl Pérez failed in that mission. He found out easily enough to whom he should go with his request. He had only to ask one of the guards or to go to the security office. But approaching a guard or going to the office of the authorities was beyond him. Guards were the ones to be avoided at all costs, he had learned in the last twenty years. And going to an office had been restricted to interrogations.

"I don't think there are any cots left," he told Dottie.

Her next assignment was for him to go back to the line for social services to find out if their names had been moved up on the list for an interview and what it would take for that to happen. "We need to find your wife as soon as possible," she told him. But he couldn't remember which line they had waited in for social services the afternoon before. Back and forth he wandered between the lines through the hot morning, his bell-bottoms flapping and his Hawaiian shirt soaked through with sweat. Then he forgot about social services altogether, remembering only that it was important to find his wife as soon as possible. But what did she look like if she didn't look like the old woman who was sitting under the banyan tree reading? He tried to remember her as he had every day for twenty years. It was not as easy recalling the face he had created with so many other faces around him now. He tried to remember her hair, cut short five years ago, her teeth, her tits, her toes, ten of them. One two three . . .

I'm moving away from reality, he thought with a frightening clarity. But that was impossible, since he didn't know what reality was at the moment. He was tired. He had had a bed in prison. He was hungry. They brought him food in prison. The last thing he clearly remembered was being awoken in prison and being so sure he was going to be executed. Put up against the wall and shot. He wanted to lie down on a bed and feel for his pulse. The longer Dottie stayed away, the harder it became to remember where he was and why he hadn't died.

Over by the fence in the west lot there was a man in dark sunglasses teaching English for Beginners. He rested on the ground there for a while repeating numbers in English. He left when the teacher switched to phrases. Behind the tents, a slender woman in a pink leotard led an aerobics class. She reminded him of a slender bird about take flight. But he was certain she was too young to be his wife and too fair to be his daughter. He skirted the periphery of the Orange Bowl. He saw several women with short gray hair and flowered housedresses, but none of them resembled the image he couldn't remember of his wife. One of the women smiled a sad face and offered him good day but it still wasn't his wife. Where was Dottie? Perhaps she could remember his wife for him. His mouth was dry. He needed to wait in the line for the water fountain again. In front of him, he saw Luz Paz shuffling slowly across the playing field, and his heart stopped. They were executing people here too. She was staggering and the front of her white blouse, where they had aimed at her heart, was smeared with blood.

"Buenos días," she said to him.

He pressed his hands to her bloody chest. He held her head when she fell. "Why did they shoot you?" he asked her over and over again. "Why?"

CHAPTER 17

Attempting to remove herself from Juan
Raúl Pérez's groping hands, Luz Paz sat down on the grass.
He knelt beside her and put his arm around her to support
her back, which did not need supporting. Luz Paz was bigger than Juan Raúl Pérez, but she hesitated to slug him because he seemed so fragile, and his words so strange.
"Please tell me you're not going to die," he said. "Why? Why
did they shoot you?"

She twisted and pushed him away. "Let go of me. No one
shot me. What are you talking about?" she said.

"The blood," he said, pointing to the splash on her blouse,
which had already dried to a mud-colored stain. "The blood
where they shot you."

"That's not my blood!"

There wasn't time for much commotion. Dottie had been
keeping an eye out for Juan Raúl Pérez as she waited on her
various lines. She was between them quickly, got as much
of the story as she could while helping Luz Paz to her feet,
and tried to straighten out Juan Raúl Pérez.

"Please excuse my husband, señora," she said. "He was a
political prisoner and he's still jumpy. And there is the
bloodstain on the front of your blouse."

"It's rat's blood. I just told you. I sacrificed a rat for the
soul of my little girl," Luz Paz said.

"Yes, I understand. But you can see why he thought you were injured."

"Did a rat bite you, señora?" Juan Raúl Pérez asked. "Shall I send for help?"

"Be quiet," Dottie told him. "Didn't you hear her say she sacrificed a rat for her daughter, who died?"

He had heard. He didn't understand. People killed rats, they didn't sacrifice them.

"I need to sit back down," the old woman said. "I need to rest a minute."

Dottie helped the old woman up several steps to seats in the lower deck. She sent Juan Raúl Pérez for a glass of water. The old woman was out of breath, and Dottie took her hand and waited quietly as her breathing settled to a slow rhythm.

"I'm sorry about your daughter, señora," she said. "She is lucky to have a mother to pray for her. Was it long ago?"

"A few months ago."

"How old was your daughter, señora? You said your little girl."

"Seventy-two. I guess that's old enough to die. She had a stroke. But you see, she was still my daughter, will always be my little girl."

Dottie patted the old woman's hand. Dottie couldn't imagine anyone old enough to have a little girl of seventy-two. "Well, at least she didn't suffer," she said.

The old woman snatched her hand from Dottie and turned to her. "How do you know? Why do you say that?"

Dottie wasn't sure why she had said that. "My mother had tuberculosis. She got pneumonia. It took a long time for her to die. I don't even like to think about it. She was in pain for a long time. I think from a stroke, you just fall over and die."

They sat in silence for a moment as they watched Juan Raúl Pérez approach. He had a paper cup balanced in his left hand and stared at it, mouth agape, with the concentration of a juggler. Dottie had a sip after the old woman drank.

"You'll have to give me that blouse, señora," she said, "so I can rinse the blood out before it sets too long." Before Dottie worked the sugar fields, she had done her share of laundry at the Havana Hilton. "My name is Dottie, never Dorita ever again. And this is my husband, Señor Pérez."

Juan Raúl Pérez bowed to Luz Paz. A discreet bow, a bow of a gentleman. Ridiculous, given the circumstances, Luz Paz thought. She gave her name, and he bowed again.

"I am honored to make your acquaintance, Señora Paz," he said. "I am sorry if I startled you before. When I saw the blood . . . and you seemed to be staggering."

"I'm a fat old lady with arthritis. It's a long walk."

"Yes, of course, I beg your pardon. I would still be happy to send for help."

"For help? Who do you think would come? Just let me sit for a minute to catch my breath."

Luz Paz noticed he was trembling. Compared to his healthy-looking wife, he looked skeletal. A transparent pallor lingered beneath his sunburned skull. A political prisoner, the wife had said. "Never mind. It was an honest mistake." She turned to Dottie. "I don't remember seeing either of you around here before."

"No, we just got here yesterday," Dottie said.

"Where are your cots set up?" Luz Paz asked.

"We didn't know where to get them. My husband checked today and wasn't able to get any. But we don't plan on staying here long."

"No one does."

"But my husband has relatives in the U.S."

Yes, Luz Paz thought, everyone is waiting for a rich relative to come to the rescue.

"And if they can't come for us," Dottie continued, "we're going to get a sponsor."

Now the truth comes out—the relative doesn't want them but they think some unknown sponsor does. Luz Paz saw hundreds waiting like them everyday. She felt sorry for them. "Well, perhaps I could show you where you can get cots in case you'd like to rest for a minute or two before those relatives come for you."

They didn't get a tent. Dottie displayed considerable charm for the security guard who opened the door to the storeroom, but they still didn't get a tent; there was a long waiting list. They did get two cots and at Luz Paz's invitation set them by hers in Gate 14, the large concrete hallway at the main entrance of the stadium. Gate 14 was the only gate open to the refugees, and all of them, except those with tents to set up on the peripheral stadium grounds, lived there. It was airless and crowded, but Luz Paz had a choice alcove under a ramp. Her age and connection with the gods was respected.

Dottie, who insisted on washing the blood from Luz Paz's blouse, earned her dollar for nail polish. Not from the old woman—Dottie wouldn't take any money from Luz Paz. But there were others Dottie met as she washed the blouse in the women's showers who were willing to pay a quarter to have a load of laundry washed. By the time Luz Paz's blouse dried, Dottie had a small laundry business. San Lázaro couldn't change the world but he didn't forget Luz Paz's friends. He was glad Dottie had decided to stay by the old woman. Luz Paz had been too lonely, and perhaps now she would believe that her daughter hadn't suffered. San Lázaro understood rat sacrifices when chickens were scarce. It had taken Luz Paz hours to check her rattraps with her legs so swollen and her body so grief-stricken.

CHAPTER 18

Take those clothes off, señor. There is just enough light to dry them if I wash them now."

"What?" Juan Raúl Pérez asked. For a moment he could not remember who Dottie was, let alone why she would speak to him. He had been sleeping since Dottie had set up his cot. Luz Paz had given him a clean sheet with small flowers on it. It hadn't been a comfortable sleep. He was hungry. It was hot. And although their cots were out of the way of the central traffic of Gate 14, there were still many voices and footsteps. On an overturned milk crate at the head of Luz Paz's cot were the gods of Santeria, disguised as they had been for centuries as Catholic saints. Juan Raúl Pérez eyed the bright porcelain and plastic statues with suspicion. These were the gods of the uneducated, or at least those not educated in the schools he had been. As a child, he had been both frightened and curious of Santería—he saw it as a mixture of voodoo and passion very unlike the rote rules of his catechism. It had been difficult for him to rest with the eyes of the statues so close to his sleep.

Dottie walked him over to the men's showers, quizzing him as they went.

"Did you check at social services to see if our names have been moved up on the list?" she asked.

"No," he said.

"Señor, you haven't forgotten your promise to take me with you as your cousin if your wife comes for you? You haven't forgotten our plan?"

"No, señora, I remember. But she isn't here."

"Please call me Dottie. Are you getting along with the old woman?"

"Yes, why shouldn't I?"

"Well, I just wanted to know. You practically knocked her down this morning. I understand it was a mistake, but it was strange. You should stop acting strange."

They were at the showers. She waited outside while he changed. There was a pair of track shorts and a sleeveless T-shirt reading "L'Hair," a beauty salon in Coconut Grove. This was the third change of clothing in as many days after virtually wearing the same clothes for twenty years, and it felt strange. He sat for a moment in the hope that the strange feeling from the new clothes would wear off. Yes, he had to stop acting strange, even if he was wearing strange clothes in a football stadium with a strange woman for a wife.

"You are too skinny, señor," she said when he finally exited and handed Dottie his Hawaiian shirt and blue jeans. "But you have some muscles left for an old man." She smiled and flowed away in her polka-dot dress.

Luz Paz was sitting on her cot when he returned to Gate 14. She thought of chickens when she saw Juan Raúl Pérez in his track clothes.

"You must have been in prison for many years, señor," she said.

"Yes, señora, twenty."

"I will pray for you."

"Gracias, señora. Do you know where I can get a map?"

"No. Do you know what happens to people who die of strokes?"

"No. I'm sorry, señora, I don't."

Juan Raúl Pérez lay down on his cot. No map. But at least he was sure he had been in prison for many years. Now he was in a football stadium in Miami and his wife wasn't here. He could write her another letter, perhaps one he could send her this time. He had had paper and pen the night before, but now he couldn't remember where they were. His wife would have a map. She would know where to find him.

He looked at his prone white legs till he got to his simulated-leather oxfords. They were big for him and had rubbed blisters on both heels. The shoes made him think of Sunday mornings when he and his wife and daughter went to church. His oxfords had been made of real leather then and fit his feet comfortably. They had a car, but Corpus Cristi Church wasn't far and it was pleasant to walk on Sunday mornings. He could see his wife's face clearly now, as it had looked twenty years ago. He could see his own face too. It was smiling with a full set of teeth. His thick curly hair had been pomaded back with a slight scent of peppermint. And he could see the brown leather oxfords he wore and the blue suit over a strong body of a man in his prime. It was breezy. On the steps of the church his wife laughed and held down her skirt blown up by the wind. His daughter's hand was in his. It was a lovely morning. He almost screamed in anger as someone shook his shoulders and said, "Take off those clothes now, señor."

He was still tired, and he was angry about being awakened so abruptly again. But he was used to following rules and took his clothes off where he stood. Once naked, his anger turned to shame. His skin was so white and shriveled. His body so aged and shrunken. There was no longer any hair on his head or teeth in his mouth. He wanted to reach for his pulse as he had always done when waking from his dreams but he felt such a gesture would only attract attention to his nakedness.

"This way," a man said. He had never seen the man before. He was wearing a blue suit and he was young, with a quick step. He followed him out Gate 14. It was already dark. The man led him out to the street. It was the first time Juan Raúl Pérez had been out on a Miami street. He had felt much safer in the smaller prison of freedom in the Orange Bowl. It wasn't dark enough to cover his naked body, and he was torn between wanting to stop and cover himself and doing as he was told by following the man in the blue suit. Was this someone from social services? Would he take him to his wife? He had to walk quickly to keep up with him. But as quickly as he walked, he soon lost him in the maze of numbered streets. He turned a corner finally and saw the man, standing under a streetlight leaning casually against a white wall. The man lit a cigarette.

"Please move, señor," Juan Raúl Pérez told him. "They will shoot you standing against the wall like that."

"No, señor, they will not shoot me. Even if I told them to shoot me, they would not. I will show you. Listen. Fire," the man said. "You see, no one has fired. Fire! FIRE!"

Louder he yelled it, louder and louder. FIRE! echoing through the deserted streets of night. FIRE! echoing from streetlamp to streetlamp. FIRE! echoing off the concrete walls of Gate 14.

"You know, they really should debrief these guys," security guard Esteban Santiesteban said to Luz Paz as he helped her shake Juan Raúl Pérez awake. Juan Raúl Pérez stopped screaming and sat trembling with his hand to his pulse.

A few onlookers had tried to help Luz Paz wake her neighbor from his nightmare. They dispersed as soon as the guard came.

"Are you awake now, señor?" Esteban Santiesteban said to Juan Raúl Pérez. "Are you OK?"

"Yes, señor, yes. Thank you for your help."

"No problem. You were really screaming. I'm glad it's early, you didn't wake anybody."

"What time is it?"

"Six p.m."

And Juan Raúl Pérez added "six p.m." to the numbers he counted over and over in his mind to unfreeze his nightmare.

Santiesteban turned to Luz Paz. "You know I've already

warned you about the candles and the incense, señora. I
don't want to think about what a fire would do in a place
like this."

Luz Paz licked her fingers and snuffed the candles out
with a quick pinch. She poured some rose water into the
small dish of burning incense. Esteban Santiesteban left to
finish his rounds.

Luz Paz took the silver bowl with the water in it and set it
on the floor under Juan Raúl Pérez's green army cot. "This
will capture spirits who are thirsty for your dreams," she
said. "And we will put rose petals in it to sweeten your
dreams too."

Juan Raúl Pérez slowly counted as Luz Paz plucked the
petals one by one from a withered pink rose lying at the feet
of San Lázaro.

"They play dominoes at night, señor. In the daytime too. I
will show you where. The men there look like you. Perhaps
they also have the same dreams."

He didn't want to leave without Dottie, but he followed
the old woman out Gate 14 anyway. It wasn't dark yet. He
was still in his track shorts and felt more naked in them
than he had in his dream.

CHAPTER 19

The lights were long and bright over the folding card tables in the west lot. The castanet click of dominoes crescendoed and fell through the warm night. The black dots of numbers danced from their white blocks, each marionette step placed by a quick shadow of hand. There was music from a distant radio. He couldn't see them, but Juan Raúl Pérez was certain there were people dancing somewhere. Was Dottie by the radio, and if she needed a partner, would she pull a stranger from the crowd? He hadn't seen her since the afternoon, when she had taken his clothes to wash. Perhaps she had given the clothes to someone else.

He played dominoes with the old men Luz Paz had introduced him to. They passed their stories around the domino table like a bottle of whiskey. Their scars of bravery were illuminated by the floodlights. He had no brave tale to match theirs. They had aimed rifles at Fidel Castro and led men through high mountains and wide streets. They had sabotaged the machinery of dictatorship and proclaimed words of freedom. And what had he done—been in the wrong place at the wrong time, a crime punishable by twenty years? Or had the money his brother-in-law sent regularly made him a valuable prisoner? Large sums his brother-in-law sent, according to his wife, money for bribes, money for cigarettes. None of it had ever reached him. He had begged his wife not to send money, to tell Angel not to send money, but his letters might not have reached their destination either. He wasn't sure. There was always another explanation—that he had simply been forgotten. And it was not a wise idea, in the prisons he had been in, to make oneself known.

"Twenty years, señor?" they asked him. "Twenty years you were in prison?"

"How do you know that?" he asked. Was there something in his manner of domino playing that told them twenty years? Was it the same strangeness Dottie had warned him about?

"Señora Paz said so when she introduced you."

"Yes, twenty years," he said, and prayed they'd ask him no more questions. If they did, he'd try not to hear. He tried to remember his wife's face but it was only a voice. Come here and be with us, the voice called. He had come but she wasn't here. Perhaps he hadn't made it to the other side of his dreams. He tried to remember Dottie's face, but it was only a smile. So he counted. The numbers were so easy to count here, they were only little dots, not eyes or arms, not years or hours. When the game was over, he sat and smoked the cigar he had won for winning. He blew large smoke rings from his toothless mouth and counted stars.

CHAPTER 20

Dottie lined four bottles of nail polish next to the gods on Luz Paz's milk crate. There were Flamingo Pink and Dreams of Cerise, Tropical Mango and Brass Band. It was Brass Band, a shiny copper infused with gold sparkles, that held her enchanted.

Dottie combed out Luz Paz's long white hair and gave her a manicure with Dreams of Cerise. Dottie liked Luz Paz, not that she reminded Dottie of her own grandmother but of a grandmother, and any hint of family in a strange land comforts. The old woman talked about her dead daughter, asking Dottie to repeat again and again that no, her daughter hadn't suffered when she died. While Dottie did her own nail stubs in Brass Band the idea of adopting more family came to her.

"What's your last name again, Señora Luz?" she asked Luz Paz.

"Paz," she answered.

What a shame it wasn't Pérez, Dottie thought. She wouldn't have minded adding Luz Paz as an extra relative. If Dottie's name had been moved up halfway on the waiting list for sponsors by being married, surely her name would move farther up on the list if she had a grandmother too. Just as well Luz Paz wasn't a Pérez, though—Dottie might have had to explain too much to her.

Dottie waved her hands through the air to dry the coats of gold on her hands. She had done laundry all afternoon and most of the night. That there was such an endless stream of hot water in the women's showers delighted her. Her hands were red and raw to her elbows, though, and she asked the young man she bought the nail polish from to get her hand cream for tomorrow. She had made several purchases with the money she had earned, including the nail polish, and her pockets were still heavy with quarters. She couldn't imagine how much better the real Miami was if already here in the Orange Bowl she had money, gold nails, hot water, and a new friend like Luz Paz.

Juan Raúl Pérez entered Gate 14 and watched her as she swung her hands through the air like a furious conductor of the brass band adorning her nails.

"What are you doing?" he whispered so as not to disturb Luz Paz, who was already lost in prayer by the nail polish and the gods.

"Drying my nails. What else would I be doing?"

She smiled at him, showed him her sparkling fingertips. He grunted.

"Is it because of your teeth that you hardly ever smile?" she asked.

"No," he said. Couldn't she understand twenty years in prison was enough to make a man frown with or without his teeth?

"Did you check at social services to find out about an interview to find your relative?"

"No, señora."

"Is it your teeth? Maybe you don't want to see her till you've gained some weight and gotten some teeth, or you don't think she's waited?"

"No, no, no."

"Shhh," she scolded, nodding her head towards Luz Paz. "Don't get excited. And feel my hips."

Juan Raúl Pérez stared at Dottie's Cuban-madonna hips and felt weak.

"Go on, feel my hips. My nails are wet and I can't put my hands in my pockets."

He stared at her blankly. Why was she doing this to him? "Feel my pockets, please. Oh, forget it. I just wanted you to feel how much money I made doing laundry today. It costs people two quarters at the coin laundry, so I do it for one. I had a lot of business, and there will be more tomorrow. I might make enough to buy you some teeth."

He did smile this time, relieved that it was only change in her pockets she wanted felt and not the caress of the salsa hips which had pressed against him on the boat, when the sky was blue and he had not realized he was so old.

"There," she said, "it doesn't look all that bad when you smile with your mouth empty like that."

Dottie would have slept soundly if she could have calmed down long enough to try. The lights, though dimmed, stayed on all night under Gate 14. Luz Paz murmured in her sleep and Juan Raúl Pérez snored. He seemed less strange to her now that she interpreted his bumping into Luz Paz as another bit of good luck. She lay facedown on the narrow cot and dangled her arms over the side so she wouldn't smudge her nails. It was an uncomfortable position and she was uncomfortable trying to lie still when the world seemed so much better to her than yesterday. She got up quietly and left Gate 14. Perhaps she could find another relative if she looked. Or perhaps she could find teeth.

CHAPTER 21

Felipe headed downtown on the dark side of dawn. He would have preferred South Beach, but even at this hour he was lying low. His two friends who had come with him from Cuba were already in jail. When they had first come to Miami, he and his friends had sold pot on the streets of South Beach and cocaine when they could get it. Felipe had escaped over a back-alley wall two months before, but his two friends hadn't been so quick. One was in jail in Atlanta, last he heard, awaiting deportation back to Cuba. The other was in Miami, still awaiting trial. It scared the hell out of Felipe; he had heard about the conditions of the overcrowded jails in the United States and didn't want to think about what would happen to those sent back to Cuba. Felipe got out of the drug business immediately. He wished that he had never found how easy the money was there. They hadn't been big-timers, but when they could get hold of the stuff, it wasn't difficult to sell. His friend now awaiting deportation had had seven hundred dollars of Felipe's on him when he got caught, and there had been another two hundred of Felipe's money at their apartment. He hadn't gone back to the apartment for the money or anything else. The couple they had sold the coke to had identified themselves as undercover police, and it was all too clear to him that the bullet that had whizzed by his left shoulder as he climbed that alley wall was real. He had had his three-piece white John Travolta disco suit on when he heard that bullet's whiz. The image of blood spreading over the white suit was still vivid in his mind. He pictured it spreading in concentric circles. He hadn't worn the still-lily-white suit since. The suit was too new for a stain, and he was too young to die. For six weeks after that, he slept on park benches and back alleys. When the Orange Bowl reopened he went there, cautiously at first until he was certain neither the cops nor the guards there paid him any particular attention. He felt safe there, but he still only went in the vicinity of South Beach when he was feeling especially brave. He'd duck in the nearest doorway if he saw a cop there, convinced they were still looking for him. But the only description the police had had two months before on the third suspect fleeing the scene of the crime was of a young Latin male in a three-piece white suit. Felipe couldn't have picked a better disguise.

Felipe missed South Beach desperately. He missed going dancing all night at the Electric Tropic disco and sometimes getting laid afterwards. But he missed the long afternoons the most, sitting on the seawall with his buddies watching beautiful girls in crocheted bikinis with St. Tropez tans drive by in red Mustangs. He remembered their hair blown back by the wind, their faces smiling at him. Women did smile at Felipe. He was very handsome. He had shiny dark hair that fell over his eyes at the most appropriate times. He had a child's easy smile and large dark-lashed eyes that held a practiced balance of laughter and astonishment. He had a prime-time eighteen-year-old body that never missed a beat on the disco floor.

He would get back to those St. Tropez girls in the red Mustangs. At the moment he was a businessman, and his business was doing well. He ran it from a Winn-Dixie shopping cart in the west end of the Orange Bowl. He bought his merchandise at discount stores or on the street or shoplifted when he could: cigarettes, clothes, perfume, Chiclets, soap, cheap watches with fake brand names. The week before he had made a killing on granola bars, and this week he had two hundred pairs of rubber flip-flops, which were moving well. Felipe was good at what he did. At eighteen years of age, he already had ten years of experience from the Havana black market. And except for five months in a juvenile detention hall in Cuba when he was eleven and the bullet that had missed him two months before, he had managed to stay out of trouble.

There had been rare occasions at the Orange Bowl when he had enough money saved to get out of there and get a room downtown. But a room wasn't what he had in mind. He wanted a nice apartment with a balcony overlooking the beach, and he wanted a nice car. He also saw too many things in the shop windows when he went downtown and kept buying them for himself: a Sound Delight ghetto blaster, white simulated-eelskin loafers, a heavy gold link bracelet. He justified these purchases by telling himself that he'd sell them if the price was right. He was really trying to save now. But he had had a good day and the money he had made had been burning a hole in his pocket all night. He had sold a box of Ivory soap to a new face for three dollars and fifty cents. Then he sold her a pair of men's track shorts for three dollars and later four bottles of nail polish for two dollars, pure profit, since he had gotten the shorts for free from a box of donated clothing and he had lifted the polish. She paid for everything in quarters, but it was better than the pennies and nickels he sometimes received. Tomorrow, she had told him, she wanted to buy a manicure kit she had seen in his cart. He had priced the kit at fifteen dollars for her, and she hadn't blinked an eye. And the speed with which that woman moved laundry in and out of the woman's showers made him believe she'd have more than fifteen dollars to spend tomorrow. Then around midnight she had come by again to ask him if he could get her a pair of dentures and more nail polish.

Aside from the pure profit he had garnered from Dottie,

Felipe decided Dottie was OK. He was even going to reduce that manicure kit for her to ten dollars, maybe eight; it had cost him three at Harold's Values. She was full of energy and fire. She immediately appealed to him as the mother he should have had. He was only eighteen, and although he'd never have admitted it to himself, he was very homesick. Some days he spent hours down at Mi Cafeteria over on Eighth Street talking to a fifty-year-old waitress named María who also reminded him of his mother. There were many nights he wished he'd never left Cuba. After his friends went to jail and he was left on the streets alone, his dream of being rich in the United States was frequently interrupted by longing for the life he had left behind. There he had been a big fish in a little black-market pond. Here he was nothing. He wanted to climb the steps late at night to the apartment at home in Cuba, where his mother left the pot on the stove. Where his mother kept the cookie tin filled with yellowed photos. "Before the revolution," his mother said a hundred times a day.

"Before the revolution, we had meat every day.

"Before the revolution, we used to dance.

"Before the revolution, we went to church."

Before the revolution, God had been in heaven and all had been right with the world.

Except that before the revolution, his mother had been poorer, but that's not how she remembered it, because at least she had dreams then. Felipe's father would remind her. He said that before the revolution, they had nothing but dreams. And then his father would go to bed leaving behind him the smell of shoe dye and leather glue from the shop where he worked. Felipe had no memories of life before the revolution; he hadn't been born. But that's why he had left Cuba for the U.S., because if life meant working twelve hours a day as his parents did, he wanted a shiny car to show for it. He wanted life lived in color, without a cookie tin of black-and-white memories.

The simulated-eelskin loafers echoed the fragile steps of

one man in an empty city. Miami's downtown nightlife had ended hours earlier. An all-night cafeteria off Biscayne loomed like a dilapidated bridge to the morning. A man in a well-cut suit stood on the pavement beside the cafeteria's sidewalk coffee window with three woman in evening clothes. They were laughing and speaking too loud, too fast—cocaine-induced, Felipe judged. They ignored Felipe as he stopped beside them and ordered a coffee. Just to stand next to someone in the emptiness. It helped that he stood next to a woman with pale shoulders in a blue satin dress. Her perfume was rich but not subtle, and Felipe could almost taste it as he drank his shot of Cuban coffee. They left without a word to him, but he was sure the woman had smiled in his direction. He picked up the twenty they had left for their bill before the gray-haired waitress saw it and he used it to pay their bill and his own. There was eighteen dollars change, and he tipped the waitress a dollar. Rather generous, he thought, since she hadn't been very friendly.

He found an open bar two blocks away with piped-in dance music and danced two tracks with a woman in a silver jumpsuit. The bars were nicer over on South Beach, he decided, and the women better-looking. He bought her a drink but made his exit when she asked him for another. Even if he got lucky, he didn't have any place to take her home to.

Dawn came and went with little recognition from Felipe. He noticed more cars on the street, more people on the sidewalks, and the echo from his footsteps faded.

His favorite cafeteria opened at seven, and he arrived shortly afterwards and had a large plate of eggs and sausages. María waited on him with her usual motherly fuss. How handsome he looked. How well Miami must be treating him. How nicely he was dressed. Had he been out with a date?

"No, I just got dressed up for you," he told her.

"I don't believe you," she said.

María had also come over on the boatlift, to meet her brother, who owned the cafeteria. Her life in Miami was going well. He left her a ten-dollar tip and walked back to the Orange Bowl ready for the day—it hadn't been an exciting night, but at least it hadn't cost him anything.

CHAPTER 22

Carmela Pérez sat at the kitchen table over a sheet of air-weight paper with her silver Cross pen. The pen had been a Christmas gift from Teresa three years before. She used it only to write to her husband. It was the second day in a row she had called in sick to work. The flu, she told them. She hated herself for lying. Her friend Ileana, the one who took scuba lessons, had asked her to dinner. Carmela turned down the invitation, again using the flu as her excuse. Her neighbor at the end of the block had asked if she wanted to go shopping, and again Carmela begged off. Nor did Carmela understand why she was extending her lie to people outside work; it wasn't as if she ever ran into the people she worked with in this section of town. She hated herself for being unable to cope. Hated that she now felt worse than she ever had when she really had the flu. And there was that nagging self-fulfilling prophecy she had had in her head since the boatlift began—that if she wasn't able to do the routine things now that she had been doing for so many years, she would crumble apart into more pieces than could be put together. That's why she was writing to her husband. She was going to do something constructive, something to prove that her thoughts could still be organized. She studied the blank sheet of paper and then began to erase the emptiness with her large round script.

After perfunctory opening salutations, she wrinkled up the paper and tossed it in the garbage. She took another sheet and studied the emptiness anew.

She didn't get up to open the door when she heard Angel's car turn in the driveway. And she made a big show of opening the locks after he rang the bell. If he didn't like the fact that she didn't have a gun aimed at him when the door finally swung open, it was too bad. She walked back to the kitchen without giving him the chance to voice his complaint.

He followed her and apologized. He stroked the plaster cast on his arms several times as he spoke. She accepted his apology, told him she was sorry about his arm, and once again thanked him profusely for all the efforts he had made. She made him coffee and told him how much she hoped things would now start returning to normal. He agreed and said that things would definitely start returning to normal, as soon as the new burglar-alarm system that he was having installed in her house was working. She wouldn't be able to accidentally leave the door open after its installation. He'd be able to stop worrying about her then, he said.

She didn't want him worrying. She didn't want him bothering her. She didn't say yes but it didn't matter. The Freedom from Worry/Total Protection Company arrived not ten minutes later.

"You look tired," Angel told her. "Why don't you just rest. I'll take care of them."

She tried to get back to the blank pages of the letter, but from the kitchen window she could hear Angel shouting orders. Strangers called back to him. The shouting ran through her nerves like a live current. She got up from the kitchen table. She wanted to leave the house, but the only place she could think of going to was the doctor's office, and she didn't need the doctor to tell her she really didn't have the flu.

Maybe I should visit my travel agent to browse through brochures for my fantasy vacation, she thought. Then she leaned against the wall in the hallway where she was walking and wondered if she was losing her mind. She didn't have a travel agent, let alone a fantasy vacation. Maybe she should go to the doctor to find out that she didn't have the flu but that she was losing her mind. They were still shouting outside the kitchen window, and now there were power tools, high and shrill. As she paced she remembered where the nonsense about the fantasy vacation and the travel agent had come from; she had read it in a women's magazine in the waiting room of the doctor's office. Which visit or which magazine, she didn't know.

Take a herbal bath—it's comforting, the article also recommended.

Buy yourself a piece of fun jewelry—you're worth it!

Flirt with a handsome stranger!

Start an exercise program!

The title of the article had been another imperative, she recalled: "Nerves on Edge—Take a Break!" or something along those lines. The shouting from outside the window grew louder. What kind of fun jewelry could replace a husband? she wondered. But the idea of a scented bath was appealing. Perhaps she should comfort herself until life returned to normal.

It took a few minutes to find the perfumed bath oil she had received months before during a store promotion for Chanel. Next to the tub, she laid out towels, a bathrobe, and a copy of *Hola*, which Teresa subscribed to. Then she remembered another one of the suggestions from the waiting room and set up Teresa's portable radio on the vanity. Listen to classical music—it adds class! The steamy perfumed water was lovely on her skin, and the Spanish gossip magazine, which concentrated on European royalty, offered a moment's escape. WTMI drowned out the power tools from the other side of the house. But it wasn't five minutes before she heard voices coming closer and she barely had the shower curtain pulled around before a face peered through the window—a stranger, but certainly not the type one would flirt with even in the land of magazines. Soon there were more voices and she had to don the bathrobe behind the curtain as the water ran out.

She just had time to throw on clothes in her bedroom before the voices came to that window. Nor was the possibility of starting an exercise program in the living room available. She went back to the kitchen, sat bolt upright, and wrote pages of opening salutations to her husband.

CHAPTER 23

So this is prison, Carmela thought, as Angel, smiling, gave her a tour of her now free-from-worry house.

White curlicued bars adorned all the windows and doors. With the "B" system on, a light sensor at front and back doors activated a buzzer inside the house long before a caller or burglar could ring the doorbell. Weight-sensitive netting on the roof also activated the same buzzer.

"What if a bird lights on the roof?" Carmela asked her brother.

"It'll only activate for over forty pounds."

What about a grenade or a little bomb? Carmela wondered to herself and felt that she was truly losing her mind to be considering such a possibility.

Timers of selected indoor lights, radio, and TV were rotated on and off when the "A" system was on. The "A" system also activated four newly installed floodlights from each corner of the roof.

No one could enter a door or a window even with a key without punching in a seven-digit code on the computer panel inside the front door within forty seconds or else an alarm was activated inside the house. Then a three-digit code was to be punched on the same panel within one minute of the activated timer or the company sounded an alarm at the local police station. Only a phone call within the next thirty seconds to the Freedom from Worry/Total Protection Company with the code words "Safe and Sound" and the initial seven-digit code would serve to notify the company to cancel the police call. The first two false alarms were free. After that, a graduated system of fines would be imposed for each false alarm.

A sleek Doberman pinscher snarled beneath Carmela's clothesline in the backyard. The dog, a female, was named King.

"She's mine?" Carmela asked.

"Part of the system," Angel explained.

The first free false alarm was activated by King. The police came. When Teresa came home from work she called the Freedom from Worry/Total Protection Company and made them take the snarling dog away before she left for class. The second free false alarm was activated by Angel, who came back to talk some sense into Carmela after the company called him to say they had taken away the dog. The police came again. Sunset was a fading ember when Carmela activated the third alarm of the day, which was the first fined alarm. She didn't even know she had activated the alarm. She had gone to take the clothes off the line before it got too dark and simply walked back through the open back door.

The police had changed shifts; it was a different officer who came this time, along with the FBI statistician Carmela had met two nights before. Both Officer Rhoades and Agent Pirelli were very nice to her, Carmela decided, considering the circumstances. Carmela made coffee. She was embarrassed beyond words, wishing she had taken that fantasy vacation and were far away. Officer Rhoades was kind enough to turn off the flashing lights on the patrol car while she wrote out the police report. Agent Pirelli inspected the alarm system and politely explained to Carmela that a system this complicated was more suited to Fort Knox or perhaps a jewelry store. Since she wasn't in a high-crime area, he suggested she have the system deactivated and buy herself a small noisy poodle. He smiled. She smiled and blushed. He handed her his business card when he left and told her to call him if she ever had any more trouble. He also told her she made a great cup of coffee.

She held the card in her hand for a long time after the patrol car sped off, certain that if she ever did follow waiting-room-magazine advice this was the kind of handsome stranger she'd flirt with. He had been so understanding. He had made her smile. She dropped the business card from her hand as if it had burned her palm. What is wrong with me? she wondered. Just because my husband hasn't come on the boatlift doesn't mean I'm about to flirt with strangers.

It only meant that life was as it had been before the Mariel exodus had begun. Only meant that her husband was still in prison. Only meant that she was still waiting for him.

She decided she wouldn't mention the last police visit to either Teresa or Angel. Angel would find out about it soon enough when he received the bill for the fine from the alarm company. In the meantime Carmela decided she just wouldn't leave her house anymore, thereby eliminating the possibility of more alarms and more strangers. She could see the moon through the bars of her bedroom window as she fell asleep.

CHAPTER 24

Juan Raúl Pérez woke to the sound of his wife filing through the bars of his prison cell and the smell of soldiers, bodies, and gunsmoke in the jungle. He realized at once that this could only be an awakening from a dream and not an awakening into reality, for he was no longer imprisoned by bars and his wife hadn't come to save him. There was also the fact that he had never smelled the smell of soldiers, bodies, and gunsmoke in the jungle. Perhaps he fell back to sleep, for he awoke again reassured by Dottie's presence sitting on the cot next to his with her nail file filing her golden-lacquered fingertips. The smell of death in the jungle persisted, however. He needed air. He sat up, gasping for a breath. He didn't find one; there was only the smell. He could see it emanated from a leafy tree growing next to Dottie on her cot. The tree had a face. It was an old man dressed in camouflage clothing. A matching knapsack hung from his shoulder. Juan Raúl Pérez took a deep breath of reality which left him stupefied. "Who is this man?" he finally coughed out.

"Shhh," Dottie said. "Keep your voice down, señor."

She moved over to Juan Raúl Pérez's cot and sat down. She whispered in his ear, "He's another relative. It took me two days to find one."

"Find one what?"

"A relative. You understand?"

"No, is he related to you?"

"No. I thought he'd be your father."

Juan Raúl Pérez began to tremble. He had done so well the day before, believing for hours in a row that he was awake, that he really was in the United States living in a football stadium with no execution pending. He had played dominoes most of the day, and the games he had won had given him a tiny spark of confidence. There had been minutes, tens and twenties of them, when everything made sense, even Dottie. But now the earth seemed unsteady below him again. Dottie was sitting so close to him, clean and warm, and the smell of her was fresh soap. Yet he had only to turn his head and again came the overpowering smell of soldiers and battles in the jungle.

"If this man says he is my father, he is lying," Juan Raúl Pérez whispered. His father was dead. He was sure of that. And when his father had been alive he had smelled of rose water and tobacco.

"Of course he doesn't say he's your father, he doesn't even talk. But I checked his identity papers and his name is César Armando Pérez. I explained to him about becoming part of our family"—she leaned closer to his ear—"you know, to get a sponsor, and he shook his head yes and came with me. He seemed excited about it. Really. But I do not think he can talk. That could be to our advantage, though."

She nodded towards the old man and smiled. If the old man nodded back, it was barely discernible. "Don't worry," she continued, "I've already told him that if your wife comes, he's not coming with us."

So, the old man was just another part of Dottie's plan to get a sponsor in case his wife didn't come. The old man was being adopted just as he had been.

"I wouldn't have got you up so early," Dottie said, moving close to him again. "But I want you to take him over to the showers. I tried to clean him, but they won't let me in the men's showers with him and they won't let him in the women's. You have to watch him—he wanders off at times."

"Señora, no. I can't bathe this man. He smells terrible. And I don't even know him."

"What do you want from me, señor?" Her whisper was angry, as close to a scream as a whisper could get. "I have had very little sleep in the last few days. I've spent my nights looking for another relative and all day doing laundry. I'm trying to get enough to buy you some teeth. All you've done is sleep and play dominoes. I'm just asking you to clean him up a little. You may be my ticket out of here, but you could cooperate just a little."

Her ticket out of here, of course. He moved away from her warm soap smell and her anger. "You are not very kind," he said.

"Maybe I'm not, but when I'm not lying I'm honest."

She put the nail file in her pocket and headed back back out Gate 14.

"Women," Juan Raúl Pérez thought he heard the old man sitting on the cot say.

"What did you say?" he asked him. César Armando Pérez did not answer.

"This is a farce," Juan Raúl Pérez told the old man. "I hardly even know this madwoman who has decided to adopt you as my father. I have a lovely wife and a child. They are waiting for me on the Southwest Twenty-third Street of Miami. I just haven't been strong enough to contact them yet. I was getting stronger yesterday."

The old man kept silent. The smell of him clung to the heat of Gate 14 and the heat was everywhere. Juan Raúl Pérez wanted Dottie to come back and take the old man away and leave him alone. All he wanted was to be left alone, away from all these crowds of faces. Then he grew frightened that Dottie would come back and take the old man away and leave him alone, alone with no wife, no father, and two rotting teeth in his mouth. He reached for his pulse but instead found the old man's wrist in his hand, and

Juan Raúl Pérez angrily pulled him over to the showers.

Juan Raúl Pérez waited twenty minutes in line at the men's showers. He had to pull the silent old man back by his dirty camouflage army shirt several times when he wandered from the line. He clung to the old man fiercely as he washed layers and layers of dirt from him. He cursed him and in the same breath prayed that Dottie would not abandon him. The old man grimaced as a hard jet of water and Juan Raúl Pérez's soapy hands caught him straight in the face, exposing a fine set of natural white teeth and pink gums. Juan Raúl Pérez hated him for those incongruous teeth. He could have drowned him in the shower for those teeth.

The clean bag of bones César Armando Pérez became without his layers of dirty clothes, without the balls of matting in his long white hair, shivered and remained mute.

"I guess I'll have to start calling you Papá," Juan Raúl Pérez said. The old man picked up the the knapsack he had placed on the ground and flung it back over his shoulder. Standing there naked with the camouflage knapsack, César Armando Pérez looked like an obscene gesture in a military graveyard. But when Juan Raúl Pérez grabbed his hand to move him along, the old man curled his fingers in Juan Raúl Pérez's hand like the hand of a child, fragile and trusting. Juan Raúl Pérez wrapped him in a towel and put him in the sun to dry by the ten-yard line.

"Give me his clothes," Dottie said as she hustled by on one of her laundry runs. "Here's a pair of trousers to put on him in the meantime, but I'll need them back. They're not ours. Then please bring him over to the line by the tents. They're cutting hair there."

Juan Raúl Pérez had to pull him back in the showers to put him in the trousers.

A team of hair cutters from L'Hair in Coconut Grove, on community service time for conviction of marijuana possession, trimmed Juan Raúl Pérez's few remaining strands into bald. Then they sheared Papa's great mass of long white hair into a new-wave creation: spiked on top, shaved on the sides, and feathered in the back to a ten-inch tail.

Dottie found Juan Raúl Pérez following the old man through the lower bleachers and returned Papa's clothes, now smelling like Ivory soap. She was very happy, having just come from the desk where the list for sponsors was; her plan was working. With the addition of Papa, their names were being moved up on the list.

"How can this be?" Juan Raúl Pérez asked. "Who would want to sponsor this old man? Who would want him in his house?"

"People get nervous taking strangers into their homes— but a husband and wife and grandfather? That's not strangers anymore. That's a family."

Not his family.

It wasn't yet noon when Juan Raúl Pérez took the old man to the showers to change him back into the camouflage clothing. Being married to Dottie was one thing, but chasing around the strange man posing as his father was another. It was too much for Juan Raúl Pérez. It was too much movement and too much confusion. Dottie had only been a rest stop, a way to gain a little strength before he faced whatever truth awaited. He didn't feel any stronger, but he felt that by staying he would lose the little strength he had left. He bade the old man goodbye and went to find Dottie to say goodbye to her.

CHAPTER 25

It wasn't as easy as he'd thought it would be. Nothing was with Dottie. He found her over by the west end zone with Luz Paz. They were spreading the wet clothes they had laundered over the fence to dry. The sun was shining. The breeze blew the clothes with a slow rhythm. The colors danced in the air.

He had to wait until she had moved away from Luz Paz before he could speak to her. He gave Dottie the trousers which she had loaned to Papa. She didn't question that he had left the old man over in the men's locker room. Before he could say goodbye, she insisted on giving him a cup of coffee and a pastelito from a paper bag by a box full of wet clothes.

"Eat another," she told him. "That old man had you running ragged."

"No, thank you, señora. I'm leaving."

"You really must stop calling me señora," she said. "And finish that last pastry. You're too skinny and I've already had enough."

He took the last guava confection from the bag. He was still taking orders. Like a prisoner. He put it back without tasting it and refolded the bag. "Señora, I'm saying goodbye now."

"Go ahead. I heard you. I don't blame you for leaving the old man. I didn't think he'd be so much trouble."

And then Luz Paz was there by the box looking through the pieces of wet clothing. He said no more. Perhaps Dottie hadn't understood how far away he was going. Or perhaps, like the old man, she hadn't realized he would be so much trouble. Either way, the separation was more painful to Juan Raúl Pérez walking away than to Dottie hanging laundry. She had taken good care of him the past few days. He didn't know if he would have been strong enough to function through the shock of his journey without her.

"Thank you, señora," he whispered to himself. "Thank you. I'll never forget you."

The sky was bright and blue with long sweeps of cirrus clouds overhead. He didn't look back—he only had enough courage to go in one direction. He crossed the street. He had left the Orange Bowl. He was free, as if the door to his prison cell in Cuba had just opened and he had only to walk twenty-three streets to find his new life. He headed south and stopped at the next corner to note the green-and-white street sign: N.W. First Street. He kept walking. The street ended abruptly not two blocks away and he turned west on a large thoroughfare until the next cross street where he could travel south again. When he looked up, the sign read S.W. Second Street. Could it be that easy? he wondered. Could the city of his dreams actually be laid out like a giant grid with the compass pointing in the direction of his dreams? He quickened his pace and wove through the grid to confirm the compass. The points held; not only would it be easy for him to find his reason for existence but it wouldn't take him very long if the short blocks continued.

The houses were painted pastel. Children played a game of soccer in a small front yard. On the next block a girl sat her doll on the front steps of a yellow house. He heard not a word of English, and except for the cars, sleeker and brighter-colored, he could have been transported in time and place to a suburb of Havana when he and all the world were young.

At an open door, he stopped to watch a man in an easy

chair eating from a plate in front of a TV. The phone rang. The man put his plate down and left Juan Raúl Pérez's field of vision. Juan Raúl Pérez walked on. Eighth Street surprised him, coming over his reverie with a loud vision of the future. There were no trees. The cars honked. Everything moved rapidly. The street went on without his moving. A man shouted at a woman walking from a store. Juan Raúl Pérez sat down on a bus bench. It was hot and there was no breeze on this street. His feet began to hurt in his simulated-leather oxfords which were too big and chafed against his heels. He leaned his head back on the bus bench and looked at the sky, dizzied for a moment by the loud open freedom, terrified for a moment by the wide open freedom. I could just stay here, he thought. I really am free. I could sit here for hours and no one will miss me and no one will know. A woman with large gold hoop earrings sat down on the bench beside him, and he was glad not to be alone in the awful freedom.

"Excuse me, señora, where am I?" he asked to hear her voice.

"Calle Ocho, señor. This is where the bus stops."

He thanked her and left the bench.

"Where am I?" he asked a man a block farther west on the same street.

"Calle Ocho. Are you lost? Can I help you?"

Cars rushed by in noontime traffic spurts. He knew it was too easy, to think that all roads led home when he wasn't even sure where he was. How could this be the U.S.? The storefronts all proclaimed their goods in Spanish. It even smelled like the market district in Havana except that this was new and thriving and moving by him at futuristic speed.

"Where are we?" he asked at a sidewalk coffee stand.

"Calle Ocho," the man standing next to him answered. "Are you new here from Mariel?"

Juan Raúl Pérez ordered a coffee.

"I'm sorry, I didn't mean to offend you by my question,

señor," the man said when Juan Raúl Pérez didn't answer him.

"No, señor, I was only thirsty. Yes, I arrived here from Mariel Harbor. Exactly where is this Calle Ocho, señor? And why does every one speak Spanish here?"

"This is Southwest Eighth Street, it runs east and west. You just crossed Southwest Twenty-seventh Avenue, which runs north and south."

"Ah yes, of course. Thank you. Is this Twenty-seventh Avenue anywhere near the Twenty-third Street of Miami?"

"Well, that depends where you want to go on Twenty-third Street. As I said, the streets run east and west and the avenues north and south. Courts, roads, and places also run north and south."

"Ah, thank you, señor. It's really very simple, isn't it?"

The woman placed a shot of café cubano and a tall glass of ice water beside it. Juan Raúl Pérez drank the ice water first and the woman refilled it and moved to another customer. He drank the rich sugary coffee and chased it with the cool water. He felt his pocket for a peso and found none. He wondered if he should run away without paying and end up in prison perhaps, or tell the woman he had no money.

"Señor, no, please, it is on me," said his neighbor, still standing beside him. "Welcome to Little Havana, no? But tell me, señor," his arm was around Juan Raúl Pérez's shoulder, "tell me, what do they think of us there? I wanted to stay and fight. But I had a family, young babies, a wife. I wanted to go with the Bay of Pigs invasion too. We didn't forget you. But my family—my wife said she'd leave if I went back to fight. But that was almost twenty years ago, no? Old history, I shouldn't bring it up. Señora!" The man pounded his fist on the bar. "Another coffee for my friend here!" But when he turned back, Juan Raúl Pérez had already walked away.

After several detours, he turned south back on Twenty-seventh Avenue. His feet were burning, and with each step, the shoes cut into the blisters on the back of his heels. He took his shoes off for several blocks. Then put them back on. Then took them off again. Following Seventeenth Street was Eighteenth Street. It wasn't difficult; he'd been writing to the same address for so many years now.

Twenty-third Street was shady and quiet. Even with his heart beating so hard and his head pounding and his clothes soaked through with sweat, he could see what a lovely street it was. It was exactly the street she should live on. And it wasn't far from how he had always pictured it. If there were any discrepancies between the street on which he now stood and the Twenty-third Street of his dreams, he let them go. He wouldn't remember the years of details he had painstakingly brushed on the canvas, only how at home he felt there as soon as he turned the corner and found the right house. He knew turning the corner that his fears had been groundless. She had waited. This was home.

It felt cooler here to him as his heart stopped racing. He walked slowly up and down the sidewalk opposite the lovely little white house. He took off his shoes and felt the ground rise up through his feet. It was perfect, the warm sidewalk, the cool grass, the bumps in the road where tree roots broke the surface. Each time he promised to cross the street to the same side as the house. And several times he got as far as the center of the road before casually walking back to the opposite side. Just to get a little closer. Perhaps to the car window and see if there was something of hers lying on the seat, a handkerchief, a book. Perhaps even to look in the window of the house, to see what it looked like inside the living room, the kitchen. In Cuba, there had been a radio on top of the refrigerator, dishes drying by the sink, blue flowered curtains in a neat ruffle above the sill.

He took a deep breath. He crossed the street. He ran his hand across his forehead. He knocked. Once. The alarm sounded with such a nerve-shattering roar that he was blocks away before he realized he had dropped his shoes.

CHAPTER 26

It was the fourth time in two days that the alarm had sounded from Southwest Twenty-third Street; the police didn't rush over. This gave Carmela a little extra time to frantically push in the wrong numbers on the control panel and then call in the wrong code words to the Freedom from Worry/Total Protection Company.

"Help me, Teresa!"

"No. We *want* the police to come this time. This is not a false alarm."

"He knocked on the door. We don't want the police to come when somebody knocks on the door."

"He had the house staked out, Mama. You saw him."

But he had knocked! The police would think they were lunatics. Mr. Pirelli must already think she was a lunatic. Carmela went to her bedroom to run a comb through her hair. She hadn't left the house all day. When the police knocked, Teresa answered the door and punched in the code numbers on the computer panel. It was an Officer Williams at the door. There was no one with him.

"Another false alarm?" Williams asked.

"Oh no," Teresa said. "A burglar. Come in, please."

"He was not a burglar," Carmela said. "He just walked up to the house and knocked. Maybe he had the wrong house or maybe he wanted a glass of water or something. But this alarm system is so sensitive, it went off before I could punch in the number. I'm sorry you had to come out here for nothing. We'll pay the fine, of course."

"He was a burglar!" Teresa said. "He was some kind of weirdo, and he wasn't knocking at the door, he was trying to pound it in."

"Teresa, he wasn't a weirdo," Carmela said. "There was something wrong with him, officer. He was hunched over and crippled."

"Was he wearing these shoes?" Williams asked and showed them the shoes he had picked up at the doorstep.

"Now do you believe me, Mama?" Teresa said. "You think a normal person would leave shoes on a doorstep? He was some kind of pervert."

Williams had a hard time deciding whether it was a false alarm or not. Over his third cup of coffee and second piece of coffee cake, he decided to give them the benefit of the doubt. According to both the mother and the daughter, the man had walked by the house several times over a period of an hour or so. And all the time he had been staring at the house. They had been watching TV and had seen the man through the living-room window. Neither of them had gotten a close look at him, but they both agreed he was crippled, bald, and wearing a lime-green parrot shirt and bell-bottoms. A Marielito, according to the daughter.

"I know you both said he was a stranger," Williams ventured, "but could he have been an old family acquaintance perhaps that you hadn't seen in many years? A neighbor from Cuba? Was there anything familiar about him? I don't think a burglar would have knocked on the door or even pounded on it."

"You know, there was something familiar about him," Carmela said. "I had this uncanny feeling that I had seen him before. He was a pathetic creature. He reminded me of the old beggars in Havana Square when I was a little girl."

If there had been a moment's doubt that the man who walked back and forth in front of the house had been anything more than a stranger, the shoes left on the doorstep had driven that vague thought from her head. Her husband had taken a nine narrow shoe. The shoes on the doorstep were a size eleven, extra-wide.

We have built a house. It would take a hurricane to blow our house down, but we move always in the eye of the storm. We have built a house. We have peopled it with phantoms and mirrored it with memories. The sun rises each day and beats upon the house. The wind blows. The rains come. Time erodes. Yet each day we are there to fix it. We wind the phantoms in long white bandages. We lick the blood from the mirrors. We are strong, we are weak; it does not matter. We are there. Our house will stand; its foundation is pain. They can't take our pain from us. We have suffered enough—death cannot touch us.

Yet only the dead can say this without fear. Except for Lazarus, my brother.

Oh my Love, I hope there is a house somewhere where you are still living.

CHAPTER 27

Not a good day for Dottie. Nor had it been a good night. She was still working on too little sleep and too much energy. Her gentleman husband had lost his shoes and his gentleman feet were so torn up that he could barely walk by evening. Therefore she had had to watch Papa all night while her gentleman husband played dominoes with the other gentleman. It had kept her from her laundry, which had been light. If she hadn't seen for herself that the Pérez Family had been moved up to number 132 on the sponsor list, she would have definitely gotten rid of Papa and maybe her gentleman husband too.

Getting Papa down for the night hadn't been easy. She and Luz Paz got him a cot, but he didn't seem to understand that he was supposed to lie down on it and sleep. He preferred to stand like a sentinel at the edge of their little alcove. It made everyone uncomfortable except for Luz Paz, who said she thought it sweet how the grandfather they had been so lucky to locate stood guard over the family. "Was he in the military?" Luz Paz wanted to know.

"I think so," Dottie answered, "but I'm not sure—we were separated from my father-in-law for a long time."

After Luz Paz fell asleep, Dottie got the old man on the cot and tried to tie his leg to the bed with a sheet. Juan Raúl Pérez pointed out that it would wake up everyone in Gate 14 if the old man wandered off in the night with his bed attached. They ended up with Papa's cot wedged between them. Juan Raúl Pérez slept soundly while Dottie, with one eye open, flung her arm across the old man whenever he stirred. She awoke early. Papa's bed was empty. But he hadn't gone far, he was back at his sentinel post.

Dottie traded a straw purse she had gotten from the donation box to a woman for a pair of thick cotton socks for Juan Raúl Pérez's gentleman feet. She also bought him a pair of flip-flops from Felipe's Winn-Dixie cart and another bottle of nail polish for herself. Ripe Melon the polish was entitled, but Dottie was no more proficient in English than she had been before. Felipe, whose English was limited to street jive and drug lingo, interpreted it for her as Opium Poppy. Strange, Dottie thought, she always thought poppies had a more orange cast. Neither Felipe nor his competitor, who ran his sundries from a Publix shopping cart, had yet to find her the set of dentures she had been asking for. However, both of them were eager for her to put a down payment on them. She told each of them that she'd put money down when she saw the goods.

Luz Paz applied salve and bandages to Juan Raúl Pérez's feet. Then she said a few sore-feet prayers to San Lázaro, who aside from his powers as an ancient African deity also happened to be the patron saint of skin abrasions. Dottie wasn't very sympathetic. Not only couldn't he remember where he had lost the shoes she had gotten for him, he seemed to be having trouble remembering where he was again, and Dottie thought it was high time he snapped out of it. Luz Paz told Juan Raúl Pérez that he should stay off his feet for a few days. Dottie gave him the socks and the flip-flops and told him to stay on Papa's trail. She had work to do. She had over forty dollars from doing laundry and she wasn't about to stop now. The supply of dirty clothes, however, was about to stop. She did two loads first thing, and then another an hour later, and then there was no more. She checked for competition, she went round to former customers. Everyone had plenty of clean clothes, and as it edged closer to the end of the month, everyone on government assistance began watching his pennies.

Everything was so close! She could see the slender buildings of downtown from the upper bleachers. She could feel the pulsing rhythms of Miami from the radios of the cars cruising by. They were already 132nd on the list for sponsors. And who knew, any day now, the social services desk might take Juan Raúl Pérez's information to find his relatives. And dentures might turn up at any minute. Was there nothing else to do but wait? For forty minutes, she waited impatiently on a line for a job as a driver for a party goods supplier. She didn't get the job. She didn't have a driver's license. She went over to the vendors in the west parking lot and bought coffee and chicken croquettes.

Luz Paz was sitting on her cot trying to free her arthritic feet from her white nurse's shoes. Dottie handed her lunch and told her the laundry had run out. Not that she cared about the money for herself, except to get out of this hellhole and go dancing, and to buy her husband some teeth. Maybe the señor didn't mind being confined like this, since he was used to it from being in prison, but she certainly did.

Dottie was wringing her Cuban-madonna hands by the end of her recitation. "I don't want to stay in this stadium forever, señora. When will I be free?"

"You are already free," Luz Paz said. "You could walk out of this stadium right now. But, of course, where would you go?"

"Exactly, señora. Last night I kept crossing the street back and forth to see what freedom felt like. I'm not a fool, señora, it felt the same. If our relatives don't come and we don't get a sponsor, then I need money to be free. I asked last night at social services how much apartments cost in Miami. I will be here a long time doing laundry to get that much. Maybe I was just fooling myself thinking I could wash my way out of here. It doesn't matter—now I don't even have laundry to do. The only other thing aside from laundry that I know how to do is harvest sugar cane, and I haven't seen any on this football field. The only other thing I know how to do I am saving for freedom and men like John Wayne!"

"Dotita, please calm down. Please sit down. You will not be here forever. You have not even been here for three days."

"Almost four days," Dottie said.

"Three, four, what is the difference? And John Wayne is dead."

"What?" Dottie said as tears brimmed her eyes. "John Wayne is dead, señora? This cannot be. Maybe you are thinking about Elvis Presley; he's dead. But not John Wayne."

"The cowboy movie star, John Wayne. I don't know this Elvis Presley but I know John Wayne. My daughter and I used to see his movies a long time ago in Cuba. His death was in the papers. And what do you care—you already have a good husband. If you have no more laundry to do right now, why don't you rest? You've hardly slept at all. This heat must be getting to you. And all that hot water. Sit down, please."

"It was hot in Cuba too," Dottie said, but she sat down. She put her raw hands to her face and cried.

"What is wrong, Dotita? Did you know John Wayne?"

"I don't know what's wrong," she said between sobs. "Of course I didn't know John Wayne. I haven't even seen him in a movie in twenty years."

Luz Paz was shocked by Dottie's reaction. And she felt sorry for Juan Raúl Pérez, whom she had seen earlier, flip-flopping after his father, who was more spry than the son. He was so kind and respectful to Dottie, always calling her señora. But how could the poor man just out of prison compete for a place in his wife's heart if she dreamed of John Wayne? Yes, her husband needed a new image, and quickly too, if Dottie had kept her life together while her husband was in prison by dreaming of men like John Wayne.

"Come, mi hijita, do not cry now. We must offer a sacrifice and light a candle for the soul of John Wayne."

Luz Paz didn't know if the soul of John Wayne needed a

candle but she knew the souls of dreams dying did. She crammed her edemic feet back into her white oxfords and motioned Dottie to follow. Luz Paz would have preferred to stay where she was to light a candle—she had never liked John Wayne—but the security guard had just warned her again about the fire hazards of lit candles. She would have to go up to the upper levels again where no one bothered her. She wondered if she should offer the candle to Our Lady of Mercy who as the Santería god Ochun ruled love and honey and all things sweet. Surely Ochun could make Dottie fall back in love with her toothless husband and leave John Wayne alone. But since Juan Raúl Pérez reminded her more of the crippled San Lázaro and since Lázaro was her favorite god, she decided to pray to him.

Dottie followed Luz Paz to the hidden hallways of the uppermost bleachers. Dottie tried to stop crying. And she tried to pray. She couldn't remember the last time she had offered a prayer since her mother had died. The gods had never had much use for Dottie, since she usually took care of herself so well and wasn't in need of their service. She bowed her head and tried to concentrate when Luz Paz twisted the rat's head off and poured the blood into the silver bowl. She tried to find the right words as Luz Paz lit the candle and invoked San Lázaro's help. Dottie looked up with a jolt when she heard the security guard speak.

"Señora," Esteban Santiesteban said to Luz Paz, "I have told you a hundred times not to light candles in the stadium, not even up here.

"And you too," Esteban Santiesteban said to Dottie. "Neither of you should be up here."

Dottie's tears dried. She smiled at the man. She had never before realized the power of prayer; standing before her in a football stadium in the land of her freedom was the man of her dreams—John Wayne. She rose from her knees and threw her arms around his neck. She moved her Cuban-madonna hips ever so gently, for love, for freedom as she had imagined.

CHAPTER 28

John Wayne. The English-speaking world knew him above all by his voice, the low monotone with the strangely arrhythmic drawl. Cuba knew him by voice too, the voice of the actor who dubbed his movies in Spanish, a high-pitched emotional cascade of words superimposed over the barely moving lips of John Wayne. Even though it was many years since Hollywood films had been projected in Cuba, Dottie would have known that voice anywhere. That the same voice, the essence of John Wayne as Dottie knew him, was wrapped in such a handsome package was a bonus Dottie couldn't have dared hope for. Esteban Santiesteban did sound like John Wayne's Spanish dub. That was where the resemblance to John Wayne, or rather his overvoice, ended. Security guard Esteban Santiesteban was a dark man with intelligent green eyes and a sad smile. Born in Cuba, raised in the U.S., he was now in his midthirties. He never stayed at one thing too long. He had worked as a cab driver, bartender, insurance salesman, Carvel ice cream franchise store owner, and other assorted employment since his military service. His relationships lasted about as long as his jobs did. Life was too short, he had found out in Vietnam, to put up with any long-term aggravation. It was enough to earn his way, and to feel tired at the end of each day.

"Juan Wayne," she breathed in his ear.

"I think you got me mixed up with somebody, lady."

"Oh, I know I've got you mixed up with somebody."

"Dotita, don't!" Luz Paz said. She was fumbling on her hands and knees to put the candles out. "There, Señor Police," she said. "The candles are out. You can go now."

Esteban Santiesteban had never had a woman throw herself on him like this in his life. He wasn't going anywhere.

"You are so handsome," Dottie said. He had heard that a time or two before, but it never hurt to hear again.

Dottie swayed against him with all the subtlety of a tropical hurricane. Warm waves surged through his groin. If it hadn't been for the look of terror on Luz Paz's face, Esteban Santiesteban never would have moved. Prying himself from Dottie was like pulling apart two magnets. He took a few deep breaths and waited for his reason to return. He felt embarrassed and waited to hear a giggle or two. This had to be some kind of a joke—why else would a complete stranger attack him so? He looked at Dottie's face. She was a good-looking woman, and there was no hint of practical joke in her eyes, only, yes, it was admiration, perhaps adoration.

"Has anyone ever told you that you sound like John Wayne, señor?"

No one had. And he himself was only familiar with John Wayne's English voice, and there certainly was no resemblance there; Esteban Santiesteban spoke a little too rapidly in both English and Spanish. "What's going on, señora?" he asked Luz Paz, who was quickly packing up her prayer gear.

Once it was pointed out, Luz Paz had to admit to herself that the security guard did sound like John Wayne. It was eerie, considering whose soul they had praying for, and also strange because San Lázaro was not one of the trickster gods. "Come on, Dotita," she said, "we have to go now. It's only some trick of our imagination. We shouldn't be up here. Let's go."

"A trick, Señora Paz? More like some kind of reincarnation. You of all people shouldn't doubt the power of prayer."

"No, Dotita. John Wayne hasn't been dead that long. This is not the answer to your prayers. This is just some security guard who follows me around telling me to put out my candles and to stop praying."

"I never told you to stop praying, señora, you know that. I just can't have any fires. Now what's really going on?"

The voice. His voice.

"I can explain everything," Dottie said. "Is there someplace private we can go to talk?"

"No, Dotita. Your husband. Think of your husband. He loves you very much."

"No, señora, he doesn't. He probably won't even mind."

"Yes he would," Luz Paz said. "And this man has already met your husband. He helped him the night you first came when your husband woke up screaming."

So she had a husband. Nothing is ever as good as it seems, Esteban Santiesteban thought. It was that skinny old man who had been screaming. He had seen him since playing dominoes. Esteban Santiesteban didn't like any of the domino players. They wanted him to sit around listening to their war stories and prison reminiscences, but as soon as he even mentioned his own Vietnam experiences, they acted as if his war were child's play. Some of them said they had never heard of Vietnam. It was probably a very unhappy marriage, he decided.

"Will you at least let me explain, señor?" Dottie asked.

Esteban Santiesteban looked into her full dark eyes. There were tears there.

"Yes, of course." Even as he said it, he had a feeling that this was going to require more caution than he was capable of.

"How do you feel about freedom?" Dottie moaned. She was taking her breast out of the top of her dress and placing it in Esteban Santiesteban's hand. He fondled it as he thought about Dottie's question. They were in one of the press rooms, now a rarely used temporary security office which he had the key for.

"I like freedom," he said. He wanted to tell her about how he had fought for freedom and the United States in Vietnam, but words weren't coming easily at the moment. Would she think his war was child's play also? He moved his hand under the blue polka-dot dress and found the courage to begin. "I had two tours of duty in Vietnam," he said. "I fought for freedom."

"Oh yes, talk to me," Dottie breathed. "The voice. Talk to me." She ran her stubby fingers ever so gently over his eagle belt buckle. She had gotten his shirt off almost before he had time to lock the door. She didn't like men in uniforms, and he would look far better naked.

"My freedom hero," she said. "My United States freedom hero."

CHAPTER 29

No, she didn't blame San Lázaro; she blamed herself. She should have been praying to Ochun or maybe Chango, but not Lázaro. What did Lázaro know about love?

Luz Paz was frantic. She circled around her cot as fast as her swollen feet could carry her. Several times she stopped in front of her milk cart of gods with the intention of kneeling down to pray, but it seemed she had already screwed things up enough by praying. That look in Dotita's eyes when she heard John Wayne's voice! No, she couldn't afford to chance any more prayers, Luz Paz decided. Gods help those who help themselves. She shuffled out Gate 14.

She found a volunteer from St. Anne's Church distributing used clothing and canned goods, who promised her that he'd ask back at the parish for dentures. But he didn't seem optimistic. In the south lot she saw Juan Raúl Pérez pursuing his father, and Luz Paz ducked behind a tent to avoid him. She was afraid he'd ask where his wife was, and she didn't want to be the one to tell him that after his twenty years in prison, his wife had just run off with another younger, more handsome man, and that she, inadvertently, had arranged their meeting.

Her arthritic joints seemed to swell with each degree of heat. She found Felipe in the west lot and gave him ten dollars as a down payment for a set of dentures. She also gave him one of her old Cuban coins she had brought with her on the boat. Everyone knew Cuban pesos were worthless outside of Cuba, but this one was gold, and if the gold was real maybe he could get a few dollars for it. What else could she do? Aside from a few more old coins, she had no other money except a ten-dollar bill. She told Felipe that if he found the dentures she'd give him cash for them, but the truth was she'd have to let him hold her statues as collateral until she could see if her nephew would give her the money. It would be difficult giving up her statues even temporarily, but she saw no other alternative. And when she got back to her cot and knelt before the milk cart, she let the gods know that unless they came up with a better plan they might soon be pushed through the Orange Bowl among stale granola bars in a supermarket shopping cart.

CHAPTER 30

Juan Raúl Pérez had come up with no satisfactory reason why what sounded like a prison bell would have gone off when he knocked on the door to the house he had dreamed of for twenty years. The only thing he could come up with was that he had imagined that alarm, that his heart had been racing so fast, his emotion had been so charged, that he had detonated some type of mind-scream that he had interpreted as a prison alarm bell. Didn't such a monumental knock deserve a trumpet blast, a shout of joy? Perhaps he hadn't even knocked. Perhaps his mind had shrieked so with emotion that he had heard that terrible sound and run before he even knocked.

What was even more disconcerting was the still life of the house on the Twenty-third Street of Miami which he now held in his heart. He could no longer bring it into view without imagining spotlights in the eaves, bolt locks on the doors, bars on the windows. He had to stop calling it to mind or else soon he would imagine rows of barbed wire around the yard, an armed guard tower against the sky. In prison he had envisioned sunlight through an open window, and now in sunlight he could only see bars. Better to try not to think at all of the Southwest Twenty-third Street of his dreams. If social services came for information so they could locate his relatives, he would give them Angel's name. It would be better to learn the truth gently from a face he could barely remember. All he had now was the security he thought was Dottie and the ancient war relic which was Papa. Juan Raúl Pérez was grateful for the both of them. If Dottie wanted him to spend his days chasing the old man through a football stadium and showering him down whenever the jungle smell crept back up on him, it was fine with him. Whatever she wanted. Juan Raúl Pérez even harbored a notion that perhaps he could get the old man to talk, fix him up a little, make him a more presentable father.

"Come back here!" Juan Raúl Pérez called as Papa marched through the aerobics class.

"Where are you?" Juan Raúl Pérez called as Papa wove through the orange bleachers.

"Who are you?" Juan Raúl Pérez asked when he had corralled him into a stadium seat. "Who are you? What is your name? How did you come here?"

But if the old man heard, it did not matter; César Armando Pérez had long since passed the point where he was capable of saying where he had been and who he was. The only thing which could be supposed from his clothing and his knapsack was that the old man had once been a soldier. And if Papa had once been part of the bomb Cuban politics are made of, it had exploded long before, leaving only a shell and the smell of gunsmoke in the air.

"Where are you?" Juan Raúl Pérez called in desperation not to lose the old man for good, not to lose Dottie.

CHAPTER 31

Felipe Pérez sat on the seawall at South Beach until sunset. He was too happy to be lying low anymore. He had on a new bathing suit which left little to the imagination about his longing for a girl with a St. Tropez tan. He still had two crisp hundred-dollar bills in his brand-new black leather disco pouch. What a day! It had started slowly; nobody had even wanted a granola bar, which he blamed on the heat, strong enough to seep through the foil wrappers and render the bars a sticky pulp. Then after his lunch of a half-dozen Raisin Crisp granola bars which were far from crisp, he was about to go back to his cot for a little siesta when the crazy old Santería lady had practically attacked him and overturned his Winn-Dixie shopping cart. "Do you have any teeth?" she asked. "I need to buy a set of dentures immediately."

It occurred to him to then that he really should check out this denture scene. Not only did this old lady look like she was willing to fork over whatever she had for a set, but Dottie had asked him several times.

He hadn't found any teeth with the ten dollars in cash and the small gold coin Luz Paz had given him. But then he had stopped looking for teeth after Patti's Pawnshop had given him an estimate of seventy dollars for the coin. Paradise Jewelers had given him an estimate of two hundred and twenty-five dollars, and over on Third Street, the South Florida Coin Exchange had given him two hundred and seventy. He didn't want to waste the whole afternoon trying to get a better price. And the clerk there had looked it up in a catalogue, so Felipe felt confident that they weren't ripping him off. The coin was gold, no bigger than a quarter, with a profile of the great Cuban poet and liberator José Martí on one side over the imprint "Patria Libertad." On the other side beneath a crest were the words "República de Cuba, 4 Pesos, 1916."

He had only taken the coin as down payment because the old woman just had the ten dollars cash. Four pesos was small change in Cuban money, and Cuban money wasn't worth the paper it was printed on in the U.S. But this was gold and it was old, so he had followed his hunch and taken it to the pawnshop. He hadn't thought it would be worth more than maybe five or ten dollars for the gold content. But what did he know about rare coins? He had never seen one before.

Now if he could only find a girl worth his time, Felipe wouldn't mind spending the two hundred he had left on her. There was plenty more where it came from; the old lady had had a bag full of them. She hadn't seemed to have a clue to their value, and Felipe saw no reason to tell her. What would an old woman do with so much money?

Felipe had been calculating all afternoon. If Luz Paz had twenty coins, that was almost five and a half thousand dollars. If she only had ten, it was over two and a half thousand, and he had glimpsed a load in her drawstring purse.

"You don't know what you're missing!" Felipe called to a woman in a string bikini who had ignored his hello as she walked by.

"Fuck off," she answered over her shoulder in English, a phrase Felipe already knew in English.

There hadn't been one all afternoon who had known what she was missing, Felipe bemoaned. He had gotten a few smiles, and three woman on beach towels had given him the time of day. He decided it was easier to pick up girls when you weren't working solo, or at least it had seemed that way when he had been hanging out with Orlando and Hector.

It was getting late, the beach was thinning out, and Felipe saw a cop half a block away. Felipe pulled on his clothes over his new bathing suit and headed across the street to Mannie's Bar.

The crowd had changed, Felipe thought, both on the beach and at Mannie's. Or maybe he just hadn't been to South Beach in so long. There was only one person he recognized, a barmaid named Josette who was too skinny for his taste, although Hector used to think she was cute. But Hector was in an Atlanta jail awaiting deportation.

"Hey, stranger," she hailed Felipe. "Haven't seen you in a long time. Orlando was in here yesterday looking for you."

Felipe froze. Orlando was supposed in be in the Dade County jail awaiting trial. And what did Josette know about it, anyway?

"Orlando who?" he said.

"You know, Orlando—one of the guys you used to come in here with all the time. He's out of jail."

"Oh, that Orlando. I wondered why I hadn't seen him around. You say he was in jail?"

"Yeah, some nickel-and-dime shit. Don't know if they didn't have enough on him or if they just let him out. You know they've been doing that. Jails are so crowded, only keeping the heavies in."

"Good. I'm glad he's out. You tell him I said hello if you see him."

Felipe drank a beer in record time and left. He headed over to Washington Avenue and got a taxi. He wanted to be back in time to talk with Luz Paz about their upcoming business deal. He'd tell her he could only get two dollars a pop for the coins and that he had a line on a set of teeth which cost a hundred. He'd even really find a set of dentures for the coins, have them sent over if he had to. She'd be happy and he'd be on his way.

He didn't know why he had frozen when Josette had told him Orlando was out. He would have been happier if it were Hector out, not only because Hector had had Felipe's cut of the nine hundred on him when caught but also because he got along better with Hector. But Orlando was OK and he shouldn't have frozen—if Orlando had squealed on him, he wouldn't be going to Mannie's and asking for him. By the time the taxi let him off at the Orange Bowl, Felipe decided he'd go back to Mannie's wearing his white suit as soon as he could and try to find Orlando. If Orlando had been set free already, certainly Felipe wasn't going to be arrested after all this time. He'd even invite Orlando over to his new apartment he'd get from the coins and they'd drive around in a shiny new car to pick up some babes. But no drugs. Felipe would tell Orlando that up front. Felipe was a reformed man.

CHAPTER 32

Esteban Santiesteban was called in to work early because the Orange Bowl was closing. He had only had three hours of sleep, something which normally would have rendered him a zombie. But his adrenaline was still high, his hormones still pulsating. Who needed the sleep? He had finally met the perfect woman. Not only was she beautiful, she seemed to love him simply for his existence on earth. She loved to hear him speak. Begged him to speak. He had told her his fight for freedom and she had moaned with compassion. He had told her his heart and she had listened to his every word.

Even now alone in his drab studio apartment with the air conditioning bordering on refrigeration, he could feel her presence surrounding him like a warm bath. He didn't know how he could have thought it was a joke when she had first thrown herself on him in the upper bleachers. It was no joke. It was fate. It was love. Tonight he was going to take her to dinner and then dancing. It would be nice to take her out. They had spent yesterday till three in the morning in the security office. They hadn't exactly consummated their relationship, he reminded himself, or rather they had consummated each other with mouths and hands, but not that final meeting. He was hoping that would come tonight, assuming the only reason for the delay was that neither had

had birth control. He took care of that at the drugstore on his way to work.

At seven o'clock he was back in the same room that he had left only four hours before. But this time he was there for a meeting with the head of security and thirty some other guards from rent-a-guard companies like his own. He had brought Dottie to this room because it was seldom used. They rarely had meetings, so this must be important. It must be important also to have so many guards on hand—there were rarely more than three or four on duty. The Orange Bowl was closing, and it was, according to the city commissioner speaking to them, "important for the people of Miami, important for the refugees being transferred, that this transition go as smoothly as possible. The eyes of the nation are focused on Miami, or at least they will be if we have any more bad press."

It was important, this meeting, but he could barely concentrate. Couldn't all the others in the room feel Dottie's presence here as well as he could? She had stood on the very same desk where the commissioner now sat. She had lifted her polka-dot dress up high and danced a combination salsa/cancan. They had both laughed. And on the sagging couch over by the window, she had thrown her head back, her breathing quick, her body very still. This meeting was important—where were these people being transferred to? Where was Dottie being transferred to?

The noise at the Orange Bowl was deafening. By eight o'clock, work crews moved in and were jackhammering everything and anything metal. Leaking roofs and falling rafters could no longer wait. Even if the refugees were moved out immediately, there was still some doubt whether the stadium could be readied in time for the first Miami Dolphin exhibition game on August 9. Close to two hundred refugees were to be moved to federally funded hotels too decayed for the tourist population. That only left seven hundred more with no place to go. Another temporary shelter,

Tent City, was almost ready on the Miami River bank under the I-95 overpass. But no one was to be moved there, due to a temporary holding order: businesses near the site were suing the city to keep the refugees away. The case was randomly assigned to a U.S. District Court judge who was on vacation for the next three weeks. The Dolphins meanwhile were scrimmaging farther north on the athletic field of Biscayne College.

The jackhammers roared over the ramp at Gate 14.

The Orange Bowl throbbed with a dull heavy tension.

Esteban Santiesteban went to find Dottie. He regretted that he had done most of the talking the night before; he didn't know what she did during the day, where she went. He checked the obvious places first, the vendors in the parking lot, the lines by the women's showers, the early crowd starting to fill the west lot out from the concrete heat of Gate 14. He was hoping to avoid going to where he knew her cot was, in the alcove that housed Luz Paz's saints and the man he had helped shake from his nightmare days before, the man that now mattered as her husband. He was plagued with questions as he went: people asking if they were going to be sent back to Cuba, to jail, to the Krome Avenue Processing Center, to Arkansas. It was his job to quell such rumors, to keep everyone calm, and by doing so prevent both panic and a mass exodus to the streets. He answered their questions. No, they were all to be transferred to another holding area nearby. He tried to avoid further details, since no one knew exactly where or what that holding area might be. Their questions made him even more anxious to find Dottie. Was she also worrying that she'd be sent back to Cuba? Was she upset, crying? He had to find her quickly, reassure her. If her husband was there, he'd do something official—ask her if she'd seen any suspicious candles being lit and whisper to her to meet him somewhere. He was almost in a run to get to her. When he saw her and stopped, he was only several cots away. Luz Paz was on her knees in front of her milk crate. Dottie and

Juan Raúl Pérez were sitting on a cot with Papa between them. She was leaning forward over a bowl of water on the ground. She came up with a wet rag in her hand. "Please, Papa," Esteban Santiesteban heard Dottie say. "Please let me just wash off your face. Please, Papa." She said more. Esteban Santiesteban didn't listen. Dottie's husband was on the other side, holding the old man's hands down, but gently, with care.

If Esteban Santiesteban had come upon Dottie and her husband embracing, it would not have been as intimate as the scene in front of him. The husband and wife caring for an elderly parent (was it her father or his?) who was as reluctant to have his face washed as a squirming child.

Esteban Santiesteban started walking backwards, unable to take his eyes from her, wishing for a minute that his own face were dirty. He had once gone with a married woman in Denver, when he had a truck route through there. The affair lasted a sweet three months, but the woman in Denver had been a disillusioned soul looking for something she couldn't find at home, and he had been a temporary solution as good as the next. But Dottie—oh, he had been so sure that Dottie had been looking for him. In this world. In this universe. He had never felt that way about a woman before.

Luz Paz looked up and shot him a glance of obvious hatred. He took a few more steps backwards. Dottie, following Luz Paz's gaze, looked up then too. She didn't seem surprised. She winked at him. But he didn't want a wink at the moment. She said something to her husband and came to Esteban Santiesteban as if it were the most normal thing in the world that he should be standing there. She walked right up to him and said hello.

"I just wanted to check about the candles," he said. "I, ah, just wanted to make sure there were no fires."

"Just us," she said. "I thought about you all night."

It was what he would have wanted to hear. But not with her husband so near. Neither of them was speaking loud enough to be overheard, but her husband was looking at them.

"I also wanted to tell you that you're not going to be sent back to Cuba."

"You'll make sure nothing happens to me, won't you?"

She shouldn't be asking that with her family so close. "I'll do what I can."

"Well, see you at seven tonight then, at the back gate where we said we'd meet. Perhaps it isn't a good idea for you to come to talk to me here when my family is with me."

"You still want to go?"

"Yes!"

"OK," he said. "See you later."

Esteban Santisteban turned to go, but Dottie grabbed him from behind, held him from moving. He stood still, embarrassed she had done this to him in front of her family. But the smell was wrong, and looking down at the arms holding him he saw they were the claws of the old man. Before he could fling the old man from his back, Dottie screamed at Papa, "Get off him. Leave him be and don't ever do that again." The old man immediately loosened his grip and walked away just as casually as Dottie had approached. Esteban Santiesteban left quickly, as Dottie apologized to him and scolded her husband that he should watch the old man more carefully. Esteban Santiesteban must have heard her words wrong as he walked away, though. It sounded as if she said, "If Papa ever goes at somebody like that again, we'll have to get rid of him," but she couldn't have said that.

CHAPTER 33

Dottie did two free loads of laundry for Eladia Soto, to have Eladia do her hair and makeup. Eladia would have done it for free. She hadn't plied her beautician's trade in many years and she wanted the practice. Dottie wanted to do more laundry; she had it in her mind that the more laundry she did for Eladia, the better her hair would turn out, but that was all the laundry Eladia had.

Dottie wasn't worried about the Orange Bowl's closing. She had been when Juan Raúl Pérez had awakened her early with a panic in his voice different from his other panics. She had thought then that it was the end of the world, a world she had just found. But as the morning wore on and she questioned her way through the rumors, it seemed a fortuitous thing. They weren't just closing down the Orange Bowl, they were speeding things up, and it was about time. They were finding people jobs and transferring them to hotels on Miami Beach. She pictured the hotels as luxurious monuments to capitalist affluence. Once she was out there, there'd be no stopping her. There would be a lifetime of John Waynes, an Elvis Presley for a change of pace.

It had been nice, the night before, it had been the closest thing to her dreams since she had arrived. She wanted days more of foreplay. She had waited so long, had rushed so many times, that now she wanted time. These were no longer the Cuban-madonna hips of convenience. She was more than looking forward to her evening of dining and dancing with Juan Wayne. It was about time dreams came true. To have Juan Raúl Pérez follow her around through her excitement was a pain in the ass. And now wherever Juan Raúl Pérez went, Papa followed. She had to calm Juan Raúl Pérez down several times, he was convinced that the Orange Bowl's closing meant their shipment back to Cuba, he wasn't buying her luxury-hotel theory. She could almost hear a low moan of fear coming from him. He was also grabbing at his wrist again, an annoying habit she noted whenever he got particularly nervous. Then he hadn't wanted to take the old man to the showers, and she had had to clean the old man off herself as best she could with a basin of soapy water and a washcloth. Not to mention Papa jumping on Juan Wayne's back. "He probably thought he was taking you back to Cuba," Juan Raúl Pérez had told her. "He was wearing a military uniform."

She did hope he wouldn't be wearing his uniform tonight. "He's just a security guard," she told Juan Raúl Pérez, "and a friend of mine."

But she didn't blow their cover, no, not even to Esteban Santiesteban. She had made a promise to Juan Raúl Pérez, and as long as he upheld his end, she wouldn't renege. She'd even adopt a hundred more Pérezes if it'd get her out of this hellhole an hour sooner.

"Please leave me alone for a little while, señor. Papa is like an old dog underfoot. Take him for a walk or something."

After her hair and makeup were finished she went to cruise the donation boxes for a new dress. She wanted to greet her first evening in freedom with all the flair she could find.

CHAPTER 34

The moment Felipe took the drawstring purse full of old coins from Luz Paz, he hated her. Intensely.

She also tried to give him seventy-five cents she had made doing laundry, but he wouldn't take it. He didn't want the old woman's hard-earned laundry money, he just wanted the coins she was too stupid to know were worth anything. She trusted him. Her desperation sickened him.

"I know these are only worth a few dollars, but please, at least take them in good faith," she told him. "At least see if you can get the teeth. It was all my fault, and now he even has the nerve to walk right up to her, bold as can be, in front of her husband and his father. I should have prayed to Ochun and not Lázaro. Maybe I made Ochun angry."

Felipe never knew what Santería mumbo jumbo she always rambled on about.

"Well, señora, I could take them on good faith and see if I could locate some. But I can't promise you anything; dentures are hard to come by."

"God will reward you. Even if you can't get them, thank you for trying. I have to go pray now that she doesn't run off with him. Please hurry—you know, they are closing the Orange Bowl." She placed the purse in his hand and shuffled off.

When Felipe first heard the rumors of the Orange Bowl's closing earlier that morning, he had almost gone to find her and steal the coins. He was glad he had waited; it had been so much easier this way. But it made him sick to take them from her now. She was just like all the rest of the old Cubans, he thought, just like his own family and all the others he had left behind, living on bad promises and misplaced trust. Victims. He could smell them a mile away. He hadn't thought it would be this easy, though.

He counted the coins over in a stall in the men's room. There were fourteen of them. Fourteen times two hundred and seventy was over thirty-seven hundred dollars. And there were five other coins, smaller but maybe worth something. One of them dated back to 1898. He felt good fortune enveloping him like a girl with a smile and a St. Tropez tan. He'd get a very nice apartment far away from all these stupid people. There would be red Mustangs lined up at his door.

CHAPTER 35

The life-sized San Lázaro spent all morning outside Zayres in the Westchester Shopping Center. It was hot. He was scantily clad in a purple loincloth. At his feet in the Plexiglas-enclosed trailer attached to the battered '64 Impala were thousands of pennies which people slipped through the small slits in the glass. Two dogs, slightly smaller than life size and of indeterminate breed, were also at his feet. The dogs traveled with him wherever he went, perpetually frozen in joyous yaps, one to each side of his crutches. There were not many shoppers at the shopping center to bless. He moved on, heading east over to the Orange Bowl, where there were many refugees in need of his blessing.

The '64 Impala moved down Coral Way slowly in due respect for the crippled saint who marched through eternity bent over crutches with two dogs yapping at his feet. The Impala was also burdened by the weight of the trailer containing the prayers which accompanied the thousands of pennies thrown at his feet.

Despite his kind face and crippled leg, despite his sad eyes and leper's skin, San Lázaro was not the average altruistic do-gooder deity. That there were pennies at his feet and not hundred-dollar bills did not mean he had less power than saints in large basilicas with crowns of gold and sapphires.

San Lázaro preferred pennies. Pennies were the offerings of the poor. He did not turn away the rich who still remembered to give to the poor, but they were wise to convert their larger bills to pennies when they needed a favor from him. Even the rich must humble themselves to receive the embrace of the leper. And the poor who had not a penny to leave for San Lázaro could leave him a glass of water. It had been hot in Africa, it had been hot in Cuba, it was hot in Miami; he accepted a glass of water gladly.

He passed many other San Lázaros on his way to the Orange Bowl. Some of them wore hand-embroidered robes with fresh-cut flowers at their feet. Some of them were naked where the sun had melted the purple plastic loincloth. But whatever the size and economic status of each San Lázaro, behind his kind face and healing blood was the perpetually resurrected ancient power of Babalú-Ayé. For those who could not embrace the leper, for those who would not leave a glass of water for all that is holy and thirsty, for those who would steal a penny from the hand of a poor man, his power was majestic and dark. His power was white and blinding. His power was the blood of the slaves stolen from their homes. His power worked the sugar plantations under hot Cuban sun, madonna hands ripped open by slavery and servitude. The blood from his kind leper sores was primordial and powerful. His crippled legs had traversed many poor villages and many dark slums. His power turned the corner at Northwest Sixteenth Street at the entrance of the Orange Bowl enclosed in Plexiglas behind the battered '64 Impala, just as Felipe crossed the street.

Thump thump, went San Lázaro with the drums of Babalú-Ayé beating in his heart. And Felipe was down. *Thump thump,* went San Lázaro, and Felipe's forehead bled as he lapsed into unconsciousness.

CHAPTER 36

San Lázaro's driver wanted to take Felipe to the hospital. He wanted to call the paramedics, the police, the immigration authorities, his insurance company. Saint on the back of his car or not, there was protocol to follow in Miami. He had been driving San Lázaro for fifteen years, ever since his wife had had a miraculous recovery from a stroke, and he had never had an accident. Neither he nor San Lázaro was a rich man, he declared to the crowd gathering at the sidewalk just in case the fallen man had any ideas about suing him. He and his wife lived on their social security since he had retired as a maintenance worker at the Hialeah racetrack. When the Plexiglas trailer got too heavy he turned over every single one of San Lázaro's pennies to the charity of his wife's choice: the Catholic Charities Relief Fund, Muscular Dystrophy, Immaculata School for Girls, the Republican National Campaign Fund, the Jackson Memorial Burn Unit—he had receipts for them all, he told them.

"It wasn't your fault!" yelled Linda María Pérez from her four-foot-high vantage point in the portable Café Cubano/ Lunch stand parked not twenty yards away. "I could see the whole thing from here. He came running out from over there with a little suitcase not looking where he was going. I almost called to him—it's Felipe, he sold me nail-polish remover last week. He ran right into your trailer, I'd swear it in a court of law!"

Dottie was at the portable coffee stand too, but she hadn't seen a thing. But hearing Felipe's name made her wonder if it wasn't the same Felipe who sold her nail polish and laundry soap. She hurried her way through the onlookers. Luz Paz was kneeling, bent over Felipe on the street.

"Señora Paz, is he all right?" Dottie asked, kneeling beside her.

"I don't know. He's out, and his head is bleeding."

"I'll go get a guard to call an ambulance."

"No. Wait, Dotita, I think he's coming to. And if you call the authorities they'll take him to Jackson Hospital, and he could end up anywhere after that. One man went to Jackson from here and ended up in Texas after he was released."

Felipe was coming to, mumbling vague obscenities.

"This is better," Luz Paz said. "He's talking. Let's carry him back inside."

Dottie motioned to two men beside her to help with Felipe.

"No need to call the police," Luz Paz announced to the crowd. "He's fine."

"I feel personally responsible for this accident," Luz Paz told Dottie after they had laid Felipe on Juan Raúl Pérez's cot and set about to bathe his wound. "He was on an errand for me. You see, here in his pocket were the coins I gave him to buy a set of teeth to replace your husband's missing ones." She placed the coins on the table along with Felipe's wallet. She took off his shoes and socks.

"Why, señora? What made you do that?"

"Why are you all dressed up like you are? Are you going to run off with the guard? That's why I did it, Dotita. I didn't want you to leave your family. I felt sorry for your husband. I thought you would love him more if he had teeth. I shouldn't have interfered again. It was stupid of me. Look what happened: the poor boy is bleeding, your husband has

no teeth, and you're still going to run off with your hero."
"If I was going to run off with him, a set of dentures for
my husband wouldn't stop me, señora. I'm only dressed up
like this because I have some job interviews this evening
and I wanted to look decent for them. And you shouldn't
give your money away like that." Dottie fingered the coins.
They looked old, not worth much. She looked through
Felipe's wallet. He had a U.S. driver's license; she had never
seen one before. "Oh, look, his name is Pérez," she said.
"Felipe's last name is Pérez."

Luz Paz watched over Felipe while Dottie went to wait in
line at the social services desk to inform them that the Pérez
Family now included a child. By the time she returned, Luz
Paz's faith had been restored. San Lázaro had let Dottie
almost fall in love with John Wayne so she could send
Felipe out to find teeth and be struck down by Babalú-Ayé
himself so that Dottie could be reunited with her lost son
who had come months before on another boat. Dottie had
never before doubted the old woman's sanity, but she kept
her mouth shut. She could understand social services believing her—Dottie not only told a convincing lie, but there
was never the same person twice at the social services desk.
Dottie could only surmise Luz Paz believed her because
people believed what they wanted to believe. And Dottie
valued Luz Paz's friendship too much to let her know she
was being deceived.

Flies hovered and landed, their wings too weighted by the
hot sticky air to move when swatted at. A dark promise of
rain dulled the flaming sky for an hour or so but then
moved on without leaving a drop of water.
Juan Raúl Pérez hadn't seen Dottie in hours. He needed
to find her so she could tell him again that everything was
all right, tell him that they weren't going to be shipped back
to Cuba. Two busloads had left not forty minutes earlier.
Some said, as Dottie had earlier predicted, that the buses

had only taken them to hotels on Miami Beach. But others said the buses were bound for Atlanta, from where the passengers would be deported to Cuba. There had been other rumors too—that they were all being sent to prisons in the U.S., that they were going to be dumped into the streets, where they would be left to fend for themselves.

With Papa close behind as he had been all day, he checked back at their cots. But this time she was there. Her transformation was staggering. Dottie's Cuban-madonna hair was teased and curled into a massive ebony lion's mane. It not only surrounded her face but stuck a foot into the surrounding air. Jet-black eyeliner tried to make her large round eyes into long almonds, and many layers of mascara had turned her delicate lashes into wrought-iron railings. The black eyeliner also formed a small beauty mark, à la Marilyn, above Dottie's fire-engine-red lips. She had found a red Lycra jumpsuit in the donation box. It wasn't her size, but it stretched.

Perhaps on someone else, the effect would have been cheap, but Dottie had the capacity to elevate cheap to beautiful.

"Where are you going? Are we leaving now? Why are you dressed like that?" He plopped Papa on his cot and almost sat on the body stretched out on his own cot.

"Who is this man?" Juan Raúl Pérez asked.

"Your son," Dottie said.

Felipe's head was swaddled in the white bandages Luz Paz had applied. His chest was wrapped in an Ace bandage. He was sleeping soundly. Luz Paz had done her share of village nursing years before. She had felt his ribs one by one, and none seemed broken. His breathing was regular and his belly wasn't swelling. The gash on his forehead was superficial, although it had bled copiously at first.

"Yes," Dottie said, "our very own son. Isn't it wonderful?" Dottie was holding her now strangely sculpted head at just the right angle to suggest equal portions of humility and pride. Her eyes shone beneath her black eyeliner. Juan Raúl Pérez wondered for a moment if Dottie's transformation wasn't due to some kind of burning insanity and not her new red clothes or her makeup or hair. No, nothing seemed as it was or should be. He checked the cot where Papa still sat camouflaged. Then he put his hand to the handsome young cheek of Felipe to make doubly sure it wasn't a chameleon transformation of the old man.

"Hey, don't fucking touch," Felipe said sleepily and drifted back off.

"I don't have a son," Juan Raúl Pérez said. His voice was level and calm, but he was sweating heavily and felt his eyes trapped between anger and tears. He could barely focus. If Dottie now had a son for her family sponsorship program, would she still need a husband? Being part of Dottie's family had seemed his only ground since the Twenty-third Street of his dreams had disappeared. The day's rumors of being sent back to prison or being left out on street had done little to ease his mind.

"We do now, señor. Luz Paz and I went through his pockets, only because he had some old coins of hers on him. He was on an errand for her. He has a Florida driver's license and his last name is Pérez."

"This is madness, señora. I've seen this boy—he sells rubber sandals like the ones you got for me from a shopping cart. Why is he now our son? Why did he have Luz Paz's money? What is he doing on my bed?"

"Luz Paz sent him to buy you some teeth."

"Stop! Leave my teeth out of this. I don't care about them. Why is he on my bed?"

"You are being very ungrateful, señor. Luz Paz has been very kind to us. This boy got hit by a truck doing an errand for her and she feels personally responsible. When I told her we'd like to adopt him, you know, watch over him, she was very much relieved. And having a son will help us be sponsored."

"Where is Luz Paz? I need to talk with her. And all of this

doesn't explain why you are dressed so differently."

"Luz Paz will be back in a minute. She went to get more bandages. And I'm only dressed like this because I have some job interviews this evening and I didn't want to look like a dishrag." She was going to tell him she had met an old friend and was going to go to dinner with him. After all, there was really nothing between Juan Raúl Pérez and herself except in front of everybody else. But he seemed too shaky now for the truth. "I need you to watch both Papa and your son while I have my interviews later. Luz Paz told me she'd help you."

"This is madness. Do you understand that?"

"No. I asked him when he was awake if he wanted to stay with us and be our son and he said yes as long as we didn't turn him over to the authorities. Isn't he handsome? He took my hand and told me that he'd be a good son."

"Señora, how big is this family going to get?"

"We are seventh on the list for sponsors at this very moment. I've already told social services that we found our son. We are seventh on the list now because we have a child and because they have moved so many people out of here already. Yesterday there was over a hundred before us on that list. Could you at least cooperate? They are closing the Orange Bowl in the next few days, and I'd like to be out of here before that happens."

"Yes. Yes, I'm going to try to cooperate. I think I understand." He also understood Dottie still needed him.

"Isn't he a good-looking boy?"

"Yes, señora."

"You'd better take Papa now and go get a cot if you don't want to sleep on the floor."

CHAPTER 37

Two more buses arrived at the Orange Bowl after dinner, but this time no one would board. The Orange Bowl wasn't much, but it was better than a bus trip to nowhere. Too many rumors had circulated throughout the day, too many questions had been left unanswered. A dozen or so people set up a makeshift barricade at the front gate. They threw rocks and bottles and cans at the buses.

The police were called and two squad cars arrived. Both kept their distance. There were now about fifty people shouting by the barricade. Too many police cars might have brought more.

The powers-that-were ordered the incident kept as low-key as possible. Miami had had enough bad press during a series of riots in May, and the city was still volatile. It would be better to wait. And it would rain soon. The sunset was obscured by low dark clouds. Rain could disperse an angry crowd quicker than an army.

But the rain didn't come and the waiting didn't disperse the crowd. Where there had been fifty, there were now eighty, then one hundred and fifty, then two hundred and fifty. More barricades were erected. Then a car was overturned and set afire. The guards left on the inside moved as quietly as possible to the outside. The fire department arrived with police backup. The Orange Bowl "disturbance" was on.

Juan Raúl Pérez couldn't find a cot. The storeroom where they were usually kept was locked and he couldn't find a guard to open it. The extra cots which were sometimes scattered here and there had been taken to use in the barricades, but Juan Raúl Pérez hadn't made it as far as the front entrance to learn that yet. And he lost Papa. One minute Papa had been right behind him and the next time he turned, the old man was gone.

"Li-ber-ty. Li-ber-ty," he heard the crowds chanting at the front gate as he searched. He saw the car burning. He didn't know why the people were shouting. He didn't know why the car was burning. He didn't see Papa, and he moved away quickly to find him.

It was relatively quiet under the bleachers, where Luz Paz prayed over the sleeping Felipe. Why wasn't it Dottie watching over her son? Perhaps Dottie was somewhere with Papa.

"Señora, where is Señora Dottie? And have you seen my father?"

"No, señor. I haven't seen the old man. I thought you went with him to get another cot. And your wife went on a job interview."

"They are fighting out on the street, señora. There are fire trucks and police. I don't know where the old man is." His voice was rising. "She told me that while she was gone I should watch the old man and the son. I can't find him. I don't know where he's gone!" He had to shout now to be heard over his beating heart. "Are they coming for us? Who will watch the boy if they come for us?"

"Calm down, señor. Watch the boy and I'll go look for your father. Just sit here and watch him."

But he couldn't do that. He was afraid of getting caught in the ruckus outside. Afraid the police would take him to prison. Afraid that they had already taken Papa. But he couldn't send Luz Paz out there.

"No, I'll go look for him, señora." He didn't know if he could make it. His muscles were twitching. He didn't know if he could walk without falling. He took a deep gulp of the airless heat beneath Gate 14 and turned. He started walking. One step. Two steps. Three. Four.

It wasn't the noise that woke him, nor the lights which had been turned on full everywhere in the stadium because of the disturbance. It was the Winn-Dixie shopping cart. He sat up on the side of the bed murmuring, shit shit shit. His head felt like every hangover he had ever had all rolled into one. It took him several tries to get up on his feet.

"Get out of my way," he mumbled to Luz Paz as she tried to restrain him.

"You're hurt. You have to lie down." She was no match for him.

"Sorry, señora, I have business."

Every step jarred Felipe's throbbing head and aching ribs. He couldn't remember where he had left his shopping cart, and he was determined to find it and return to his former way of life before he had decided to rob Luz Paz, before San Lázaro had knocked him down. He was grateful no one had turned him over to the authorities and even more grateful to Dottie for telling him she'd watch over him like an adopted son. He was homesick and repentant, just as he had been after his brush with the authorities two months before. He had carelessly abandoned his cart when he had attempted to leave the Orange Bowl with Luz Paz's coins earlier in the afternoon. The cart held a forty-dollar box of Seiko watches which might net two or three hundred dollars, dozens of pairs of flip-flops, a gross of Marianna nail polish which yesterday he had planned on selling to Dottie but now wanted to give to her as a present. And there were many other sundries in the shopping cart which he would now need as an honest businessman. He continued his search, aching and reforming as he went.

CHAPTER 38

Throughout the day, Esteban Santiesteban vacillated between canceling his date with Dottie and trying to find out the best restaurant in town to take her to. He knew it would be her first night out on the town, and he wanted it to be memorable. He called his nephew from the pay phone, he asked the other guards, what were the best places in town to go dancing? To eat? How much did they cost? He wanted to take her home afterwards. He wanted to erase the family scene he had witnessed that morning.

He was asked to work late but he refused and left for home at five o'clock. He had already made up his mind before he left. He didn't want to break up her family. He didn't want her to cheat on her husband. He didn't want to love her. The road to hell is paved with good intentions—he had made up his mind, he was on the road to hell. He stopped at his bank's automated teller on the way home and withdrew three hundred dollars for his journey. He was far from a rich man, but the road to hell wasn't a trip he often made, and he had a feeling it was going to cost.

He laid out his best suit and showered. His studio apartment, always meticulously neat, now seemed too shabby to take her home to. His cleanliness couldn't hide the cracks in the jalousie windows or the faded patches in the green shag carpet. But there were plenty of nice hotels, and he'd have enough money for a room with a view of Biscayne Bay. At seven o'clock when he picked her up at a back exit, the Orange Bowl melee was only embryonic. If any questions came to mind when he passed the two buses and patrol car around front, he forgot them when he saw Dottie.

"Talk to me, Juan Wayne," she said as she got in his secondhand Ford (Buy American) Pinto. "I've been waiting all day for you to talk to me."

He had dinner reservations at the Golden Pelican on Key Biscayne at eight. He took her the scenic route through the diminishing rush-hour traffic. She was the first person he had ever allowed to ride in his passenger seat without a seat belt. She sat close. It felt dangerous.

They had drinks on the patio and a window view for dinner. He had never felt so proud to be seen with a woman. Heads turned as she passed. The stretch jumpsuit molded to her every Cuban-madonna curve. Her face was exotic, no hint of domesticity now.

He was talking too much, both from nerves and to answer her questions. He had meant to ask her about her family, to find out if it had been her father he had seen, what her husband had been imprisoned for, if perhaps her husband was mean to her, was a horrible person, no longer went to bed with her. But instead he was now telling her what it was like to live in the United States.

He selected the wine by price; twenty-six dollars seemed reasonably expensive. He ordered swordfish. She had the surf and turf and ate each bite with an enjoyment that scared him.

"You're not being sarcastic or anything when you call me Juan Wayne, are you?"

"No," Dottie said. She squeezed his knee beneath the table. They went back out on the patio for dessert: Tía María over chocolate ice cream. He had had several places recommended to him for dancing. He had never been to any of them and decided the safest thing to do was to go to all of them.

Perhaps the object of her affection wasn't Esteban Santiesteban. Perhaps it was the lights from downtown Miami high-stepping across Biscayne Bay. Perhaps it was freedom. A new life. A dream. But it was love. At Casanova's the bass was so loud she had hardly to move, the music moved her. She didn't notice that no one in the crowd was over twenty-five, she felt barely eighteen herself. At Scaramouch, tiny lights twinkled from every darkened corner. On the dance floor, a fog machine limited visibility to inches; she couldn't even see her shiny patent-leather pumps. She felt as if she were dancing on the clouds, high up over the lovely darkness and the lights of the city. At the Village Inn, a band called Skin Tight sang "Roll Over Beethoven," and the floor cleared around her as much to watch her dance as to avoid her whirling power. She asked the band if they knew "Hound Dog." They did.

"I want a whiskey," she told Esteban Santiesteban when the set was over. "I want a whiskey like they drink in the movies."

She had two. The firewater burned her mouth, her throat, her stomach, and then suddenly left her feeling good. The music turned around her. She smiled at her face in the mirror behind the bar.

"What is it?" she asked the frowning face of Esteban Santiesteban in the same mirror. "Why are you looking so unhappy all of a sudden?"

She spun around on her bar stool to him as he called something in English to a bouncer and uniformed cop at the side door several feet away.

"Nothing," Esteban Santiesteban said. "They were only talking about some kind of scuffle at the Orange Bowl earlier when they tried to relocate some people. It's under control now."

"How big a scuffle?" she asked, the whiskey rising in her throat like bile.

"Nothing big. The cop said it was on the eleven-o'clock news and it's under control now. Don't worry, Dottie, I won't let them take you anywhere you don't want to go."

"I hope they haven't relocated anyone. I want to go home."

"Where?"

"To the Orange Bowl."

"It was just a disturbance, not a riot or anything. It's over now. Don't let it spoil our night."

"My family is there! My son was sick when I left. I want to make sure they're still there."

"Your son?"

CHAPTER 39

Felipe found his Winn-Dixie shopping cart behind one of the barricades, where it had been commandeered for the cause. As the supply of bottles, rocks, and cans dwindled, sundries from the shopping cart were thrown. Several reporters and one officer were wearing the watches that had been thrown in their direction. There were flip-flops everywhere. The Marianna nail polish was, of all the items in Felipe's cart, proving to be the most valuable to the cause. Each bottle was an exquisite miniature Molotov cocktail. When aimed at the fiery car, they exploded with a small vengeance, spewing molten pinks and reds some distance.

"Get your fucking hands off my stuff!" Felipe told the two men standing with his cart.

"Sorry," the larger of the two answered. His name was Villaverde. "Sorry—if this was yours. But it's ours now—not for personal use but for our demonstration." He tossed another two bottles of the liquid bougainvillea flames. Felipe was rummaging through what was left in his cart.

"My watches! Where are my watches?"

"We have no need of watches; they were used to throw."

"They were Seiko watches!"

"There were twenty or thirty of them in a box; I'm sure they couldn't have been very valuable."

"They were expensive recreations, you son of a bitch."
Villaverde hated the younger postrevolution generation.
Freedom was an abstract concept to them, and they clung
to their meager possessions ferociously. He had often tried
to tell them the little they had wasn't worth possessing, that
they'd have so much more if they were free, but they
couldn't imagine life not rationed in long lines. He had
tried to organize them twice in the hills of Cuba. Both times
one of them had traduced him and Villaverde had spent
time in jail.

"You little bastard, I'm a son of a what?" he said to Felipe
and swung.

Felipe went down. The last thing he remembered before
losing consciousness was a polite voice saying, "Please be
reasonable. He is young. He is my son."

"Señor, I don't want to tell you the names he called my
mother!" Villaverde told Juan Raúl Pérez.

"I am sorry for that, señor. I spent twenty years in prison.
I'm afraid I wasn't around to help bring the boy up right."

"I am sorry. I was a prisoner also. We took his things for
our demonstration, señor, not for our personal use."

"I understand, but these things are his livelihood. He has
a right to fight for them."

Later, Felipe remembered somebody counting, counting
his ribs perhaps or his breathing.

The SWAT team infiltrated quietly through the back of
the stadium. They hesitated using tear gas with the media so
close at hand and instead hosed the demonstrators with
water. They were caught off-guard by the initial burst of
refreshing water.

"It's raining!" one of the demonstrators joyfully yelled.

"No," said another, "it's over."

Order was restored in less than twenty minutes. The
burning car was extinguished. The stadium lights were
dimmed.

Villaverde helped Juan Raúl Pérez carry Felipe back to his cot. Juan Raúl Pérez continued his search for Papá. He looked in bleachers and fields, in shadowy corridors and locker rooms. He took so many steps that he lost count and had to start over several times. Eight hundred and thirty-one steps brought him to a dark ramp on the upper deck. A flashlight lit Juan Raúl Pérez's face.

"Don't fire!" a strange voice screamed when the light hit his face. Juan Raúl Pérez dove to the ground, catching the side of his head on one of the orange plastic seats as he fell.

"Jesus Christ! Why did you say that? I wasn't going to shoot him," a SWAT team member told the old man in camouflage clothing who had been silently following him around since his arrival over the back fence hours before. Papa remained mute, and he wondered if the old man had really uttered "Don't fire!" or if he had just imagined it.

"Shit," he said to Papa. "He's not moving. Let's get him downstairs."

CHAPTER 40

Juan Raúl Pérez didn't feel any pain. But he decided never to move again. He wanted only to lie there on the concrete or wherever they were carrying him to. Maybe he had been executed. Maybe he was dead, he didn't know.

"Where am I?" he asked the concerned Cuban-madonna face hovering over his own. He never recalled a face looking as beautiful as Dottie's did at that moment. He also felt relieved. Here he was finally executed and it didn't feel that bad at all, only distant, and the distance felt lovely. It wasn't so bad being distant from the crowd. He also felt distant from his confusion and exhaustion and the pain in his forehead where he had knocked against the seat as he fell. The skin beneath his eyebrow was beginning to swell and his forehead was already swollen. Dottie wished she had some ice to put on it, but there were police and guards about and she thought it better to stay where she was.

"Where am I, señora?"

"You are lying on my cot in the Orange Bowl in the United States and we are here with you. Your son is on your cot and Papa is on his own cot," said Dottie. Her face was aflame with the reflection from her red jumpsuit.

What a beautiful, incredibly beautiful face she has, he thought. "Señora," Juan Raúl Pérez said, "I love you. You are a peasant and you always know exactly where you are on this earth." Then he fell into a distant sleep.

Dottie wasn't sure if this was an insult, but she let it alone. If it wasn't an insult, she didn't want to know about the love part.

It was just as well she had no cot to sleep on. She stayed awake most of the night to guard her family. She wasn't letting any of her chances for freedom slip away.

PART TWO

~~~~~~

FREEDOM
AUGUST 1980

In the morning, you would stretch your way to the edge of the bed. You would pull on your long robe as you sat there, and then rise, spreading the folds of the robe from you like a bird taking flight. You opened the window. Light filled the room.

But before I would picture that gentle flight, I imagined you lying beneath me. I thought, if I am longing for her so badly, she must be longing for me too. Sometimes when the memory of your face passed before my eyes unexpectedly—I thought, she is thinking of me now. For several years you stayed locked tightly in my arms until desire drove me from my mind. I had to let you go. I had to drive you to the airport again, kiss you softly, and watch the plane take off.

And yet freeing you from my arms gave me a certain freedom. I could imagine your new life, pieced together from your letters: the apartment off Red Road, the duplex in Hialeah, the house on Twenty-third Street, Teresa's confirmation, the letter you wrote that afternoon from the beach.

But now I don't know where you are and I am lost—I am unprepared for this freedom.

CHAPTER 41

Father Joseph Aiden couldn't understand his parishioners' accents when they did speak English. He couldn't even understand their sins. Once in the confessional, he thought a woman confessed to being a communist spy. He made her repeat it three times before telling her that for penance she must report her position to the authorities and say a rosary every day for five years. The penitent, Beatrice Gómez, thought it rather a stern punishment for confessing that sometimes she missed Cuba so much that she prayed for all communists to die. She made sure it was to old Father Martínez that she confessed the same sin to the next week. He heard her confession in Spanish and told her to say one Ave Maria.

Father Aiden also thought one of his weekly penitents was a drug dealer, but since the man spoke nothing but Spanish, Father Aiden couldn't be sure and thought it a sly way of forcing forgiveness from him.

No, it hadn't been Father Aiden's idea to sponsor any of the Mariel refugees, although the archdiocese was encouraging it and many other neighboring parishes and civic organizations had been doing so since April. The idea to house refugees at the Church of the Resurrection had come from the parish's Lay Council, who also came up with a special collection fund to finance the project. He knew his opposition was in vain once he saw the first-graders holding bake sales on the church steps and contributing their milk money for the newly arrived huddled masses. Yet since the end of May, when the parish had started sponsoring several Mariel refugees, he was glad of it. He had been a parish priest for over thirty years, and these last few months had been the first time that he really felt that he was saving souls. Here was the chance to teach the native tongue and old-fashioned American values to those fresh off the boat— *before* they were corrupted into thinking that they didn't need English to survive in Miami, *before* they figured out that Miami wasn't part of the real United States.

Behind Father Aiden's desk in his study were a crucifix on the wall and the flag in a stand. His blue eyes sparkled with the task of conversion on hand while Father Martínez ushered the new family of refugees into the room. Father Aiden rose from his desk and smiled. The smile froze on his face.

Felipe's forehead was crisscrossed with Band-Aids. The dark circles ringing his eyes and the three-piece white suit gave him the look of a gangster from the thirties. When Father Aiden shook his hand, Felipe grunted. The man in the camouflage suit introduced as Grandfather appeared more vegetable than human. The overweight Mrs. Pérez was dressed in a red body suit so indecently tight that he could see the outlines of her underwear.

"We were all Catholic and could be again if we had to, Father," Dottie said as she shook Father Aiden's hand.

Father Martínez translated, and Father Aiden wondered if his own words sounded as garbled to his listeners.

"The United States is founded on the principle of freedom, Mrs. Pérez, and whatever your beliefs they will be respected," Father Aiden said.

Juan Raúl Pérez shook Father Aiden's hand and bowed. Father Aiden felt he should avert his eyes from the man, but it was difficult not to look. One side of Juan Raúl Pérez's face and his entire forehead were swollen beyond proportion. Combined with the bald head and the sunken mouth, he gave the impression of a wizened baby with a birth defect. Dottie had already explained to Father Martínez that her husband had been injured saving a policeman during the Orange Bowl disturbance the night before.

The housekeeper from the rectory had put out sandwiches and soft drinks. Father Martínez seated the guests and passed the refreshments.

"This family's history is very sad," Father Martínez said to Father Aiden.

"I can see that," Father Aiden said.

CHAPTER 42

Felipe's ribs ached. The cut on his forehead
was superficial. The brunt of his confrontation with San
Lázaro and later with the first of Villaverde had taken him
squarely in the chest, and although nothing was broken,
muscles were torn and dark bruises blossomed. It hurt
when he took a deep breath. It hurt when he moved. He was
glad he felt like shit, because he couldn't have taken refor-
mation any other way.

He checked his face in the bathroom mirror. A little Marianna cover stick hid the dark circles under his eyes. He
replaced Luz Paz's crisscrossed Band-Aid design with two
small strips high on his forehead and combed his hair to
cover it. Not that he was going anywhere. Not that he felt
like going anywhere. He replaced his suit with a pair of
cut-offs, rewound the Ace bandage over his ribs, and carefully lowered himself onto the bed. The room was a
sparsely furnished dormitory cubicle with two twin beds
and two crucifixes. He had to wonder if it was worth it. He
had only meant to be good for a while, till he felt better, not
to be assigned a bed in the priests' house with Papa for a
roommate. Dottie had warned him to guard Papa with his
life. Felipe had just wanted to be good for a while, not to be
punished.

Aside from his family's apartment in Havana, this was

the dullest place he had ever spent the night. Even the Orange Bowl hadn't been so dull. He couldn't help thinking that if he had looked both ways before crossing the street the day before, he would now be in a beautiful apartment somewhere with a girl with a St. Tropez tan lying in his arms, loving him. Well, at least he wasn't in jail.

Papa lay on the other twin bed with wide eyes that Felipe was sure would never close in the dim light of the table lamp. He told the old man to turn off the light so he wouldn't have to see his face. But Papa didn't move, so Felipe had to do it himself. Felipe turned on the ghetto blaster on the night table between them as low as possible. Then he realized that even that low, he might not be able to hear Papa if Papa should get up and wander off into the night. He had lost Papa twice already since Dottie's warning. Without the radio on, the silence intensified the gaze of the old man. Felipe was sure the night would never pass, was sure days of nights passed while he waited in the darkness where the wide eyes of the old man opened up more darkness and more silence. Cursing the pain in his ribs, Felipe finally pushed his own twin bed over to the door and fell asleep guarding it. There was no other way out of the room except a clean second-floor drop through the window.

Dottie put ice on Juan Raúl Pérez's forehead and fed him aspirin that she had gotten from Father Martínez. Their room was in the church hall. It was a long narrow space, running almost the length of the building, and had been used as a storeroom until two months before, when the Church of the Resurrection started sponsoring refugees. The room had high side windows and no air-conditioning vents, but there were several electric fans. Juan Raúl Pérez watched the fans nod their heads this way and that, now a breeze, gone a breeze.

Dottie's voice floated on the breeze from the fan. "We're free!" she said. "Our plan worked. And I think Father Aiden liked us."

She walked the length of the room, touching the donated furniture as she went: a dresser painted white, a bamboo chair with green cushions, a brass floor lamp with a pleated shade. The room had the musty odor of an antique store.

"Do you think you will feel strong enough to work tomorrow? What good luck to have jobs just like that. Maybe you should wait, though—your head looks painful. I am just glad you were able to make it this far." There was a small desk. Dottie sat at it and opened the drawers.

"You and I eat in here," she said, looking over at a pink Formica table. "Papa and Felipe eat with the priests. The cabinets in the bingo kitchen across the hall are full of canned food left for us, and Father Martínez showed me how to use the stove there."

He watched the moon through the leaves of a banyan tree outside the window. He was falling asleep. He had volunteered to sleep on the floor, because this was the room married couples stayed in and there was only one bed. But Dottie, sympathetic to his injuries, had refused his offer. He was glad. His aching head outweighed his gallantry at the moment. There had been straw matting in prison. This was the first real bed he had slept in in twenty years. The first fresh pillow in twenty years. He was wearing stripped pajama bottoms Dottie had found laundered and folded in the dresser. The sheets were white and clean and the soft cotton was gentle on his skin. The fans nodded their heads, here a breeze, there.

There was a pay phone across the street at the high school. Her call was answered on the first ring.

"Are you OK?" Esteban Santiesteban asked.

"Oh yes. It's wonderful here. But I can't make it for lunch tomorrow."

"Why not? Didn't you have a good time dancing before we had to go?"

"It was the best time I've had in the U.S., but I have a job tomorrow. I'm going to sell flowers, and I start tomorrow."

"Sell flowers?"

"Yes. Work in a florist's. I'm very excited. I know it's going to be wonderful. I never would have thought of working in a flower shop."

"How about dinner then?"

"I don't know what my hours will be. I have to go now. I'll call you tomorrow. Say hello to Luz Paz for me when you go to work tomorrow."

"Wait! Don't you want to talk for a minute?"

"No, not now. I'm tired."

She wished there were separate beds as she crawled between the sheets; Juan Raúl was sleeping on his back and emitting a noise between a snore and a moan. But the rhythm of the annoying sound sent her quickly to sleep.

CHAPTER 43

Perhaps because he was free.

Perhaps because the aspirin and the ice the night before had dulled his pain.

Perhaps because he had so often dreamed of waking up in clean sheets with his arm around his wife.

Whatever the reason, the next morning Juan Raúl Pérez awoke with an erection. It had been years since he had awoken with an erection and it took him several minutes to identify his condition as something real and not from a dream or a memory. Warmth glowed in the air. The smell of close flesh gave the warmth a thick tension. A throbbing pulsing edge removed it from anything remotely resembling sleep, or dream. Femaleness enfolded him. Indeed, when he opened his eyes his arm was around Dottie.

He was sorry he had opened his eyes—it wasn't his wife his arm was around!

He removed his arm. He inched his way away from Dottie. He got as far as the wall and could go no farther. What was she doing in the bed? How dare she sleep in the bed when she had said she'd sleep on the floor? Or had she only said he could sleep in the bed, not that she would sleep elsewhere? A woman like Dottie wouldn't care who she got into bed with, he decided.

Given the space, Dottie was a messy sleeper: one foot

hung off the bed, the other leg bent toward her stomach in a tangle of cover. Her hair was spread out everywhere, entangling the pillow and her arms. Juan Raúl Pérez noted this with displeasure. She was an unrefined, crude, messy woman who lied and schemed and attracted strange people like Papa and foul-mouthed punks like Felipe. But even this harangue didn't take away his erection. He put his hand down to feel the strange sensation. It felt like the only part of him that was strong, that had substance. That was real.

It repulsed him, the very idea of waking up with his arms around a strange woman disgusted him—it wasn't adultery, it was sacrilege. His teeth started chattering. He carefully moved to the foot of the bed and got up.

Juan Raúl Pérez made his decision as he stood in the shower beneath buckets of cold water. He would find out the truth, as quickly and quietly as possible. Dottie was free now; he had no more obligations to her or to the rest of the family she had created. He could no longer wait for strength when his throbbing member was pointed in another direction. Only the truth could give him a chance at freedom. He would find out the truth as soon as he could. He felt purity descend upon him. All else descended too, and he was erection-free by the time he was dressed.

Dottie woke to the sound of someone shouting from outside the door and then pounding. "Señor, Señora, come quickly! Please open the door."

Dottie got up and opened the door. It took Father Martínez a moment to remember why he had come. In her tattered white slip, Dottie appeared to him to be more naked than clothed. "Your father-in-law is in the tree outside your window. You'd better come quickly," he said. "Father Aiden can't get him down, and he wants to call the fire department."

It was one of the altar boys coming into church for early mass who had spotted Papa in the tree.

"I told you to watch him," Dottie yelled at Felipe. And

then to Papa, "You ungrateful bastard. Get down from there."

"Señora, you cannot speak like that in public," Father Martínez said."

"Tell her she can't parade around like that in her pajamas in public!" Father Aiden told Father Martínez to translate. He did.

"It is a slip, not pajamas," Dottie told Father Martínez to relay to Father Aiden.

During translation, Juan Raúl Pérez appeared. Papa came immediately down from the tree and stood beside him. But Dottie was still the center of attention.

"You are not allowed to walk around dressed that way, and your father is not allowed in the tree," Father Aiden told Dottie via Father Martínez.

"He is not my father," Dottie said.

"My father is an old man, please forgive him," Juan Raúl Pérez said to Father Martínez. "He is used to sleeping with us. We will move him into our room right away. I am sorry for the disturbance."

"Where were you, Señor Hard-on?" Dottie whispered as she went by Juan Raúl Pérez.

How had she known? he wondered, looking down. She was so crude, she probably had a homing device for that sort of thing.

"Hey, I'm not sleeping in the priests' house by myself," Felipe said. "I'm going to get my stuff."

"Tell them," Father Aiden told Father Martínez, "tell them they should at least try to speak English."

CHAPTER 44

Victor Castro (no relation) was a tall stocky man in his early sixties. He had come to the United States with his wife, son, and two daughters in 1961. It hadn't been easy for Victor Castro, and he planned on returning to Cuba the minute it was liberated.

For many years now, Victor Castro had sold flowers from the back of an aging yellow truck. Early each day, he went down to the wholesale market by the train tracks and bought a supply of flowers for the day. It was not an enjoyable business for him—he was not a good salesman, and flowers didn't agree with his allergies. Nor was it a lucrative one, at least not until the Mariel boatlift supplied him with a cheap and seemingly inexhaustible labor pool. He still bought the flowers; the refugees sold them and he took the profits. It hadn't been easy for Victor Castro when he had first come over, and damned if he was going to make it any easier for anybody else.

Baby-pink carnations were on special that morning. He also got a good deal on long-stemmed roses that wouldn't last another day. Then he got the usual greenery and cheaper flowers and went to pick up the day's labor supply. There were two waiting outside St. Anne's, a mother and daughter who had sold for him for weeks now. There were over a dozen men waiting on Douglas Avenue by the airport, both new and old faces. They were a disheveled crew, sleeping by the river docks or behind the airport warehouses. There were a few more by Flagler Dog Track. At the Church of the Resurrection, there were half a dozen more, two regulars and a new family of four. The new family wasn't going to last long, Castro judged—not only was the woman in heels and the son with an attitude, but a guy with a weird-shaped head and a geezer in a camouflage suit were not going to sell a lot of flowers.

He arbitrarily assigned them street corners. He made sure to tell his vendors that he had rented these corners from the government. It wasn't true—the corners were free to anyone, and he didn't even have a vending license. But the cops didn't check and the refugees were either too oblivious or too frightened to question anything with the word "government" near it. He hadn't been challenged yet except by the Moonies, but they didn't come out till night. Before dropping them off at the corners, he sold them flowers to sell. How they got home was their business.

The Church of the Resurrection had a fund to help first-time sellers get started, so he knew the new family would have enough money to buy a bundle right off, probably more than they could sell for the next two days.

"Take some more," he told Dottie. "I'm giving you a good corner this week, 'cause you're new. Take more ribbon too. That'll be twenty dollars each."

"What?" Felipe said. "What are you working on, a thousand percent margin?"

Oh shit, Castro thought, trouble, but not a bad guess on his profit margin by the kid. On a good day, Victor Castro could make two hundred dollars for two or three hours of work. On an average day such as today when he picked up only one round of workers he'd make half that. The vendors, when they were lucky, could clear ten to fifteen dollars a day. "Hey, you don't like it you can go somewhere else," Castro told Felipe. "I'm just trying to help out 'cause nobody gave me any breaks when I first came."

"It's fine," Dottie said. "We'll take them."

If Dottie was disappointed about selling flowers from a hot dusty median divider and not the quaint flower shop she had imagined, her first sale changed her mind—three dollars in fifteen seconds to a young woman on her way to pick up her boyfriend at the airport. Three dollars! That was equal to twelve loads of laundry and an hour of raw hands in the woman's showers at the Orange Bowl. She opened her fist and showed the crumpled bills to Felipe with a giggle. The next three sales were hers also. But sale of a double bunch fell to Felipe right after that.

Flagler and Le Jeune was a good intersection. It caught downtown traffic during the rush hours and airport traffic all day long.

The morning rush-hour traffic began its flow. In the time zone between red and green light, Dottie smiled and swished between cars. Blue cars, yellow cars, vans, and convertibles. Red roses, purple statice, baby's breath, and carnations. Green light, red light, dollars, and faces. And music from a thousand radios.

People who had never rolled down their windows for faces on the corner rolled down their windows for Dottie. This wasn't the sad-eyed face of a heavy-hearted refugee. This wasn't the face of poverty, danger, or pleading. This was a smiling face, with polka dots flying and hips swaying. Her arms were full of flowers and her feet caught the rhythms of salsa and rock.

The two others who came also from the Church of the Resurrection were Rafael Bosch, a laconic middle-aged man who studied borrowed law books at night, and Juana Calleiro, a frightened young woman who had left her husband in Cuba. Juana lived in the convent and the nuns watched her two small children while she worked. Rafael was quickly concerned that Dottie would put a dent in his earning, but it wasn't so. He wasn't making the sales she was, but the thirty dollars in his pocket by the time the rush hour slowed was far more than he usually made all day. Cars stopped for Dottie. And if one car stopped, a car behind was more likely to do the same. There was never any such residue when he worked alone with Juana, who had to be pushed to leave the curb sometimes. Dottie got the windows down, and Rafael was right behind her. Felipe wasn't doing badly himself, but he didn't move very fast with the pain in his ribs. The lights turned green much too quickly.

Juan Raúl Pérez did not sell a single flower. Nor did he try. He had enough trouble keeping Papa out of traffic and out of the vendors' way. He also ran errands for Dottie. She gave him money to buy Coca-Colas at the Texaco station at the corner. Up the street at La Rosa bakery he bought pastries and coffee for the sellers.

Two blocks away at a local farmacia, Juan Raúl Pérez captured Papa in an old wooden phone booth. It was close in the phone booth with Papa. Juan Raúl Pérez hyperventilated enough courage to open the telephone directory, turn to the section marked P, and let his fingers crawl to the pages for Pérez. He lost focus several times and had to stop to slow his breathing down. There were no Carmela Pérezes listed, and of the dozen C. Pérezes, none of them was on Twenty-third Street. He carefully copied all twelve or so addresses and phone numbers on a crumpled sheet of legal paper from his pocket. Juan Raúl Pérez did not try to call any of the phone numbers. His courage was spent. He did buy a small street map before leaving the store.

At one o'clock when the lunch-hour traffic thinned, they had lunch at Burger King. They had already sold a day's worth of flowers, including the portions for Papa and Juan Raúl Pérez. Juan Raúl Pérez and Papa, Rafael, and Juana all headed for the bus home after lunch. Dottie and Felipe waited until they were out of sight before they went off to find flowers at a better price to sell for the afternoon.

At the bus station, Juan Raúl Pérez braved another trip

through the telephone book which hung on metal chains below the public phone. There were many Angel Díazes and even more A. Díazes. They didn't do him any good, as he didn't know Angel's address. In the yellow pages, he checked under furniture stores. It didn't matter there that he knew neither the name or address of his brother-in-law's store. On the first page of listings, there was a half-page ad for "Angel's Taste of Cuba," which included a poorly reproduced head photo of Angel Díaz himself. There was even a little map in the corner giving the location and directions from the expressways. He ripped the page out quickly and hid it in his pocket. He waited till he was alone back in his room at the church before he examined it further. He read every line and examined each sentence. There were store hours and the guarantee of the lowest prices in town and the largest selection of Cuban-style furniture in the U.S. What was Cuban-style furniture? he wondered. His and Carmela's had been Mediterranean, he recalled. And there was the shadowy photo of the grinning man Angel could have grown into. The face had grown larger and squarer. But it was his wife's brother's face. Juan Raúl Pérez had never received a letter from Angel while he was in prison. But there was always news of him from Carmela and sometimes a postscript in Angel's own hurried scrawl: "Have enclosed one hundred dollars. Maybe you can buy some extra food." Or "I am working with a lawyer who is working with a lawyer in Havana to obtain your release. Enclosed fifty for cigarettes." The money was long gone from the envelope by the time Juan Raúl Pérez got the letters.

Yes, Juan Raúl Pérez decided, he would contact Angel. His brother-in-law would either lead him to Carmela or tell him the truth about her status. Whatever happened, Angel would help him. He was not only family but he had lived with Carmela and him for four years from the time he was ten when his parents had died. Angel would give him a job even if Carmela was remarried or dead. Best not to think of it; he would know soon enough.

Surely Dottie no longer needed him. He could see that when she and Felipe came home from selling flowers at eight that night. She was brimming with good fortune, and her newfound freedom graced her every movement. He tried not to notice how radiant she looked. He was still disgusted from his morning's erection.

She got two mattresses to lay on the floor for Papa and Felipe, carrying them over from the rectory with a priest Juan Raúl Pérez had never seen before. In the hall, she told Juan Raúl Pérez they would have to sleep together in the big bed since she didn't want either Papa or Felipe to know they weren't married. He objected. He would prefer to sleep on the floor.

"It was just a piss hard-on," she answered. "Don't take it personally."

He was silent after that. It didn't matter. He'd be out of her life tomorrow. No, she didn't need him at all. She had made seventy-four dollars, not including Felipe's share, which she said they'd split equally between the two of them and made him promise not to tell anyone else. He told her to hold his share for him.

There were no flowers in the room, but Juan Raúl Pérez could smell them from Dottie's skin as she slept: roses and carnations, and the almost absent sweet dried air of baby's breath.

CHAPTER 45

"Get those fuckers away from here," Angel
Díaz told his sales manager. Two Marielitos had been hanging around outside for ten minutes. Angel could see them
through the store windows, and so could everyone else. It
looked bad. Bad for business. "Call the police if you have
to," Angel said. "I don't want them around.

Having neglected his business in the past four months for
his trips to Key West during the boatlift, Angel now had a
warehouse full of back stock he needed to move. A Taste of
Cuba was having a big sale with full-page ads in both the
Herald and the *News*. The store was crowded. Even Angel
was out on the selling floor, something he preferred not to
do. But at least it was less trying during big sales: people
were less hesitant with the large red tags displaying the dollars saved per item for a limited time only.

The Marielitos were gone by the time the sales manager
got out to the sidewalk to shoo them away. Late in the afternoon they came back, and Angel sent the manager back out
to get rid of them.

A voice behind him asked, "Angel?"

"I'll be with you in a minute."

"Angel Díaz?"

Angel spun around and saw one of the Marielitos. "I can't
have you people hanging out here. I'm very busy right
now."

"You've grown up."

"What? What do you want, mister?"

"I guess you don't recognize me."

"No, I guess I don't, and I don't have time to play games right now."

But the Marielito just stood there.

"Here, you want money? Take five dollars," Angel said. "Buy yourself food and don't come back here again."

"But I'm your brother-in-law, Juan Raúl Pérez, remember?"

Angel didn't know whether to slap the guy or laugh.

"What the hell are you talking about, mister?" He stared at the toothless man's strange head.

"It's me, Angel. I suppose I've aged a bit."

"And your head?"

"An accident at the Orange Bowl."

"Right." But something clicked just then; Teresa had described the burglar to Angel as a weirdo in an oversized parrot shirt, and that's what this weirdo was wearing. It certainly wasn't his brother-in-law. Juan was a tall well-built man with black bushy hair, a round face, an authoritative voice. The man standing before him was small and malformed. He was also rail-thin, and his voice wasn't even close.

"Why don't you come into my office?" Angel said. He would ask him a few questions before he called the police, questions like what the fuck did this man know about his brother-in-law that he was doing such a bad job at impersonating. He hoped this man was crazy, an escapee from a lunatic asylum, because he had a horrible feeling as he showed the man into his office that his brother-in-law was dead and that this impostor knew it. Impostors don't impersonate the living. It's too risky.

Angel closed the door to his office and gestured the man to the chair in front of his desk.

"I've come to find out the truth," Juan Raúl Pérez said.

"Oh, have you now? Why don't you relax for a minute first? Cigarette?"

"Thanks."

Angel watched the man light the cigarette with trembling hands. An old alkie maybe to have hands that trembled so? What did he want? Money? Instant family? Angel saw that the man was watching him fumble as he tried to light his own cigarette with his broken hand. Won't hurt to let the guy know right from the start that he didn't take any shit. "Broke my arm," Angel said. "Bashing some guy's head in." He got the cigarette lit.

"I'm sorry," Juan Raúl Pérez said. "Nothing to do with my family, I hope."

His family! What a set of balls. One wall of Angel's office was a window. He looked out it and was glad it was there. This way he wouldn't kill the guy in front of witnesses. "When'd you get out?" Angel asked.

"About a week ago. No, it was a week and a half, I guess. I was somewhat confused when I first got out."

He had to think about it! He wasn't even sure when he got out. "They released you from El Muro?"

"No," Juan Raúl Pérez said. "I was never there. I was in Calvario, you know that. You are Angel Díaz, aren't you?"

Angel ignored the question, took a deep breath, and did his best to stay calm. "What the hell were you doing over on Twenty-third Street last week?"

"So she still lives there. How is she? And is Teresa all right?"

Angel could have kicked himself for mentioning Twenty-third Street. He was giving this guy too much information—how else would he know the impostor had been to Twenty-third Street if someone hadn't told him? He took a long drag on his Marlboro and took the offensive: "My sister moved a long time ago. If you were Juan Pérez you would know that."

"Who else would I be?"

"I don't know. I was hoping you'd tell me that."

"I do not understand what you are saying. Where has my family moved?" Juan Raúl Pérez asked.

He didn't get an answer. He continued, "I see this is very awkward for us both and you hesitate to tell me. But I came to find out the truth. Is she alive? Of course she must be if you say she has moved. Has she remarried? Is that why you do not want to tell me? And Teresa, where is she?"

Angel wanted to scream at him to cut the shit. What a set of brass balls on this guy. If he really wanted to work his way into the family then he shouldn't have run off when Carmela's burglar alarm had gone off. Her husband would have had no reason to run off. And he shouldn't have been stupid enough to forget his shoes he had taken off to tiptoe around. Pretty hard to fake a shoe size. But then the man sitting across from him didn't know Carmela had already seen him and didn't know who the hell he was.

"You tell me what you want," Angel said. "And then tell me what you know about Juan Pérez."

"What? I have already told you what I want. You can tell me the truth, whatever it is."

He was getting nervous, Angel could see that. The man had let his cigarette burn out in the ashtray and he was starting to sweat, twisting his hands, clutching at his wrist. It made Angel want to slap him. Angel calmed himself. No use killing this guy before he got any information out of him.

"You want a glass of water?" Angel asked. It was time he called the police.

"Yes, please."

"Excuse me for a minute," Angel said. "Here, take another cigarette. I'll be right back."

Angel went into his secretary's office and told her to call the police. It was too complicated to tell her about the impostor sitting in his office, so he just told her to tell the cops there was a burglar. It was the wrong thing to tell her. Her door was open and she started screaming: "Oh my God. Oh my God, a burglary. Nine-one-one. I'm calling right now, Mr. Díaz. Should we evacuate?"

Evacuate? Shit. "Keep your voice down," Angel said. He

heard more shouting. As he went out the secretary's door he saw the other Marielito in the camouflage suit. The old man was running and knocked over an armoire and a chair in his path. The customers were scattering. A salesmen went for the old man. "Leave him alone," Juan Raúl Pérez shouted and grabbed César Armando Pérez. "Come on, Papa, come on!"

Anticipating the possibility of gunfire, several customers had hit the floor. Their prone bodies and the fallen armoire blocked Angel's path. He screamed after them, "The police will get you, you scum. Don't you ever go near my sister again!"

After the police the secretary had called left A Taste of Cuba, Angel was on the phone with his lawyer. Angel didn't tell the police or the lawyer that he had also told the secretary to call in a burglary-in-progress at Carmela's house.

Angel told the lawyer what shits the police had been. Then he filled the lawyer in on the details as he saw them. While he waited for the private investigators the lawyer was sending over, he called Flavia. He had already sent his sales manager over to cruise Carmela's house to make sure the police were there and to watch the house when they left. One of the PIs would take over that task as soon as it could be arranged. Angel wanted the house watched and Carmela trailed if she went out in case the imposter decided to make a move. In the meantime he had his secretary call the house every twenty minutes to make small talk.

Angel had to wait fourteen rings, count them, fourteen, before Flavia answered the line.

"He may be dead," he told her.

"Who?"

"Carmela's husband. My brother-in-law. Who else have I been looking for for twenty years?"

"Oh, Angel, I'm sorry. Does Carmela know?"

"No, Flavia. And nobody's going to tell her until I figure out how to handle this."

"How did you find out?"

"There's more to it than that, Flavia. These two guys were here a little while ago. I don't know if they personally bumped Juan off or if one of them was his cellmate and got the information that way. The guy was so stupid, I should have killed him for just being stupid. He was trying to impersonate my brother-in-law, and he brought his father with him. Juan Pérez's father died twenty years ago."

CHAPTER 46

Juan Raúl Pérez asked the man at the café cubano window to call a taxi for him. He had twenty dollars in his pocket that Dottie had given him that morning. He hoped it would be enough to take him to the Twenty-third Street of his dreams. Maybe Carmela had moved, as Angel had told him; maybe a neighbor would know where she had gone. But at all costs he needed to secure her place in the universe. He counted his pulse for the ten-minute taxi ride and assigned it 154 beats per minute. He got out several blocks from his destination; he needed to compose himself before he got any closer.

"I have to stop and sit here a minute, Papa," he said. "I can hardly breathe."

He wanted to believe that it was only that Angel hadn't recognized him. He barely recognized himself some mornings when he shaved. But there was something about the look on Angel's face, a look that denied reality unless it was on his own terms. He remembered the same look on Angel's face when Carmela once said her father had had too much to drink at the party the night he drove the car off the road. Ten years old and bold as can be, he called Carmela a liar. And one day when he had given Angel a tour of the newspaper, Angel had announced to him on the way home in the car: "You can stop trying to take the place of my father.

Maybe my father was only a coal merchant and you think you're a big shot, but my father was a great man." Juan Rául Pérez had told the boy that he wasn't trying to take his father's place, that no one could do that. But the boy had only sat stiffly with that same look on his face.

"Maybe that's who he expected to rise from the grave," Juan Raúl Pérez told Papa. "Maybe he was waiting for his father."

He sat on a stone beneath a tree until his pulse got down to 110. He wanted water. "Is there a canteen in that knapsack?" he asked Papa without expecting a reply. He rose, but the old man pulled him back by his shoulder and handed him a camouflage canteen. He drank rapidly. The water calmed his heart and gave him strength. He handed the rest back to the old man and waited while he drank. Then he walked boldly up the center of the road: one two three four . . .

His bravado ended less than a hundred steps away when he turned the corner and saw the police car in Carmela's driveway. There was a policewoman writing on a clipboard. There was a man in a white short-sleeved shirt. They were both facing Carmela with their backs to him. But he could see Carmela, and it was Carmela. She was alive. Living. Breathing. But how could she have changed so little? How could she look so much like herself and different from how he had imagined her? Papa pulled him from behind. Was it Angel who had called the police? Would they arrest him here and throw him in jail the way they did in Cuba? No, it wouldn't do for him to be arrested again after he was already free. Were there police in Miami who wore short-sleeved white shirts instead of uniforms? He thought she glanced at him a moment. But if she recognized him, she pretended she didn't. Not with the police so close. No, it wouldn't do for him to be sent to jail after he had come so far. After he had seen her face, her beautiful face.

The man in the white shirt put his hand on Carmela's shoulder. It took Juan Raúl Pérez's breath away. Papa tugged at him again. Juan Raúl Pérez ducked behind a car and peered through the car's window. Papa tugged harder, but he could not leave now even if it did mean going to jail. The man dropped his hand from Carmela's shoulder and the air returned to Juan Raúl Pérez's soul. In a minute both the policewoman and the man got into the police car. Carmela walked into the house, but the police car didn't move. Papa pulled Juan Raúl Pérez by his shirt and pulled him around the corner and half the way home.

CHAPTER 47

In the space of a half hour, she had gotten over half a dozen phone calls.

The first one was from Angel telling her that he had arranged for her to have her first gun lesson tomorrow, telling her that she had promised to have a lesson. She didn't remember promising, but she wasn't sure. She didn't know if she simply lacked the strength to fight Angel anymore or if she thought the quickest way around him now was just to say yes to whatever he requested.

Then she got a phone call from Angel's secretary asking her how she was. She hardly knew the secretary and didn't remember her ever calling the house before. Then the secretary called back and told her about the big sale at the store, asking if Carmela wanted any furniture. Then the secretary called back to ask if she had seen Angel. Then if she had seen Angel again. Then that she had found Angel. Then Angel called to ask for Teresa. And then just as she sat back in her chair to watch TV, she saw the police car drive up in the driveway. Officer Rhoades was at the wheel—Carmela had met her twice from previous visits—and Pirelli was in the passenger seat. Had she become so inured to the alarm system that she hadn't heard it go off this time? She shut off the TV and was out on the front grass before they knocked on the door. The lights were flashing from the roof of the car. Was the siren sounding too but Carmela couldn't hear it?

"Everything OK?" Pirelli asked.

"Yes. The alarm didn't go off, did it?"

"Not that I know of. Headquarters got a phone call from a woman who said her house was being broken into at this address."

"It wasn't me," Carmela said. "I don't know what you're talking about."

"You're sure, Mrs. Pérez?" Officer Rhoades asked. "I know you're having a hard time, and I know I came down pretty hard on you last time I was here. But I just want you to know you can get in a lot of trouble calling in a false report to the police. Do you want me to check through your house?" Officer Rhoades took her clipboard and started writing.

"No," Carmela said. "I mean, you can come in if you want to and have a cup of coffee."

"We didn't come for coffee," Rhoades said, still writing.

"I didn't call the police," Carmela said. "I didn't hear the alarm go off. I'm not crazy."

"No one said you were, Mrs. Pérez," Pirelli said. He put his hand on her shoulder. It was a kind, simple gesture, but it made her jump. He let his arm drop.

Carmela saw two Marielitos turning the corner at the end of the street. One of them was wearing a Hawaiian shirt like the one who had knocked on her door that day. Should she tell the police? But he had only knocked on her door that day. She turned her head and they were gone. She was seeing things. She was going crazy. What was going on? Why the phone calls from Angel and his secretary? Why the police? She felt she had suddenly become a bit player in a life which had once been her own.

"Are you all right, Mrs. Pérez?" Pirelli said. "Do you want us to sit with you a minute? Do you want to call your daughter?"

"No. I just don't know what's going on. And I don't know

who called you. I would know if someone was breaking into my house, wouldn't I? I mean, I would hear the alarm go off, right?"

"Do you think you should see a doctor?" Rhoades asked.

"Yes, certainly," Carmela said. She thinks I'm crazy. They both think I'm crazy. Yes, it was no use arguing. Yes. Yes. Yes. "Can I go now, officers?" Yes, she needed to see a doctor. She felt ill standing there on the front lawn in the afternoon sun with the lights from the patrol car flashing. "Can I go back inside the house?"

She wasn't inside the house a minute and the patrol car was still in her driveway when Angel called again to ask if Teresa was home yet. Carmela didn't tell him the police were there. They were gone fifteen minutes later when Flavia called to ask how she was. An hour later Angel called. And she could have sworn Javier Mateo, the manager from Angel's store, was driving back and forth in front of the house, but she could have been seeing things again. In the early evening, Angel appeared at the door and said his condo was being sprayed for bugs, could he sleep on the living-room couch.

"Yes, Angel, certainly."

Strange, since he always slept at Flavia's anyway. Had they fought? She didn't ask. "Your secretary called the house all afternoon," she said.

"She's a pain in the ass, isn't she?" Angel said. "I might have to get rid of her." Never, Angel thought. The secretary was a jewel to have called the police for him and given this address when he had asked her to.

Before they went off duty at the change of shift, Officer Rhoades and Officer González came by Pirelli's temporary office to ask if he'd like to go for drinks with several of them. Pirelli declined. He liked to keep his professional life separate from his personal life, which wasn't difficult; he had been divorced for fifteen years and didn't have a personal life.

"I'm sorry," Pirelli said, glancing at the computer terminal on the desk, "I've still got a mountain of work here tonight."

"Sure," Rhoades said. "Hope I didn't mess up your stats reporting that Pérez business as misinformation this afternoon."

"Of course not," Pirelli said. "We both decided it was the kind thing to do."

"Remember Pérez with the alarm system on Twenty-third?" Rhoades said to González as they were leaving.

González remembered it well, he'd been there a few times himself.

"She's lost it." Rhoades said. "It was really sad; she didn't even bother with the alarm this time. She called in a break-in at her house. There was nobody there and she denied the whole thing. Pirelli was with me. I reported it as misinformation and let it go. I felt bad for her."

Pirelli got up and got himself a cup of coffee. He skipped the sugared doughnut sitting in a box next to the Mr. Coffee. His military trimness was starting to give way, and he didn't like it. Too many years on the road. Too many fast-food dinners. He got back to the computer. He doubted he'd ever see Carmela Pérez again. His on-the-scene crime reports were done. He and his three-person unit would be meeting with the politicians and local community leaders for the next week. Barring no further breakdown in the South Florida network and no other crime crises in the nation, he'd be off to L.A. to investigate gang wars and then tentatively to Oklahoma, where there had been continuing problems with the police and Native Americans.

He had felt sorry for Carmela Pérez that afternoon and was sorry he hadn't asked Rhoades to keep him informed if there were any more calls from Twenty-third Street—as long as he was still in town. But it really wasn't any of his business now.

CHAPTER 48

The smell of formaldehyde and acetone filled the room. Dottie waved her hands in the air to dry her nail polish. Her toes, separated by thick wads of cotton, stuck out in five different directions.

"I'm just not used to doing this anymore," she bemoaned. "You lose the knack." To compensate for the awkwardness in her hands, she lacquered everything in the general area of each nail. Then when her crimson appendages dried, she painstakingly erased all unwanted color with Q-Tips dipped in nail-polish remover.

"You missed dinner," she told Juan Raúl Pérez without looking up from her toes. "Sorry you got stuck with him all day. I got you both hamburgers, over there on the table. We had another good day, though."

Papa took his paper plate and sat on the bed by the door. Felipe was stretched out on his own bed with eyes closed and disco from the radio close to his ear.

"Careful of my nails!" Dottie said when Juan Raúl Pérez sat down on their bed. It was difficult to eat his McDonald's burger with the smell of her nail polish. Each bite tasted pungent and bitter.

"You should see how much I made today," she whispered.

He put down his hamburger. "I think I will get those teeth, my Love," he said.

He had never called her anything but "señora" before, and she looked up to see his face. He wasn't paying any attention to her, just staring off in space.

"Good," she said. She thought a hamburger wouldn't be difficult to gum, and the bread they used was so soft.

"How about my hair?"

"You don't have any."

"Do you think I should get one of those toupees they make for men? I used to have dark hair, very wavy."

"Oh no, they're horrible. First you should gain some weight. Then grow a beard, that's all. Bald men look good with beards."

A beard, yes, it would cover a multitude of sins and give the impression that he could still grow hair. He had seen her! She was alive. The policeman with the white shirt had put his hand on her shoulder and she had almost jumped away from him—perhaps she had remained faithful.

Had there been a flicker of recognition in her eyes? Was it fear he'd get arrested by the police for some reason he couldn't fathom (he certainly had never fathomed his arrest and prison sentence) that made Carmela not call out to him?

He finished his meal, her face before his eyes. His wife of letters from Twenty-third Street. His wife of twenty years ago. She was without the extra weight and the gray years he had aged her with, without the tired shuffle and old flowered dress he had dreamed her in. How could she change so little in the time he had changed so much? The graceful corolla of dark hair surrounded a slightly sad but lovely face.

"You look kind of crazy, señor," Dottie said. "Are you OK?"

"Yes, señora, thank you, I'm fine." But he took the ice wrapped in the towel that she gave him and put it on his forehead. And he swallowed the aspirin she handed him. He did feel strange.

The best thing would be to change every-thing: my life, your life, the lives in between. The life which is lived. The life which is dream.

Here I am ready to change your life as if you were still a player in my dreams. As if I hadn't seen your face today. I don't even seem to be able to change my own life, it just seems to get changed for me.

The best thing would be to have only one life: a life for living or a life for dreaming. The best thing would be to have only one life, the dream not separate from the life, the coun-try, the house without bars where you rise in the morning.

Between the prison and the life, memories of myself reach for your hand, but of course I see now that it wasn't you at all. You are much younger. Your eyes are more sad. You are in the living more gracious than the humblest of my dreams.

The next time you see me I will be a strong man. Will that be different from your dreams?

The best thing would be to live not wandering as I do be-tween worlds.

When I tried to sleep tonight, my Love, I dreamed of the man in the white shirt. And so I will not sleep tonight; there are enough problems with police in my waking hours. Would they have arrested me today if I had called out your name? If I had run to your arms? I pace through the darkness while you sleep, surrounding you with love, removing barri-ers between us. I saw your face today. Could you not see mine? Could you not feel that I would be happy if only to sit at your feet and worship as a stranger, not even to trouble you with the burden of dreams? Or to see what I have shrunk to.

CHAPTER 49

She dreamed that people were surrounding her house. She woke before dawn, frightened and tired. She wanted to get up, make herself coffee, walk around to shake the dream off, but Angel was sleeping in her living room. The same dream came back when she fell back asleep, but now people were moving in a crazy zigzag in front of the house.

Teresa and Angel had already left when she got up. It was after nine. She no longer had to call in to work each day. She had a note from her doctor excusing her for another five days. "It's nerves," the doctor had told her again. "It's understandable in your circumstances." But he had written "influenza" on the note, at her request; she didn't want anyone to know how she had fallen apart. She had been so strong since April, but now she had fallen apart.

She couldn't shake the dream. Not coffee nor toast nor a shower nor an *I Love Lucy* rerun could let her shake off the feeling that people were still zigzagging in front of the house. But the street through the living-room window above the TV was still.

Angel came by at eleven to take her to the gun lesson she had promised to go to somewhere in her memory where she couldn't recall. He was full of newspaper headlines for the long ride out to the end of Kendall: murders and drug wars and rising crime rates from the prison population that Fidel Castro had unleashed in Miami. She felt as if she weren't really outside in Angel's luxury car, only the scenery moving beside her like a trick of motion from the movies.

"Now this is a Beretta twenty-five caliber your brother and I have picked out for you. I use this model for a lot of ladies," said Hy Matthews, her instructor at the shooting range.

"Don't do this to me, Angel," she said. "You've already installed the alarm system on the house and I won't be needing a gun too."

"Take the gun, Carmela," Angel said. "The alarm won't help you when you're outside the house."

"Don't I need a permit or something?"

"This is Miami, don't worry about it," Matthews said. "Now go on, take it. It's a pretty little thing, isn't it? Lightweight and won't throw you back halfway 'cross the state every time you pull the trigger. Don't worry, I don't have it loaded yet."

He placed the small gun in her hand and pointed out and named all its parts. "Now see how good that feels. And it's not louder than necessary in order to bring the neighbors running."

They were in an office in the back of a building that had once been a roller-skating rink. There was cheap wood paneling on the walls and a shelf of trophies. The door was closed, but she could still hear the guns from the practice range. *Pop pop pop*—not like real guns. Matthews explained proper loading and safety. He pulled charts down from a roller on the wall. *Pop pop pop*, Carmela heard. "Perhaps we can do this some other time," she said.

"You told me you'd feel more comfortable with a gun if you knew how to use it," Angel said.

"But this wasn't what I had in mind, and I already have the alarm system."

"One thing has nothing to do with the other, and it's not going to hurt to try." She could hear the impatience in

Angel's voice. "It'll give you some confidence," he continued.

The pops were louder outside the office. At the end of her enclosed practice lane was an outline of a man with numbered circles radiating from his heart. She thought there would be headphones, on TV they wore headphones to muffle the noise, but instead she was given a set of disposable sponge earplugs. They were green, the only color in the place. Matthews had to move close to give her his instructions, almost whispering in her ear.

Carmela took the stance instructed and pulled the trigger as much to get the stranger away from her ear as in the hope of satisfying Angel enough to leave her in peace.

Pop, went the sharp gasp in her slender hands. *Pop. Pop.*

"Thattagirl!" Matthews shouted. "Now try really aiming for this man who's coming at you now. Make it life or death with each shot."

He kept up a constant shout of directions and praise. She missed the mark more often than not. The sweat dripped from her short black hair. The sweat dripped from her soft doe eyes. The sweat dripped from her lovely arms. She crippled the right leg on the target and shot the fingers from his hands. She tore the bowels from his abdomen. She severed his aorta and ripped his heart from his chest. She shot the eyes into darkness and his memory into hell.

CHAPTER 50

It was Dottie's finest flower day. So this was capitalism. No wonder everyone worked so hard. To have such freedom in the streets and to be paid for it, paid for carrying flowers in the street, listening to the music from the radios, watching the fashions on the women in the beautiful cars, being smiled at by the men.

"Don't your feet hurt you in those shoes, señora?" Victor Castro had asked in the truck that morning. She had waited twenty years to be free in those shoes—they hardly hurt at all.

She paid thirty dollars each morning to Castro for the flowers, ten each for the three of them, and Felipe paid another ten for his own. She didn't like giving Castro the money, but it kept them on the corner he rented from the government. Castro overcharged, to put it mildly, but she and Felipe had outsmarted him from the first day. They sold Castro's flowers first and then went and bought their own flowers to sell in the afternoon. That's when they made their real money. They bought most of them from a small flower shop on Eighth Street across from the cemetery. It was only blocks away. "No problem," the owner had told Dottie. "It wasn't easy for me when I first came. I'm happy to give somebody else a break." Since Castro didn't come back and Juana and Rafael had already been moved to the corner by Sears, no one was the wiser.

The light turned red. She sashayed from the curb. A man in a Pinto rolled down his window. "I've called every florist in town," Esteban Santiesteban said. "You told me you'd call yesterday. I finally went to the church."

"You went to the church? Who do you think you are? I've got a family to think about. You shouldn't even be here."

"I went to the church to find out where you were. I didn't know if something happened to you."

"Unless you have a place for my family to live, you don't screw up where I live. I forgot to call you. I was very busy."

"Doing what? This? I thought you said you had a real job at a florist's."

It was impossible for him to comprehend her having forgotten to call him when all he thought about was her. The light turned green. Horns started blowing.

"What's wrong with doing this?" Dottie asked.

"It's like begging, you know, going up to a car when they can't go anywhere and begging for money."

If there hadn't been flowers in her arms, she would have slapped him, she was so angry. How dare he accuse her of anything but working hard? How dare he try to take the joy from her first job in the land of her dreams?

"I have five-inch high heels on my feet. My feet are killing me. Do beggars wear high heels? I don't need you. Get out of my life. You shouldn't have gone to the church and you shouldn't be here. There are plenty more John Waynes in the United States. You don't even look like John Wayne." She was glad she was still a U.S. virgin.

The horns.

"I'll park over there and meet you in the bank parking lot," he said and drove off. He waited forty minutes in the parking lot. He knew she saw him, but she wouldn't come over, not in front of her son and her husband and the old man. He had nothing against her family, he only wanted her to know how concerned he'd been, how lonely, how much he cared for her. He got back in his car and drove around the block again and back through the intersection. He rolled down the window, said he wanted to buy flowers.

She never even looked at him. The son finally came by, handed him flowers, and took a twenty without giving him change. He drove on. He drove home. He was making a fool of himself. Life was too short to a spend it aggravated and miserable, but he couldn't help it.

Felipe folded the twenty into his pocket. Not bad for six carnations from an asshole trying to flirt with Dottie. It was a good place to meet members of the opposite sex. He was only sorry the intersection wasn't closer to the beach so the women would be wearing string bikinis. Selling flowers was the perfect excuse to approach a car with a beautiful woman in it. Felipe was feeling much better, almost his old self. He handed a long-stemmed red rose to a girl with blond hair in a sleek Porsche. "On the house," he told her. "You're beautiful."

The Porsche was back again when the light turned red. He walked over to the car, and without a word, she handed him a small envelope filled with coke. Then she was gone. Well, if he couldn't get laid, he might as well get high. He did a line from the envelope in the bathroom at Burger King and was sure he could pick up thirty for what remained. "Roses, carnations, coke," he said when he stuck his head into the car of a startled stewardess on her way to work.

"Get your goddam head out of my car!"

"OK, just thought you might want Coca-Cola, lady. I buy it at the Texaco, you don't have to buy."

The bitch. She had looked so inviting. He didn't try it again, though. He'd save the rest for later.

The next morning Felipe was gone. Along with the four hundred and eight dollars Dottie had placed under her pillow before she had gone to sleep. A note on the dresser read: "Be back later. If I'm not at the corner I'll meet you back here tonight. I've taken the money to get Father some teeth. I know how much they mean to him."

CHAPTER 51

When the first flames of sunrise cleared away the night, Felipe had awoken. There was no use trying to get back to sleep. He did the last of the coke and got dressed. Sure, the money wasn't bad selling flowers, more than he used to make at the Orange Bowl with his shopping cart. He wasn't making half of what Dottie made, though. But that wasn't the whole story. He had come with Dottie so she wouldn't turn him over to the authorities. But to live in a priest's house and then in a storeroom of a church hall with all these old people wasn't living. The night before he had helped Juan Raúl Pérez shower Papa and the touch of the old man's loose skin on his cocained euphoria had revolted him. It was just too hard for Felipe to stay reformed now that he felt better.

"Did you talk to him before he left?" Dottie asked as she shook Juan Raúl Pérez awake. "Did you give him the money?"

"Who?"

"Felipe. The money was under the pillow I was sleeping on. How could he get it if you didn't give it to him?"

She handed Juan Raúl Pérez the note while she removed the pillow, the sheets, and the mattress and then got on her hands and knees to look under the bed.

"He stole it," Juan Raúl Pérez said. "He must have taken it while you were sleeping. Get up off the floor, señora. He stole it—it's right here in the note. He probably tried to do the same with Luz Paz."

"No, don't be ridiculous. Luz Paz had given him some money to try to get you some teeth. And if he was stealing our money, why would he leave a note? There's no cause to worry."

But she was worried. His radio was gone, but some of his clothes still hung from the back of the door.

"We should call the police, señora. He stole your money."

"*Our* money. You get half for watching Papa. He'll be back. This is probably just a mix-up."

"You are deceiving yourself. I am going to tell Father Aiden the truth. We will call the police."

"Would he leave a note if he was going to steal our money? Would he leave a note saying he was taking it? And do you want to call the police so they can find out he's really not our son and we can both be sent to prison or back to Cuba? Maybe you are used to prison, señor, but I'm not."

They went in the truck to sell flowers. The day remained bright and blue. But towards one, the breeze died and the heat descended, vapid and motionless. Afternoon sailors on Biscayne Bay forgot about trying to sail anywhere and dove from their bows into the crystal water. Pop-tops hissed around town and air conditioners were switched to full blast. The cars on Flagler and Le Jeune seemed to cut Dottie's very air off. The flowers drooped in her arms. Her polka dots clung to her body. She did feel as if she were begging. "Let's just go back now," Dottie said. "I don't think he's going to meet us here. Maybe he's already home."

"There they go now," the cashier at the Texaco station told the private detective who was posing as a man who needed a fan belt and thought he might buy some flowers while he was waiting. He did need the fan belt. "You'd better run if you want to catch them."

"Too hot to run anywhere today. Guess I'll have to catch them tomorrow on my way to work," the PI said. "I'll just sit here in your air conditioning for a moment if you don't mind. Let me have a pack of Kools, please. Make it a carton."

The cigarettes and the fan belt would go on the expense sheet.

"Must be hard for these people coming over like this. You said they have no relatives here? They sleep at the church?"

"Did I? Well, at least they have each other."

"The flowers are fresh?"

"Fresh each day. Lots of people buy from them. A lot. You can tell they'll make something out of themselves the way they work."

"They don't overcharge or anything? I mean, they have to be tempted, not having anything themselves."

"My husband and I didn't have anything when we came twenty years ago. Go price them yourself."

Oops, wrong approach, the detective thought and moved in another direction.

"No, I believe you. I'm glad they're so hardworking and honest. They look like nice people, know what I mean?"

"Oh, a very nice family. I didn't see the son here today, he's hardly more than a boy. Bright smile. The grandfather is a little senile, but Mr. Pérez watches over him. And the wife works like a dog. I can see them from the window here. They buy sodas here all the time."

"Well, I'll definitely buy flowers from them tomorrow then. Let me check on the fan belt."

His beeper went off five minutes later—just his partner, staked out on Twenty-third Street, but there was no news there.

No one the detective knew at immigration had known a thing about the Pérez family. But he didn't think they would. They were months behind with the paperwork, and even if the lawyer who had hired him got a tracer it would

probably take weeks. He left that up to the law firm to follow through along with formal inquiries with the Cuban
government. But the rest had moved along fairly easily. The
Orange Bowl was virtually closed, so he had gone to Tent
City yesterday. He had started with the furniture-store
owner's description of the old man with punk hair and camouflage clothes. A lot of people there remembered the Pérez
family. Saying he was looking for lost relatives, he had
questioned several people Dottie had done laundry for until
Eladia Soto, the beautician, told him the Pérez family had
been sponsored by one of the Catholic churches. She didn't
know which. A few phone calls from the yellow-page listings connected him with the Church of the Resurrection.
The clerk at the rectory had told him on the phone that they
sold flowers on the street. From there, it had only taken a
half tank of gas to find them.

CHAPTER 52

Felipe hot-wired a Chevy station wagon in back of a school a mile from the church. He watched the owner get out of the car with books, an attaché case, and a pile of loose papers—probably a teacher on his way for a full day of work. He had learned from Orlando that it was best to steal a car when you could get a running start. Hospital parking lots and movie houses gave you more of a head start than a 7-Eleven lot. The car was big, solid, a U.S. of A. car, and he thought it would get him a good trade-in for a sportier model. But by noon he hadn't been able to sell it. He got four estimates, none of them over six hundred. "It's a gas guzzler," they told him. The only place shady enough to do business without a title offered him just eighty dollars, which Felipe refused. He got nervous and stole a license plate off a junker up on cinder blocks in the back of a boatyard. The car looked like it hadn't been moved in months; nobody'd miss the plate for a while. He put the new license on the Chevy station wagon.

He had no definite plans. Maybe he'd head to N.Y. or L.A. He'd never been to either place, but anywhere had to be better than Miami and the Church of the Resurrection. The new license gave him time on the car, and the note he had left with Dottie would cover him at that end till he got out of town.

His ribs were starting to ache again, and he wasn't wearing his elasticized bandage. He was also very hungry, so he drove over to Mi Cafeteria.

"Oye, Guapo," called María through the clattering lunch crowd. He liked how she called him Guapo, "handsome," out loud like that.

"My favorite mom—how you been?"

"Yeah, don't mom me. If I was your mom you'd be in a lot of trouble that I didn't hear from you in a week. I was starting to get worried, especially after all the problems they were having at the Orange Bowl. Follow me, I've got a seat for you at the counter. Are you out of there yet? Moved over to Tent City?"

"Don't worry, Mom, that football team coming in asked me stay and play with them. Signed me up for a million."

"Be serious now. Are you working, Guapo? You know, my brother's looking for a cook. It's not much—short-order—but it's something, and my brother treats people right."

"Hey, do I look like a cook? Really, don't worry about me. I'm already out of the Orange Bowl. Got a little place over in the residential section. It's nice."

"And work? You still selling cheap watches?"

"No, I've been working for a flower importer. I should have brought you some. Going to open a shop soon. Even got a car. Just a work car, you know. It's parked around the corner. I'll take you for a ride after lunch."

"Thanks, Guapo, but I'm on till three. And I've got to get back to work now. You want the steak with black beans and rice?"

"Sure. Who's the new waitress?" He had been watching her since he walked in.

"Isabel. Isn't she sweet? Not married, Guapo, and I don't think she's got a boyfriend. She's my brother's brother-in-law's cousin. Maybe she'd like to go for a ride. She gets off in a half hour."

"Introduce me, OK?"

"Sure, in a minute. I've got to get back."

Felipe decided that Isabel looked more like a nurse than a waitress, so clean-looking. Her dark curly hair was short and neat. No St. Tropez tan; her skin was white, with a few freckles over the bridge of her nose. There were curves beneath the starch in her uniform. And her mouth was a little too large, sweet and round.

"You look like a nurse, not a waitress," Felipe told her ten minutes later when María introduced them.

"I wouldn't mind being a nurse," she said. She was smiling but nervous, sponging the same spot on the counter that she had already cleaned twice.

"See, I got you pegged already," Felipe said. "You going to school to be a nurse or something?"

"No, not yet. But I wouldn't mind. I wanted to be a nurse when I was a little girl. Not sure what I really want now."

"Look, Mom tells me you get off work in a little while. Maybe you'd like to take a ride, go over to Coconut Grove?"

"She's not your mom."

"Shhh, don't tell her that."

Isabel laughed. Her freckles lighting up, her white teeth sparkling off the starched white waitress uniform. "Really, I don't even know you or anything. Thanks but I don't think so."

"Come on. We're practically related. You're a cousin to María's brother-in-law and I'm her adopted son. That makes us third or fourth cousins once removed by marriage or something like that."

Isabel laughed again.

"You're pretty when you smile, Isabel."

"Thanks, but really, I don't think so."

"Well, that's better than no."

The cook yelled out an order and Isabel left Felipe to his lunch. She made sure she caught María in the kitchen. Felipe was very handsome and he had made her laugh so easily. But Miami, well, she had heard too many things about the dangers of Miami since arriving on the boatlift four months before to go wandering off with a stranger. "Tell me about this guy, María. He seems nice, but I don't know. He asked me to drive over to Coconut Grove with him."

"What are you waiting for? He's a nice boy. He comes in here all the time. And look at that suit. If I were twenty years, well, thirty years younger, I'd go for him myself. And it's not as if he asked you for a midnight rendezvous. It's only twelve-thirty, it's just for a ride in the sunshine."

Isabel still didn't look convinced, and María continued, "He really is nice, a lot of tough breaks, but he's very enterprising, sells flowers, probably from a street corner, but he's too proud to say so. Look, I'll tell you what kind of guy he is. He used to come in here with these two guys, polite but kind of smart-ass underneath, then he stopped coming in here with them. I asked him where his friends were and he said he wasn't hanging out with them anymore. 'Too heavy for me, Mom,' he told me. 'I'm a good boy.' See what I mean? He's a nice guy, Isabel. And you're not going out with anybody now anyway."

Felipe opened the car door for her and waited till she was settled before closing it. He apologized for the station wagon, his work truck he called it, but it was immaculately clean. Very polite, Isabel noted. She liked that. A lot of guys nowadays weren't polite like that. And he hardly talked about himself at all; a lot of guys nowadays were always bragging about themselves. All he said was that he had a flower shop and lived in a quiet neighborhood. Nothing fancy, he told her. And he asked her a lot of nice questions without getting too personal: what kind of music did she like, did she like rock and roll, salsa, disco? Did she dance? Was the radio too loud? Did she want to change the station?

She noticed the Band-Aid on his forehead when he pushed back his hair.

"You have a cut on your forehead," she said. "Looks bruised around there, too."

"Help me, nurse, I'm dying," Felipe said with feigned discomfort and a broad smile. "It's just a scratch, really, but thanks for asking."

It was a hot afternoon, but picture-postcard-perfect with

a high blue sky and leafy shadows woven through the sunlight. Felipe took her to an outdoor café in Coconut Grove. The streets were lazily crowded and they walked up Commodore Plaza stopping at the store windows before they turned the corner to Main Highway and the café. Isabel couldn't remember the name of the café. It had a wooden terrace built up from the sidewalk with white tables under a yellow-and-white-striped awning; the police made her describe what it looked like later. No, he wasn't drinking heavily. They both had margaritas and watched the people pass. Well, maybe they had two margaritas, they were there for a few hours, and he had a glass of water too and maybe a beer. She wasn't positive. But she remembered that he wasn't drunk. He had been really nice. Mostly they talked about music and he told her he eventually wanted to have his own men's shop, exclusive, high style, latest fashions. He liked style, he told her, and he was wearing a beautiful suit. She was still in her waitress uniform and felt a little self-conscious and she told him that. "But we match perfectly and you look wonderful in white. I hope I always see you in white. You'd have style in a flour sack," he told her. He started making these comments, Isabel said, no, not nasty or loud, about the people passing in the street. How this guy really needed a fashion consultation, and that guy looked like he was going to a rodeo and that that woman had style but was dressed too old-fashioned. They drove over to Rickenbacker Causeway then, no wait, she said, they walked around a little first, then drove over to the causeway and stopped the car on the side by the bay. It really was hot, she wished she had a bathing suit. He told her he'd drive her back to her place for a bathing suit, said he knew a great place to swim. So they went over to her place off Northwest Seventh Street. He didn't hassle her at all about waiting in the car while she ran up the stairs to the apartment she shared with her mother and aunt, but they were still not home from work yet and she didn't want him up there with her alone. She put her suit on with a white shift over it and grabbed two towels. He said he didn't have his bathing suit with him and they stopped at that little shopping center across the street from the dog track and he ran into a shop and got one. That's the only time he acted a little strange, and it really wasn't all that strange if you think about it and if you were in the boatlift you'd understand, she said, I mean, I knew he was a Marielito when I met him. I could tell by his accent, it was Cuban Spanish not Cuban-American Spanish, and some of the expressions he used, but he didn't bring it up and he had been doing most of the talking.

He got in the car and didn't start it up right away. He turned to her and said, "Why didn't you want me to come up to your apartment? You said you lived with your mother and your aunt. You didn't want me to meet them? Is it because I'm a Marielito?"

"Look," Isabel told him, "I hate that word. And as it just so happens, I came over on the boatlift too, and so did my mother. No one was home, that's why I didn't want you to come up. They'll be home in an hour or so. I left them a note. You're more than welcome to meet them when you drop me off."

But it was better after that, Isabel told the detective, because they seemed to have so much more in common. They talked about Cuba, about how the world was waiting for them in the U.S. He seemed a little bitter, no, not even bitter, he just mentioned how the people here could have everything and didn't even know it.

They drove over to this place on the beach, farther up than South Beach, by the Fontainebleau. The whole place was very luxurious. Isabel hadn't been in any of the big hotels, she didn't even know you could use the beach there. They had a pitcher of beer on this back patio, like an outdoor cabaña. The waiter had a French accent. When Felipe came out in his bathing suit, he had some bruises on his chest. He said he had had an accident with one of the crates of flowers from his shop.

"Look," she told the detective, "I kind of knew he didn't own a flower shop from what María said, but I didn't say anything to him because María had said he was proud. But he did talk about flowers then, the different kinds, and he sounded like he knew something. I figured he just worked in a flower shop."

"He was a street vendor," the detective said. "We found receipts in his pocket from a store where he bought flowers. We're tracing them now."

The water was warm. The sky was magnificent. There were hardly any people down by the water. He asked her if he could take her to dinner later. She said yes. He'd been such a gentleman. They kissed in the water. There was hardly anyone swimming. He ran his hands down her body. But that's it. He didn't try to pull her suit off or anything. They kissed again sitting by the water. Isabel was a little giggly from the last beer and she hadn't had anything to eat since ten that morning. He wanted to go back to her place so she could get dressed for dinner. He said he wanted to take her someplace elegant, with a lot of flowers, and asked her if she had a nice white dress to wear.

"I was stalling for time," Isabel told the policeman for the twentieth time. "I had no idea we were riding around in a stolen car. I was still light-headed. I usually don't drink, and after the margaritas, that beer made me feel dizzy. I wasn't sure my mother was home yet so I asked him to drive around down by the beach. He didn't seem happy about it at first, said he was getting hungry, but we were getting along well. Then he said he had this friend he wanted to show me off to."

"Did he say what friend?"

"No, I don't think so."

"Was his friend's name Orlando?"

"I don't know. I think it was the girl who later said the name Orlando. I told you this already."

"Well, you're going to tell me again. Go ahead."

"This is all kind of hazy now," Isabel said, "because we

were talking and laughing and driving slowly to look at the people and the radio was up. No, I don't know what street it was. I was still dizzy from the beer. There were these people sitting on the seawall. And this one girl in a bikini sitting there yelled, 'Felipe, Orlando's been looking for you.' "

"So you don't know if this Orlando was the same person Felipe wanted to show you off to?"

"No, I told you I don't know. Felipe told the girl, 'You tell him I'm looking for him, too.'

" 'Well, he's right down at Mannie's, hotshot,' she said.

"A couple of blocks down, he parked the car and asked me if I minded waiting a second. I asked him why. He said that I was too high-class for Mannie's and said that if his friend was there, he'd bring him out to meet me.

"I said fine. I mean, I was stalling for time, as I said. And I still wasn't feeling steady enough to be walking into my house and introducing him to my mother and my aunt. And there were loads of people around, kids, old people, and we were right on the road by the beach. Then he got out and walked across the street to this bar called Mannie's. I didn't hear anything. But a lot of people had ghetto blasters going and I had the radio in the car going.

"Not even five minutes went by before he came back out. I wasn't paying too much attention. I was wondering if that girl in the bikini had been his old girlfriend or something and I was starting to fall asleep just sitting there in the car. It was warm. He came over to the passenger door where I was sitting. I thought he was kidding—he said, 'Help me, please, I'm hurt.' "

"And you just sat there?"

"No, I told you I thought he was kidding. Like before when I mentioned the cut on his forehead. I started laughing. I told him that I didn't have my white uniform on. The window was open. He said, 'Move over, I'm hurt. You drive.' "

"He didn't mention Orlando's name then or any other name?"

"No, I told you. He never said anything else. Just slumped over there with his head still halfway in the window, right next to mine. Then he slid out and down. The people on the wall started screaming to call the cops. I had to get out on the driver's side because he was jammed between the other door and the curb. He had put his suit on over his bathing suit before he got out of the car. This guy started helping me pull him up and we all saw this blood on the white vest. I kept thinking a knife was going to fall out."

"What makes you think he was knifed, miss?"

Isabel was crying again. She could barely get the words out. "I don't know. I told you I never heard a shot. The people standing around said he was dead. I was sitting here on the sidewalk with my bathing suit on and his head on my lap. He didn't say anything. I just kept looking around. The sun wasn't down yet. I kept thinking what a beautiful day it was, that nobody should be stabbed on such a beautiful day."

"He was shot, miss. You can go now. We've already checked with María Bayona where you work and she confirms you didn't know Felipe Pérez before today. We may contact you with more questions later. Your mother's been waiting out in the lobby."

"But why did somebody shoot him? He was so nice."

"Miss, this nice person you picked up sold more than flowers. He sold drugs. He was flashing around a lot of money in the bar and one of his friends thought he owed him some. You really should be more careful choosing your friends from now on."

CHAPTER 53

Dottie had seen death before, but never so perfect.
She had seen her mother die of pneumonia, but her face
had been mottled for days before her death and her counte-
nance was already haggard and drawn far beyond her
thirty-seven years. That's why she kept the photo of her
mother, taken two years before she died, so close to her always. When the image of the mottled face, purple and gasping for air and then suddenly still, came to her, she cast it
out from her eye with a glance at the smiling photo.

Her first lover's body lay riddled with bullets on the street
during the university riots. She hadn't been fifty yards from
him when he died. She had watched her friends drag the
body over to where she waited. Parts of his face were missing. Even now, recalling him when he was alive, she could
never see all of his face. When her next lover had been
shipped back in a coffin to his mother's house after the Bay
of Pigs invasion, she had opened the coffin herself. She had
been so sure there had been a mistake. She could recall his
face alive and smiling even if at her last glance it had been
so dead. And there had been other faces which swam before
her eyes in the waiting room of the hospital before they
brought her in to see Felipe's body, but not one had been so
perfect in death. She wished Juan Raúl Pérez had been with
her. But there was only Father Martínez and Father Aiden

and a nun she had never met before who had patted her hand in the car on the way over.

Dottie had been angry when she returned home that afternoon to find Felipe wasn't back. She couldn't stand just sitting there in the room with Juan Raúl Pérez's I-told-you-so eyes and Papa marching up and down in the army boots with the ridiculous knapsack on his back. "Get out of here," she had screamed at Juan Raúl Pérez. "I can take care of this myself, and I can't stand the sight of either of you."

They were gone awhile when Father Aiden had knocked on the door with Father Martínez to translate. They asked her if she and Felipe bought flowers from the shop on Eighth Street across from the cemetery. She almost said no. She thought they were in trouble with Victor Castro. So she just stood there. Then they told her the police had found receipts in Felipe's pocket and the shop owner remembered the mother and son from the Church of the Resurrection well. The shop owner had given them a discount because they lived at the church.

"So what if we did?" Dottie had said, but she was thinking Felipe must have been arrested if the cops had gone through his pockets. Then they told her that Felipe was dead. When she got hysterical, Father Aiden had waited in the room without a word to her while Father Martínez went to get the nun to pat her hand.

Why hadn't Juan Raúl Pérez and Papa returned? It wasn't true, she couldn't take care of herself. She wanted her family with her as they showed her behind the curtain where Felipe lay dead. She didn't want the nun who was a stranger holding her hand. There were so many strangers at the hospital.

"Wake up, mi hijito," Dottie said. "Wake up. You are too handsome to be dead. You are too young to have taken a wrong turn into a bullet in your gut. Men fight. You're just a boy, mi hijito, you should be selling flowers."

If she had had a son, she was sure he would be so handsome like this. Death had only paled his face, darkened his lips. A lock of hair still fell over the Band-Aid on his forehead. A white sheet was pulled to his chin. How handsome he would look in a tuxedo, Dottie thought. Wake up, Felipe. Wake up. It is not right that freedom should make your face so pale. So perfect.

The nun led Dottie's great Cuban-madonna sobs out from the little curtained room, held her hand while the homicide detective asked her so many questions.

"Did you see how perfect he looked?" Dottie asked them. "You could see how perfect he looked."

It was already dark when they returned home. They sat with her in the same room Father Aiden had first welcomed them to freedom in. Father Aiden made her drink a glass of wine. "You are very kind," Dottie said. "I can go back to my room now, though. You don't have to sit with me. My husband will be back any minute now. You see, he has to walk his father like this so he'll be tired enough to sleep through the night. My father-in-law is like a child, you know. If one of us doesn't walk him then he can't sleep and he wanders off. Like that first night we were here and he was in the tree in the morning." She knew she was sounding crazy but she didn't care. If she stopped talking about nothing she'd only start asking again if Felipe hadn't looked perfect.

"And they won't know where I am when they come home and I'm not there."

"No, Rafael is waiting for them and will send them here when they come. We don't want you to be alone. Don't worry about it."

It was after ten when Rafael ushered Juan Raúl Pérez and Papa through the door. Rafael had only told them they were wanted in Father Aiden's office. When Juan Raúl Pérez saw Dottie crying, his only thought was that Felipe was in jail and Dottie had confessed to their deception. He was relieved. He had walked almost to Carmela's house and turned back on Twenty-second Street. He knew he had to tell Dottie before he went to Carmela and he knew he'd be going soon.

Dottie flung herself into his arms before he said a word.

"He's dead," she said. "He looked so perfect."

"Who?" he asked.

"Our son."

"Who?"

"Felipe, our son."

CHAPTER 54

Only a lovers' quarrel, Esteban Santiesteban told himself. He stood in front of the mirror searching
for any resemblance to John Wayne.

"Damn," he told the mirror, "I'm better-looking than
John Wayne ever was." But just in case, he wore his secu-
rity-guard uniform with nightstick, gun, and eagle belt
buckle. It was what he had been wearing when Dottie had
first thrown her arms around him.

Only a lovers' quarrel. He had to get to her and apologize.
Depending on how that went, he would either ask her to
divorce her husband and marry him, or be content as her
lover and take whatever bone she'd throw him.

He drove to Le Jeune and Flagler, but there were strangers there this morning. They didn't know where Señora
Pérez was, none of the Pérezes had shown up for work
today. He bought flowers from them, two dozen red roses.
He would take them to Dottie. He would tell her he had
bought them from the vendors and apologize for his
thoughtless words.

He went to the rectory office at the Church of the Resurrection. It was a stupid thing to do, he knew that. He knew it
would probably just further aggravate Dottie; she had already told him not to come to the church again. But he
couldn't stop himself. If she would only grant him a few

words, he could clear the whole thing up. He practiced what he would tell her over and over again, adding and deleting, imagining her responses. The clerk who had treated him as just another face when he had asked for the Pérez family two days before now seemed to treat him like an honored guest. "Oh yes," the clerk said, "a friend of the Pérez family, I remember you from the other day. Let me show you over to their room. I'm sure they'll be glad to receive you."

"A friend of the family," the clerk announced when Juan Raúl Pérez answered the door. It was not the face Esteban Santiesteban had imagined would open the door, but he went in anyway.

A friend of whose family? Juan Raúl Pérez wondered as he thanked the clerk and showed the man in. A friend of Felipe's family from Cuba? Probably not; the visitor was wearing a dark uniform with a night stick and a holstered gun. It was more likely a police friend of Angel's sent to intimidate him. But why the roses? Perhaps a friend of Felipe's from the Orange Bowl who had already heard the news. What else could it be? Did he know Felipe wasn't their real son?

Juan Raúl Pérez bowed nervously several times and thanked the man for the flowers. The man seemed shy about giving them to him, so he took them from him and put them on Felipe's mattress.

How strange, Esteban Santiesteban thought. Did her husband think he had brought them for him? He had been so focused on his apology that he hadn't even thought about what he'd say to her husband if she wasn't home. Maybe she was just in the bathroom and would appear at any moment.

"And this is my father," Juan Raúl Pérez said, pointing to Papa, on the other mattress. The strange old man who had grabbed him from behind last week in the Orange Bowl appeared to be sleeping now. Juan Raúl Pérez offered the visitor a seat.

"Do you remember me, señor, from the Orange Bowl?" Esteban Santiesteban asked.

"Yes, of course, I'm sorry," Juan Raúl Pérez said and smiled as he recalled the security guard who had been so kind, helping Luz Paz wake him one night from a bad dream. "Yes, I remember you from the Orange Bowl. You were so helpful to me that night, just as you are so kind to bring the flowers now."

"Sure," Esteban Santiesteban said. He glanced around the room. Dottie's red jumpsuit was thrown across the back of a chair and there were bottles of nail polish on the desk. Aside from the two mattresses on the floor, there was a double bed. Well, at least they couldn't be having any amorous nights with the old man and the son also sharing the room. Yet, somehow, again, the arrangement seemed more intimate than a romantic nook.

Juan Raúl Pérez didn't know what to say. He certainly wasn't going to sentimentalize Felipe's memory the way Dottie was doing.

"The flowers are very beautiful," Juan Raúl Pérez said. "This whole thing has been a very great tragedy for the señora."

So he did know about the two of them, Santiesteban thought. But what a strange way to put it. And there seemed to be no anger in the man's voice. "A tragedy, señor?"

"Well, what else could one call it?"

"It just happened. There was nothing we could do about it."

"Well, yes, there was nothing we could do about it, but it didn't just happen. It wasn't an accident or an illness."

"No, I suppose not."

"I'm sorry, I shouldn't have mentioned that. I do not know what you know about the situation and I have taken it too far."

"That's OK, señor," Esteban Santiesteban said. He wasn't sure exactly how much Dottie's husband knew either now.

"I'm sorry I have nothing to offer you to drink. I could get you some water," Juan Raúl Pérez asked.

"No, that's all right. Is the señora around?"

"No. She's out buying a veiled hat and a dress. Who knows how long these things take."

"Well, perhaps I will be going then."

"Thank you," Juan Raúl Pérez said. "Thank you for coming. And the flowers are most kind."

Esteban Santiesteban hoped Dottie would be able to clear up his confusion on the conversation. He would call the rectory and ask if she could come to the phone. And he would apologize to Dottie for coming to the church. He shouldn't have come, he knew that.

CHAPTER 55

In the evening, Dottie returned in a taxi laden with packages. Luz Paz was now with her nephew, and Dottie had taken the bus to Coral Gables to invite her to Felipe's funeral. With her nephew's permission and Burdines credit card, Luz Paz had outfitted Dottie with proper mourning attire. Dottie had even had her hair and nails done. The nephew had watched the two descend the escalator, Dottie in black from head to toe and his aunt in white. A misplaced Goya, he thought. He felt remotely answerable for Dottie's sorrow, for the violence in the land he was now a citizen of. Her son had been an innocent young boy who sold flowers, shot down on the street by a gang of American hoodlums, Dottie said.

The funeral was set for tomorrow afternoon. Father Aiden had pulled a few strings to get the body back so quickly from the medical examiners. There would be no wake. Father Martínez would say the mass.

"We are doing his mother a favor, señor," Dottie told Juan Raúl Pérez before he had the chance to tell her someone had come by to pay condolences.

"Whose mother?"

"Felipe's. It is better not to know. If you had seen Luz Paz's poor old face crying for her dead daughter."

"But why do you think it is better not to know?"

"She started talking about her daughter. She said it wasn't natural for a child to die before the parents. I invited her to the funeral, but she said she couldn't bear it because she remembered Felipe so well. But I think it's because her own daughter died that she doesn't want to come. It was very sad. At least Felipe's mother has been spared."

It had never entered Juan Raúl Pérez's mind that Felipe had a real mother somewhere. Had he stolen his real mother's money too?

"Did you shower Papa?" Dottie asked.

"Yes, doesn't he smell clean?"

"His clothes are so wrinkled."

"He wouldn't let me take them off, so I washed him with them on."

"Well, there's nothing we can do. He's got a mind of his own, I think."

"It is always better to know, señor," Juan Raúl Pérez said.

"You didn't see Luz Paz's face, señor." Dottie took off her new black dress, careful not to disturb the stiff curls piled high atop her head. She rolled her black stockings down from beneath her new black slip. Her new inch-long ceramic nails made her hands feel as if they weren't her own. Her composure, which she had clung to all day in front of Luz Paz and her nephew, was quickly disintegrating. In front of Juan Raúl Pérez and Papa's lizard eyes, she no longer had the armor of grieving Cuban-madonna mother for a boy she hardly knew. But she was grief-stricken, for all the faces she had seen in death that were not perfect and for all the perfect faces of sons she never had. Tears flowed freely down her face. A great sob pounced on her as she stood there.

"I want everything to be perfect for his funeral," she said through her sobs. "You don't know how perfect he looked. I wish he had been our son except that he'd be dead now."

He walked over to her and held her. He didn't want to, but she was just standing there sobbing and he didn't know what else to do except to refrain from telling her that he was glad Felipe wasn't his son.

She turned abruptly from his arms when the sob left her. "I don't know if I can sleep here in this room," she said and started walking back and forth. "Felipe was my friend, you know. You weren't as close to him as I was. We listened to the radio together. We outsmarted Victor Castro together. Look, there are roses on his bed. How sweet."

"And Felipe outsmarted us and somebody else outsmarted him."

Another sob escaped. It hung in her throat like a crouched beast and burst with fury. Juan Raúl Pérez did not move to hold her this time. Did not move a muscle until she sat quieted in a chair with her hands holding her face.

"Señora, whatever brief and fond memories you have of Felipe cannot erase the events of yesterday. Felipe stole your money, and a car, and then managed to get himself shot in some kind of drug deal from what you've told me. You think he was your friend and I am sorry you are upset, but don't make him into a hero. Perhaps they will ask us to leave here because of what he did."

"Where would we go, señor? Please don't leave me. I didn't think you'd ever come back last night. Please, you're not going to leave me now."

He looked at her face and hated her large tear-swollen features.

"Señora, I think it is time we came to an agreement. We were acting as a family to get out of the Orange Bowl. We're out now and Felipe is dead. I will stay with you until I'm sure the church won't ask us to leave, and if they do, I'll wait until you and Papa have another place to live. And I will stay in case the police contact the immigration officials and find out we have lied to them about being a family. I don't know what you told the police last night and I don't want to know."

"You should have been there with me. You shouldn't have made me go to the hospital myself."

"I wasn't here, señora. I'm sorry I wasn't with you, but you sent us away earlier and I did not know."

"And why should the authorities know we lied?"

"He wasn't our son. You are not my wife. Papa is not my father. I will stay with you in case there's any trouble because of that. I won't leave you by yourself to take the blame or explain yourself. But after that I must go."

"I don't need you. I can handle this myself if I have to."

"You are upset, señora. I will stay until this mess is over."

"If they do ask us to leave, maybe Luz Paz's nephew knows someplace we could go. I didn't ask her but I could."

"No, señora. Let it rest. I just want you to know that we are no longer a family unit. And tonight I will sleep in Felipe's bed."

"You could try to find out about your wife also. Maybe she could still take us in."

"Please just leave her out of this. And there is no 'us' anymore. I said I wouldn't leave you till this was all cleared up. Leave it at that."

"If your philosophy is that it's always better to know, señor, than why don't you try to contact her now?"

"And what—introduce her to this madness? What should I tell her? Excuse me, this is my cousin you never heard of, or maybe just tell her that you are an old friend and that Papa is another friend? And then what? Excuse ourselves because we have to go to another friend's funeral, but if the police ask, dear wife, please tell them it's our son's, not a friend's, funeral. I will not do that to her. Nor to my daughter."

She walked over to the mattress where Papa was and sat down. "It is not my fault Felipe died, señor. It's not my fault if they kick us out of here." She was sobbing again. She sat on the edge of Felipe's mattress and stroked a rosebud as if it were a small child.

It was true, he thought, it was not her fault that Felipe had died. Nor was it her fault that he hadn't been strong enough to contact his wife. He didn't know why he felt so much stronger now. It was as if Felipe's death had pointed out to him the difference between dreams and reality.

"The roses are from a friend of Felipe's from the Orange Bowl," Juan Raúl Pérez said.

"Who?"

"I don't know his name—a security guard. He came by to pay his condolences."

"What security guard?" she asked, knowing exactly what security guard it was, the only one she knew.

"He didn't leave his name. He brought the roses this afternoon while you were out. He was very polite."

"I'm sure he was," Dottie said. "I'm going to check on the funeral arrangements at the rectory now."

She took several laundry quarters (the only money she had left since Felipe had taken theirs) and left. But she headed in the opposite direction from the rectory, up the block to the pay phone at the school. She was really going to give Esteban Santiesteban a piece of her mind now. First he had called her a beggar. And then he had come to the church for the second time. What if she really was married? Who was he to jeopardize her relationship with her husband and her family? What was the use of almost having an affair with someone who couldn't even be discreet? And now to come to her house after Felipe died. Never trust a man in a uniform even if he sounded like John Wayne. Yes, the real John Wayne sometimes wore a uniform, but she liked it better when he had worn cowboy clothes.

But by the time she got to the pay phone, she wasn't angry anymore. She was tired. She just wanted to rid herself of the possibility of further complications in her already complicated life. There would be better John Waynes out there when she was ready for them. There would be many of them to chose from. Felipe was dead. It was very sad.

"Just leave me alone," she told Esteban Santiesteban. "Don't ever come to my home again. My son is dead. It is very sad."

Esteban Santiesteban felt terrible. What a thoughtless fool he'd been. Life was too short to become involved with a woman whose life was so sad. But he couldn't help himself; he loved her. He would have to go to her now to apologize for his thoughtless visit.

CHAPTER 56

You don't know, Flavia, she's really cold, really distant. Like the private gun lessons that I took time off from work to bring her to and that cost me a fortune. Do you know, she never even thanked me."

"What do you want her to do? Get down on her knees?"

"No. I just want to help her. I know she's going through a hard time. And she doesn't even know some weirdo's trying to impersonate her husband. I keep getting this horrible feeling like the lawyer's going to call and say Juan died in prison two months ago. The lawyer is supposed to call any minute. Then we can go to lunch."

"If it's not too late. I told you on the phone that I have band practice later this afternoon for tomorrow's festival."

Angel studied the small black-and-white photo with its scalloped edges which he had taken when he left the house in the morning. Yesterday he had sent over an eight-by-ten studio portrait of his brother-in-law taken twenty five years ago, and to Angel's eyes it showed no resemblance to the impostor in the parrot shirt. Today the agency wanted a photo of Juan Raúl Pérez's father, and he had sent over two pictures in the morning. The photo he now held in his hand was a slightly blurred amateur snap of Juan Raúl Pérez and his father, Héctor. Héctor in no way resembled the man dressed in camouflage. And at first glance there was nothing that struck Angel about the fifteen-year-old Juan Raúl Pérez about whose shoulder Héctor's arm was tossed. Angel didn't like looking at the open eyes of the slender boy. Father and son were standing at a seaside arcade. They both wore summer suits and panama hats. Angel hadn't known Cuba then. The photo had been taken at a time when the world was right, Angel thought, but he didn't know what that meant. And the thought sat on his heart like an ache.

"Let me see it," Flavia said. "Too bad it's a little fuzzy."

"I sent two better ones over this morning."

"We should do like police artists do," she said.

"Don't touch it. Carmela doesn't even know I took these."

But while Angel took the next few phone calls Flavia took the photos to the copy machine in the back and Xeroxed several copies, lighter and darker. She sat with pencil, eraser, and white-out. Flavia couldn't draw, and each rendition was more cartoonish than the last. The masterpiece she finally handed Angel while he spoke on the phone with his warehouse was on a very pale Xerox. She had whited out Héctor's hat and given him hair that stuck straight up. Then she had penciled his suit with her own rendition of paisley camouflage. But it still didn't resemble the man Angel had seen. But the faint Xerox of the boy Flavia hadn't retouched at all held Angel's eyes in a faraway grip. He hung up the phone. "Jesus Christ," Angel said. "It could be him. It could be him, Flavia. I'm not positive, but it could be."

"It's the father!" Flavia said. "I made it look like the father. So he didn't die after all?"

"No. It's the son. I'd have to see him again, but I think it's him."

Angel's secretary put through the lawyer's call a few minutes later.

"You know, I didn't believe you when you first told me the story," the lawyer said. "A lot of people have been disappointed with the relatives who have come over, and I thought maybe that was the case. But the initial report shows that you're right, it isn't him. Now, we don't have any of the tracers from immigration or the Cuban government or the prison you say he was in—that'll take a while—so I can't tell you if he's alive or dead. But the legwork by the PI's points in your direction. They weren't one hundred percent sure that the Juan Pérez in the photo you sent wasn't the one who paid you a visit. But the photo of the father you sent over this morning clinched it for them. They said there was no possibility that the camouflaged man was the Hector Pérez in the photo. The investigator interviewed several people at Tent City who knew them in the Orange Bowl, and they were sure it was Juan Pérez's father and not the wife's. Yes—wife, I'm getting to that. That's the other thing, the Juan Pérez who came to see you is married, has been for a while and has an eighteen-year-old son. There is always the possibility that your Juan Pérez was leading a double life, getting letters in and out of prison by bribing a guard, or something to that effect. Possible but highly unlikely, since the guards are rotated and the prison system in general there is far more isolated from the public than prisons here. But the father doesn't fit into that picture. How he got your name and why he came to you I don't know, unless he thought you were somebody else. We won't know till we talk to him. As I said, this is only a preliminary report based on the agency's legwork. The whole family are street peddlers. Church of the Resurrection sponsored them. I can have somebody go right over now and talk with them if you want."

"Let me think about that first," Angel said. He was still looking at the Xerox in his hand.

"Want us to call off the tracers at immigration?"

"No, keep those going."

"How about the watch on your sister's house?"

"Keep that on."

"I'll send this prelim report over to you tomorrow."

Angel was pale when he hung up the phone.

"It doesn't make sense, Flavia. They say it's not him. And I hope to God it's not him either. 'Cause if it is, he's a bigamist with an eighteen-year-old son and a wife who's not Carmela. Resurrection Church sponsored them. I'm going over there now."

Flavia called her manager to say she wouldn't be able to make practice. She wasn't going to let Angel go alone.

CHAPTER 57

Felipe's funeral wasn't scheduled until two in the afternoon, but Dottie had everyone ready well in advance.

The imitation seersucker suit Dottie had gotten for Juan Raúl Pérez off the rack in Burdines almost fit. He wore it without complaint. They were burying something between them that never should have been there. The sooner it was buried the better, and whatever she wanted him to wear when it was buried was fine with him.

Dottie told him he looked good. "I made sure to get something old-fashioned to go with you. But I forgot you only have those rubber sandals."

Juan Raúl Pérez felt comfortable in the suit, even if it wasn't the navy suit he had imagined himself wearing in freedom. He decided he should wear it when he went back to Southwest Twenty-third Street.

They sat on folding wooden chairs on the lawn outside the church hall to dry off Papa. He had refused to take his clothes off again for his shower. It was all they could do to get him to leave his knapsack in the room. And Dottie felt too cramped in the storeroom. There was air outside, if not a breeze, and shadow from the banyan tree. Dottie's bouffant hairdo, so perfect the day before, now fell across her forehead like an oversized crown. The black dress melted to her body, forming a dark outline.

The egg-sized bump on Juan Raúl Pérez's forehead was now only the size of a quarter and the swollen area around his eye had gone down but was now a pale green bruise. He had started growing a beard, but Dottie made him shave for the funeral.

Papa's clothes were drying wrinkled, and his hair stood straight out.

All that was missing from the family portrait was Felipe, but there was no more shade beneath the tree.

Juana came by and shyly offered her condolences.

Rafael came by to tell them how sorry he was. "There will be plenty of flowers there for him. We have seen to that."

Father Aiden came by but could only pat them on the shoulders before he left since there was no one there to translate for him. He resolved he'd learn a few words of Spanish for future funerals. And maybe for the holidays.

Dottie used a paper plate to fan her face.

"I'm sorry I got us into this mess, señor. I thought about it all night. It seemed like such a good idea at first. And it did get us out of that orange cage. Orange fences. Orange Bowl."

"I have been in worse places, señora."

"How long does mourning last? I suppose we are still chained here and to each other for a few days still. Shit. Papa's gone. You can't even try to have a conversation. He couldn't have gone far. I was looking at him as we spoke. Please, señor, go for him. I am too tired now." Dottie moved her chair several inches over where the shade from the tree had moved. Juan Raúl Pérez wiped the sweat from his forehead with the back of his sleeve and went to find Papa.

He was still searching through the back parking lot when Dottie saw Angel and Flavia approaching. They had gone to the rectory first and been directed to the church hall.

"Excuse me," Angel said. "I am looking for Juan Pérez."

"I'm sorry, but he's walking his father. He'll be back soon. Are you here for my son's funeral?"

"I'm sorry, we didn't know your son had died," Flavia said. "We'd better go, Angel. You were right. These aren't the right people. And she said 'his' father? It is Juan Pérez's father, no, señora?"

The question put her on immediate guard. "Yes, of course it's his father. Who are you?"

"Señor, if I could just talk to him for a second," Angel said. "A case of mistaken identity, I'm sure. He came to see me the other day."

Juan Raúl Pérez walked back from the parking lot. "Angel," he said softly. "Angelito," he said clearly.

If only he hadn't called him Angelito. It was what his brother-in-law had called him as a child. No one else called him that, not even his sister. It annoyed Angel then and it still annoyed him now. There was no doubt now to Angel. The suit helped, and the face no longer swollen. "Your husband?" Angel said to Dottie. "Is this man your husband?"

"Yes, of course he's my husband. Is there a problem? If you're looking for the other Señor Pérez, I'm afraid he's wandered off for a moment. And our son is dead."

Angel heard nothing after Dottie's confirmation that the man he had searched twenty years for was her husband. Why she was lying about the father, he didn't know or care. But it was his brother-in-law, the man his sister was also married to, his sister who had waited twenty years. His sister had been right to wait those twenty years. Angel had never doubted that before; it was the way it should be. It was the least anyone could do for a man who had given them their freedom. Oh, it was him, everything which had once been refined and educated from old Havana days in country clubs.

"Angelito," Juan Raúl Pérez said. "I am glad you came. You had some doubts. I've changed, I know. But you recognize me now. Maybe it would be better to talk inside."

It was like hitting a cardboard box, Angel thought as his fist met Juan Raúl Pérez's gut. Like an empty cardboard box. It just caved in. He tried to stop his fist as soon as he felt the cardboard collapse, not because his anger was in check, but because it felt so strange striking something with his left fist. It was Flavia who gasped when the blow stuck, not Juan Raúl Pérez. As the cardboard collapsed to the ground, Angel bent forward and then froze when something hit the top of his head and bounced off. It was a stick. It had only stung, but he didn't know where it had come from.

When Dottie rolled Juan Raúl Pérez over to his back and he opened his eyes, he could see very clearly the dark relief of Papa in the tree. There was Dottie bending towards him. Angel and the other woman were looking up at the sky.

Dottie lifted Juan Raúl Pérez from the ground by his armpits. He vomited the second he stood and would have gone down again with the force of the expulsion if Dottie hadn't been holding him. She deposited him on the folding chair.

Angel looked into the tree and saw only leaves.

"Someone's up in the tree," Flavia said. "But I can't see him."

"No shit," Angel said.

"Oh, grow up. I'm here on your side, remember?" Flavia said.

"I can explain everything," Juan Raúl Pérez wheezed.

"Papa, come down from that tree and stop throwing things," Dottie scolded. "Get down. We spent all morning keeping you clean."

"Who are you?" she asked Angel. "Why did you hit him like that?"

Angel didn't move, anticipating a pounce or another missile from his unseen enemy in the tree. "Excuse me, Juan," he said. "I am at a disadvantage. I didn't bring a camouflaged bodyguard with me to throw sticks at you."

"What about your fist?" Dottie said. "You are a bully to hit him like that. Is that how you broke your other arm? Come, Papa, please. I don't want to have to shower you again. I don't want the priest to see you up there either."

"You're sure it's him?" Flavia asked.

"He's coming down from the tree," said Dottie.

Angel's anger was rising again as he saw the old man coaxed down from the tree by Dottie. He wanted to hit the old man too, who walked over to one of the folding chairs and sat down as if nothing had happened.

"Come on, Angel, let's just go," Flavia said. But he wasn't going anywhere.

"Why did you come to my office, Juan? Did you think you could have both wives?"

"Who are you, señor?" asked Dottie. "Are you from the police? What's going on?"

"That's what I'd like to know, señora. Your husband used to be married to my sister. I'm afraid he didn't take the time to divorce her before he married you."

"This is your wife's brother, señor?" Dottie asked.

"Yes," Juan Raúl Pérez said, clutching his stomach. "Please tell him the truth. I can barely talk."

Dottie put her hand gently on Juan Raúl Pérez and bent over to whisper in his ear, "Everything? Should I tell him everything?"

"Yes."

"Are you sure? We don't have a lot of time before the funeral."

"Yes! Please tell him you are not my wife."

Dottie smoothed her black dress and then with arms akimbo, began: "Señor, of course we are not married. It is very simple. He was afraid to call his wife because he didn't know if she had remarried or if she was dead. I was told it was easier to get a sponsor if you were a family. We had the same last names, so we adopted each other to get a sponsor. That's all. I was the wife. The man in the tree was his father and we had a son also, but he was shot down on the streets two days ago by gangsters from your country. What else could we have done? And you can tell his wife that I never slept with her husband. You should also know that I took good care of him and you should remember that if we get kicked out of here. She can have him back at any time. You could take him now but we have to go to our son's funeral. But I'll deny everything if you tell the police."

"Your story is a piece of shit, señora. I'll bet you took

good care of him. Why didn't he think we'd take good care of him? A piece of shit."

"And he went to Carmela's house," Flavia said, "so he must have known she was alive."

"Who are you?" Dottie asked. "I thought you were my husband's wife for a second, but you're too young."

"I am Angel's fiancée, señora."

"I didn't know you went to see your wife or him," Dottie said. "Why didn't you tell me that?"

"Yeah," Angel said, "why didn't you tell her that? And why didn't you tell Carmela you are married?"

"I am not married. Except to Carmela, but I didn't see her the first time I went to the house. And an alarm went off when I knocked on the door. When I went back the next time, there were police there. I only saw her a moment. It was from a distance. I don't know if she saw me or recognized me. And you, Angel, didn't want to recognize me."

"You look very different. I didn't know. I've had a private detective investigating you since I saw you. You're never going to get near Carmela, you know. You'll never find her again. I'll make sure of that, and I'm not going to listen to any more of this. We tried for twenty years to get you out of prison."

"The shoes. Why did you leave your shoes?" Flavia asked. "Carmela said her husband had small feet."

"They were too big for me. That's why I had them off, and I dropped them when the alarm went off. Why does she have an alarm?"

"To keep scum like you away from her house," Angel said.

"Take him now," Dottie said. "I can go to our son's funeral by myself if I have to. As long as you're not from the police."

"We don't want him, señora. Scum, señor, that's what you both are."

"Leave her alone. There's no reason for that language," Juan Raúl Pérez said. He spoke slowly, still clutching his stomach. "I begged you not to send bribe money, Angel. I begged Carmela. You kept me in prison for twenty years with your steady stream of bribes. And then you decide I'm no longer acceptable when you see me. I still love Carmela. If the police hadn't been at her house, I could have explained to her. And you had just finished threatening me. I need to talk with her, not you."

"You're crazy," Angel said. "Do you know that? You are fucking crazy. Carmela did see you, but she didn't recognize you. She saw you the day you tried to break in and she thought you were a beggar. And it doesn't matter, anyway; you've got another family." Angel looked over at Papa. "Did you have to bring all of Cuba with you? I'd kill him if he wasn't so pitiful. And if I ever see you again I'll kill you with or without your communist bodyguard."

"Come on, Angel, please let's go," Flavia said.

"And that goes for any of you Marielitos."

Flavia's door was barely shut when the Eldorado U-turned in a fury of burning rubber.

"Slow down, Angel. Slow down," Flavia said.

"He's a fucking madman. He practically blamed me for putting him in prison."

"He was upset, Angel, but the rest of the story is true."

"What?"

"It's the only thing that makes sense. He was wearing flip-flops, didn't you notice that? Her hair was horrible."

"What's with this fashion shit? She was a pig. He's a worm and they're both lairs. What do the flip-flops have to do with anything?"

"He had shoes but they were too big for him. That's why he had them off when he dropped them at Carmela's. That's how I know it was true."

"The shoes have nothing to do with anything!"

"All right. Calm down. What are you going to do?"

"I'm going to drop you off and then I'm going to go to Carmela's."

"What are you going to tell her?"

"I'm not going to tell her anything. And don't worry, I've come to my senses. I won't waste my energy killing him unless he bothers her. I'm just going to stay there and make sure he doesn't come around. I wish he was already dead. And I'll call the lawyer and see what should be done. I think I should buy Carmela a nice house in Fort Lauderdale or someplace. The police won't do shit."

Juan Raúl Pérez sat on the bed feeling his pulse with his fingers.

"Did he hurt your arm, señor?" Dottie asked him.

"No, my stomach. But it feels a little better now." He dropped his wrist. "Do I look like a beggar?"

"No, not in that suit. But you shouldn't have left your shoes. Those sandals don't go with the suit at all."

"I should have done a lot of things in my life."

"Well, what will you do now if she doesn't believe you either? I can't keep you, señor. I mean, after this is all over. You and I never intended to stay together for long."

"I'm not a stray, señora. I'm not yours to decide to keep or not."

"I do not mean to insult you, señor. I'm grateful that you have stayed with me during this mess and I understand that you will be leaving. We both knew this was not a permanent situation. I said that to you at the start. I am sure your wife will understand. You can go whenever you want. I will explain everything to her personally."

He tried to imagine Dottie flushed with heat with her sticky curls falling in her eyes talking to the graceful sadness of his wife. The two images side by side made him smile. But it was Carmela's face which seemed strange and Dottie's face which seemed so close to him. Dottie pushed her lacquered crown back up on her head.

CHAPTER 58

The stained-glass windows of the Church of the Resurrection captured the sunlight in a myriad of colors. On the right, Mary Magdalene and Mary the mother of James gazed with startled faces at an empty tomb. Above them hovered Jesus. On the left, Jesus with his feet back on the ground pulled a grave-wrapped Lazarus from his tomb. Behind them Mary and Martha held their hands folded in prayer. Over the central altar a large stone statue of the risen Christ soared alone.

The large church was almost empty. Esteban Santiesteban sat in the back on the side, well hidden by a pillar. Life was too short to be aggravated by the pain of a woman who didn't want him. He knew that. He didn't know why he was here torturing himself.

There were flowers in abundance. Father Martínez began the requiem mass. Rafael Bosch and another of the flower vendors wheeled the coffin on a portable stand up the aisle and placed it front and center. Dottie could almost touch the coffin from where she sat. She played the grieving mother perfectly. But with Felipe's body so close to her, her grief was no pretense.

"Not just Felipe Pérez," Father Martínez began the sermon, "but all of us are refugees seeking a safe harbor in God's love . . ."

"He shouldn't have died so young," Dottie sobbed gently

into Juan Raúl Pérez's shoulder. "That son of a bitch."
Juan Raúl Pérez tried to stifle her mouth in his shoulder.
"That little bastard. I trusted him. I hope he rots and rots
and rots!"

Juan Raúl Pérez had to lead her sobbing from the church
before the mass had ended. Papa followed behind. Felipe
was taken to be cremated without them. Juan Raúl Pérez
had signed the papers the day before. Dottie virtually collapsed when she reached their room.

Her tears are so real, Juan Raúl Pérez thought as he laid
her on the bed. She had hardly known the boy, he had stolen her money, and her tears were so real.

"I want to go back to Cuba. This freedom is nothing how I
pictured it. My dress! My dress is getting all wrinkled like
this."

Juan Raúl Pérez peeled the black dress from her pros-
trate body and hung it wet with sweat and tears on a hanger
by the window. He sat on the chair and watched her crum-
bling before him. Her body shook with the paleness of
death beneath the black lace slip. The paleness filled the
room.

"His face was so beautiful. So perfect. I had expected freedom to be so perfect. They should not have closed his coffin.
They shouldn't have shut him up like that."

"Señora. It wasn't a wake, it was a funeral. They always
close the coffin for a funeral."

"Well, they shouldn't have closed his."

He got up from the chair and paced between Papa lying
on the mattress at one end and Dottie at the other. He felt
like a shadow among shadows.

"These stupid pins are cutting into my head," Dottie
wailed. She tossed and turned on the bed. "I wonder if they
are burning him now. I feel like they are setting him on fire
now. They shouldn't burn anything so young and so sweet,
señor."

He fumbled through her fallen crown and searched for
bobby pins.

"I want to go home now. I know he stole our money, señor, but I hope he isn't burning in hell."

"You are screaming, señora. Please don't upset yourself so." He felt her falling in pieces in his hands. She had been so solid before. As solid as the concrete of his prison cell, and now she was falling through his hands in so many pale shadows.

"Ouch, you're hurting me. Why didn't I ever have a son, señor? Why didn't I ever have a child? I've been barren all my life. I'm lucky, maybe. If I had had a child he'd be burning right now. I feel very hot, señor. I feel like he's burning."

But Juan Raúl Pérez saw no fires. Where there had been bright dreams and flowers he saw only her black slip against the white sheets and her black hair medusa'd out from her agony.

"I don't want him to go to hell, señor."

He turned the fans on full-blast, their faces turning hurriedly from side to side. He went out to the bathroom and ran cold water on a towel. He dripped the wet towel back to the room and soothed the coolness over her pale body until the towel hissed with the flames of her grief. Back and forth he ran from bed to bathroom, each time taking the flames and extinguishing them under the cold tap water. Angel would have told Carmela by now, he'd remember, seeing his own face in the mirror above the sink. Don't be sad, my Love, I understand why you wouldn't want me now, though nothing is the way it seems, he told Carmela through the mirror. Nothing is the way it seems, not even this face of a beggar. He watched her tears fall down his face. He wrung the towel under the tap and hesitated in the doorway. His dream of twenty years was disintegrating in the bathroom mirror, and his immediate reality was coming apart in the bed. He returned to extinguish Dottie's burning.

"Stop doing that! You're getting me wet, señor."

He threw the towel on the floor and sat on the edge of the bed.

"I want to go home, señor. I am tired of being among strangers. Even you, señor. Even Felipe. I'm tired of being

around dead strangers too. I want to go home."
He lay beside her as she cried. And then he lay on top of her to stop her great shaking paleness and soothe the tears from her face. Where she had been so solid shook so loosely beneath him.

"Please, señora, please, you must stop talking like this."

"I want to go home. I want to go home. I want to have a dream again and I don't want this to be it! Your wife isn't the only one who shouldn't have married you. I shouldn't have either."

"Please, my Love, please don't leave me."

He tried to make himself stronger. He tried to make himself heavier on her. To condense her pale shaking dream back into a solid mass. To gather the pale shadows from the room back into her being. To make her great Cuban-madonna hips violent and samba again. To make her dance again on the open waters of passage.

"I hope they are not burning Felipe with his eyes open. Close his eyes!" she screamed.

Yes, there were eyes open. Juan Raúl Pérez saw Papa staring at their heaving bodies. The old man was standing by the door with a gun in his hands like a soldier on guard. Juan Raúl Pérez looked into the ancient eyes and the eyes were without judgment. And as Juan Raúl Pérez looked down he saw that there was no gun in the old man's hands.

"You need to wait outside," he told the old man. Papa went quickly, a soldier receiving his commands.

"His eyes!" Dottie cried, feeling Juan Raúl Pérez gathering strength inside her.

"His eyes are closed, my Love. He is beyond understanding. Only think of staying. Please don't leave me, my Love."

She slept afterwards, uneasily; waking and weeping, sleeping and waking. Then she said she felt cooler. Felt like Felipe's ashes were being thrown into the sea. Felt like he was making his way home.

Slowly. Floating.

CHAPTER 59

As Flavia's plan wove itself into a pretty bubble above her head, her steps became light and her car breezed over to her final destination. She filled in the ellipses of her mind with the lyrics of her songs. She had never stopped believing in the lyrics she sang. It was one of the reasons her audience loved her. It was one of the reasons she'd never make it outside a nightclub. Every word she sang, she believed.

After all, she told herself, she had only promised Angel not to say a word of this to anyone. That didn't prevent her from arranging an accidental meeting between Carmela and her husband before Angel contacted the lawyer and told his sister. Carmela would recognize Juan Raúl Pérez now because Flavia would announce it from the stage. They had already waited too long. Flavia knew she could have never waited like that. She was having a hard enough time for the past four months waiting for Angel to return to normal, when he had been a smiling man who cared about his family and loved her. And now that things hadn't worked out the way Angel had envisioned, she didn't know how long his bitterness would last or where it would lead. No, everyone had already waited too long. She would have preferred the accidental meeting to take place at the club, but there was always the possibility of Angel showing up there.

He wouldn't come to the festival where she was singing tomorrow. He was always uncomfortable watching her sing outside the club, which wasn't often. He never liked to see her perform in places he wasn't familiar with. He preferred being her boyfriend at the club, where the valet took special care with his car and the bartender knew his name and his drink and the owner clapped him on the shoulder and sat down with him to smoke a cigar.

"It's now or never," she sang in the silence of her silver Camaro as she drove to the church. She could almost hear the band behind her playing softly as she spoke:

"And now, ladies and gentleman, we have a very special treat for you this afternoon, and I want you to clear a space on the dance floor for two very special people, a husband and a wife . . . It's now or never, our love won't wait, tomorrow may never come . . . a man and his wife who haven't seen each other in twenty years, and we, right now, are going to unite them here . . . so darling, take me in your arms, it's now or never . . . let's have a big hand for them, she's been waiting a long time for him. He was a political prisoner in Cuba for twenty years, please step out here together . . . Tomorrow will never come, it's now or never . . . Mr. and Mrs. Juan Pérez. This song is dedicated to you . . . our love won't wait!"

She could see them rushing into each other's arms. A tear rolled down Flavia's cheek. It was going to be wonderful! She'd keep going over her speech until she had perfected the timing.

It had only taken a phone call to Angel, guarding the house at Carmela's, to volunteer to give him a break by taking Teresa and Carmela to the festival tomorrow. Teresa and Carmela had both sounded anxious to get out of the house. Flavia needed their support, she told them. She promised them a pleasant afternoon in sunshine with good music and the rest of the world. They wouldn't be alone, sorry to say; Angel had had a private investigator secretly trailing Carmela since his brother-in-law had paid him a visit, so his sister wouldn't get hurt, as he put it. So far Carmela hadn't left the house.

Next she called to complete the second stage of her plan. She spoke to Roberto, her manager and lead guitarist for the last four years. Roberto said no, they couldn't add "It's Now or Never" to the song list tomorrow. The Varadero Festival was a Cuban festival and they already had two tunes in English. She also never quite reached the climatic high note in their disco arrangement of "Now or Never." He told her his reasons. She revealed her plan and he changed his mind.

"It's cute, Flavia, I like it. The crowd is going to go wild." They subbed it for "I Got Rhythm."

The only thing left for her to think about was how to get Juan Raúl Pérez over to the festival. She wished Angel hadn't hit him earlier. She decided she'd confront Dottie and Juan directly. If he still loved Carmela as he said he did, and if the other woman didn't care if he left or not, Flavia didn't see why there would be any problem. Too bad she couldn't make the whole thing a surprise, though. She had thrown a surprise party for Angel last year on his birthday, and it had been a grand success.

It was late when she reached the church. Walking through the empty church hall in the darkness was the first time since her plan's inception that she felt a flicker of anxiety. She was alert to the possibility of sticks flying through the air.

"This is silly," she whispered aloud to herself. "That stupid old man was only trying to help Juan because Angel hit him. He was protecting him. And it was only a little stick, not a machine gun or something."

She heard no movement from the other side of the door the clerk at the rectory had earlier specified. She tapped gently on the door.

"Psst. Psst. Señor? Señora?" she called and knocked a little louder. She knocked again and with no answer turned to go over to the rectory to see if she had the right place.

Dottie answered the door before Flavia had gone ten feet. Dottie was groggy with sleep. Her hair was disheveled and the strap from her slip fell from her shoulder.

"Oh, it's you," Dottie said. "Is your boyfriend with you?"

"My fiancé. No, I came by myself."

"Señor Pérez is sleeping now, and so was I. Why don't you come back some other time."

"No. It's you I came to talk to. Really. Please, couldn't we talk for a minute somewhere where we won't wake him."

"I'm not dressed, Señorita."

"Flavia. My name is Flavia. What's yours?"

Dottie paused. "Dorita," she said. "My name is Dorita."

"Maybe you could just throw something on and we could walk outside. Is the old man around, Dorita?"

"He is sleeping too."

"I really was hoping to talk with you."

Dottie came back out with a white bedsheet thrown over her shoulders and brought Flavia to the bingo kitchen. She flipped on the lights.

"What do you want, señorita?"

"I came to apologize for Angel's behavior this afternoon."

"Fine, señorita. But you ought to tell the señor that. I hope you told his wife what I asked you to—that she can have him back anytime. I told you the truth this afternoon."

"I know that. Please sit down." Dottie remained standing. "I really do believe you," Flavia said. "Angel doesn't. He thinks you're some kind of home-wrecker who stole his sister's husband from him. His words weren't exactly that."

"You mean he thinks I'm a whore who's got him trapped between my legs."

"Something like that."

"Well, I'm not a whore, señorita, and I've never . . ." Dottie stopped before she said she had never slept with him. She had just come from sleeping in his arms, and she had opened her legs to him that afternoon.

"You don't have to tell me anything, I believe you."

"You're right, I don't have to tell you anything. But listen anyway, señorita. I am free here—well, almost—and since I'm here I don't have to fuck anyone for anything but love. And I am not in love with Señor Pérez. He has been a kind man to me. We have been through some bad times together. But I didn't know him before I got on the boat. I've known all along he had a wife and daughter. I thought they'd be on the dock waiting for him. I guess he didn't have a chance to call them from prison and let them know he was coming. I don't have any relatives here and I didn't know what to expect. He did, and I thought it would be good to know someone who had relatives here. But he was afraid to contact her. And I'm sure it wasn't easy for him when he did work up the courage to see her or his brother-in-law and have them not recognize him, although I didn't know about that till this afternoon. Twenty years is a long time. He was afraid she had remarried or moved or had another lover."

"I understand that."

"No, you don't. Neither do I. The only way I could wait for somebody for twenty years would be if I was in prison. But I dreamed of coming here for twenty years and I got shit the second I stepped off the boat."

"But he knows now that she waited for him. Why is he afraid now?"

"I don't know, señorita. Your boyfriend didn't recognize him and his wife thought he was a beggar. People have their pride. But I do think he loves her. He's got these papers he writes her letters on and then never sends them."

"Maybe he loves you."

"Maybe he does. But he told me all along that he was going back to her. He told me again yesterday. I am free now, señorita. I don't have to love someone because he loves me. And he's not the kind of man I've ever dreamed of. I want a man free to love me back. I want a man who's free like the United States is free. Señor Pérez is still a prisoner. A few days on the outside world doesn't make a man not a prisoner after he's been one for twenty years. And you can tell your fiancé that I've never had to get a man by stealing him from anyone."

"He must be a burden to you. He seems a bit depressed."

Dottie finally sat down at the table across from Flavia. She was impressed by the truthfulness in Flavia's voice. And Flavia was sincere; she believed every lyric she sang.

"He is sad all the time, señorita. And he has terrible nightmares. Do you know, I think I'm catching his sadness. I came here with all these dreams and now I'm locked in a storeroom with him and I'm sad now too."

"Why haven't you left him?"

"Why hasn't he left me?"

"His wife has waited twenty years, Dorita."

"Take him then. I told you that."

"It's not that easy. Especially with Angel around. I was thinking of arranging an accidental meeting between them, and I was hoping you'd help me."

"You want me to help you?"

"Yes. If you really want to give him a chance. And if you really don't love him."

"Just tell me what it is, señorita."

"I'll be singing at a festival tomorrow. I'll announce his name and his wife's name and they'll meet. I'll give you the address and directions and money for a taxi."

"Why don't you ask him?"

Because she wanted it to be a surprise, but she said, "Because as you said, he's got his pride."

Dottie gathered the sheet over her shoulders. The only thing she wanted to do was go home, but she didn't know where that was.

"What will become of me?"

"I'll give you money for the taxi to get home too."

"That is not what I meant."

"I'm sorry, I don't know. I guess you'll be free then. I don't think you're the kind of person who will find it difficult to be free."

"I keep the old man?"

"Sure, that's up to you."

"I don't know about the old man. I've gotten used to having family around, but he's not very good company. If there's any problem with me taking care of him, someone will have to take him."

"I'm sure something can be arranged. Tent City is open now. Listen, I'll be singing 'It's Now or Never' when I announce Mr. and Mrs. Juan Pérez. Do you know that song? It's in English."

"Yes. It's by Elvis Presley. Do you know the song 'Hound Dog'?"

"Not really. I'll call his name."

"I'll make sure he's there, señorita. He'll have to hear his own name."

In the dead of the night, Juan Raúl Pérez woke alone in the bed. He got up like a man still in a dream and found Dottie sitting in a chair in front of a fan. "Please come and lie down," he said and brought her to the bed. "Please don't leave me," he said and pulled the sheet to her shoulders. Please stay where I can find you in this strange land.

CHAPTER 60

Dottie started casting him away from her-
self as soon as she got out of bed. The difficult part had been
getting out of the bed. The sun poured gently through the
high side windows. The sound of early Sunday danced
lightly through her waking. On the street outside, people
were coming and going to mass. They greeted each other in
familiar ritual. Then from a distance came a quick slam of a
car door and the voice of a child calling to a friend. She
stretched out her legs beneath the sheet and tried to un-
tangle her arm from under Juan Raúl Pérez's head. She had
a momentary vision of him as an infant, bald, toothless,
and content to dream. She repossessed her numb arm and
saw the light catch the stubble on his chin. Wrinkles crev-
iced his face. But even with the realization that he was an
old man, older than his years, it was still hard to turn from
him. He smelled like the well-worn dreams of men she was
used to, eternally weary, yet always anxious for another
dance. She was at home in that instant, in a land filled with
promise with one of her own tribe by her side. But this was
not the right man; he didn't belong to her. Dottie had stolen
kisses before, had even stolen hearts, but that was before
she was free, when she needed to steal to survive. She
propped her legs on the floor and headed for the bathroom.
She showered and combed her hair from the tangle of yes-

terday's grief before she awakened him. She couldn't imagine how to distance herself gently. Even without tears, there was always the brute hand of destiny. It would be better, she thought, combing her hair, if he left glad to be rid of her.

"Get up!" she told him before his eyes were open. He awoke with the quick glance of the very young and very old wondering what part of the universe they had landed in this morning.

"Get up and get moving. I want to get out of here for a while. I'm tired of sitting around."

Her scolding tone reminded him which part of the universe he was in. He breathed her in lovingly. He did not have the strength that morning to worry about anything more distant than Dottie. He did not know that he would never have that strength. He had been beaten too many times. He was lucky to have escaped with his pulse. For the moment his heart gladdened to see Dottie standing there barking orders as she fought with her hair. She was solid again, contained and steady on her bare chubby feet. The white slippery ghosts of yesterday had slipped back into her layer by layer until she stood there by his bed frowning with impatience. And like any sweet and desperate lover, he attributed her solid standing to his love. His seed had healed her. His desire had made her whole again.

"Move!" she said. "Papa's gone. Find him, please, so we can go out."

He didn't move from the bed, but not from defiance. He would do whatever she asked of him, but he wanted her back in the bed again with him. "Señora, a minute?" he asked and held out his hand.

"I don't have time for lazy men. We should all get out in the open air."

Papa hadn't gone far. When Juan Raúl Pérez opened the door he was standing stiffly on the other side of it.

"Come in, Papa, you don't have to guard us."

"He'll need to be showered before we go out," Dottie said.

"Do you notice, he doesn't seem to go so far anymore?" he

said to Dottie. "Yesterday he was standing by the door too but on the inside. I got the impression he was guarding the door."

"I don't want to talk about yesterday. You can wear your suit from the funeral. I don't care how long mourning lasts, we're going to a festival on the beach. A friend gave me the name and address. I have it written down. Here it is, the Varadero Festival on Crandon Beach."

"But Varadero is a beach in Havana. I used to go there before the revolution."

"Don't get nervous. We're not going to Cuba. That's just the name."

After breakfast while Juan Raúl Pérez showered Papa, she sat on the bed wondering what she'd tell Father Martínez and the others when she returned without her husband. Maybe just tell them that he got a job somewhere out of town and that he'd be back sometime. "Got a letter from my husband today," she'd tell strangers. "He's fine." The old man would probably just wander off without Juan Raúl Pérez to go after him every few minutes. She'd be by herself then. Perhaps then she would have the time to find a better John Wayne than the security guard. Her family as she had created it was dissolving before her eyes. It didn't help that Juan Raúl Pérez was being so nice to her. Telling her he was glad she was feeling better while they sat eating toast in the bingo kitchen. Telling her, "It will get better each day. We will learn to get used to where we are."

She wanted to tell him to stop being so hopeful all of a sudden, to stop planning their lives together when she would be giving him away in a few hours or at least returning him to where he belonged.

She went to the rectory to call a taxi. Juan Raúl Pérez was sitting on the steps of the church hall drying Papa when she returned.

He opened the car door for her and Papa when the lime-green taxi pulled up. She sat staring straight ahead as tears rolled down her face.

He wanted to kiss away her tears. "You'll feel better once

you dance," he told her. "Everything is going to get better."

An hour in traffic didn't break her distance. He could only sit back and admire her self-containment. He would do whatever he had to do to keep her rooted like that with a fierce line of determination set in her jaw. He had no way of knowing it was his fate being determined in that set jaw.

He opened the car door for her and led her through the colors and the crowds. When he had first landed on this shore, he would have sunk beneath such a throng of shouting moving bodies. But today, he had Dottie by his side and felt stronger. The smell of ocean surrounded him. He took a deep breath and let the music drown the beat of his pulse.

"Papa is gone," she said.

"Don't worry about him for a few minutes. He will find us when he wants.

"Do you want to dance?" he asked after they made their way over to the center stage where the percussion screamed of Cuba and the horns heralded the afternoon.

"No," she said, "I don't feel like it now."

He didn't have to ask her again. He was already being pressed against her by the waves of dancing bodies. He had only to move his arms around her and press her madonna hips to his own. It was always Sunday in the dream. Always Sunday afternoon.

"Just this time," she said, "till the music stops." But the music didn't stop and she lost herself to the song and the sunlight and the crowd.

CHAPTER 61

Carmela was happy enough to be leaving the prison of her house and getting out from under Angel's warden eyes. He had brooded all night through long silences by her side, leaving her only to peer through the curtains at the least little noise. He kept telling her she should move to Fort Lauderdale.

"I just want to make sure that scum Marielito isn't going to come back here."

"Who are you talking about?"

"That scum burglar."

"Angel," she had said for the fortieth time, "I'm sorry we gave you that impression. He wasn't scum, just some poor old lost soul who didn't seem to know where he was going."

"Didn't know where he was going, my ass! You are too trusting. He was scum." He was peering through the living-room curtains again. "Turn the light off in here so I can see outside better."

"Angel, I really appreciate your being here, but we've got the alarm system and—"

"And the gun," he interrupted. "You still have the gun, right? Nobody's thrown this one away yet?"

"Yes, I've got the gun. Please sit down. You're making me nervous."

"Where is the gun?"

"It's in my white shoulder bag on the table in the hall. If you want to look, go ahead."

"I believe you. Don't get so jumpy. I'm just saying it's not going to do you much good where you can't reach it. It should be in here in the living room with you. You have to learn to be on guard, to protect yourself and Teresa. I can't come here every night!"

Carmela and Teresa went to mass at St. Michael's on Sunday morning, but Carmela couldn't focus in on the peace she found on other Sunday mornings. When they returned to the house, Angel was still standing by the living-room window waiting for a Mariel invasion to land at their doorstep.

"Take your gun," he reminded her when they walked out of the house an hour later. She patted the white shoulder bag she wore and waved goodbye.

Yes, she was glad to be getting away from the fortress that had once been her house. She was glad to go anywhere away from Angel. But as she sat in the passenger seat of the car seeing nothing but Teresa's clenched hands on the wheel as the traffic over the bridge thickened, she wished she weren't going to a festival at Crandon Beach. Traffic always made her nervous. The line of cars came to a standstill. Teresa turned off the car and they opened the windows. The heat poured into the car like an amorphous being. Carmela wished she were headed in the opposite direction to her job at Bal Harbour at the perfume counter where the sculpted glass bottles offered cool sanctuary and the rules of department store organization offered a calm orderly existence. She had friends there, people she liked and who liked her.

"I shouldn't have taken off work today," she said suddenly to Teresa.

"You didn't, Mama. You have off every other weekend. This is your regular day off." Teresa enunciated her words carefully.

"Oh," Carmela said. "I know. I just forgot for a minute. I'm really OK, Teresa. I'm going back to work tomorrow."

"Great. I know you said you were feeling better, but you still have plenty of sick time left if you need it. Just sit back and relax."

"I am relaxed," she lied.

The cars beeped behind them. Teresa started the car back up to a slow crawl. Carmela felt surrounded by everyone else's expectations of her. They made their way slowly and finally circled a distant parking lot twice before Teresa made her own space on a green strip of divider.

"I hope they don't tow the car away, Teresa. I don't think we're allowed to park here. I didn't think it would be this crowded. Maybe I should wait here in the car and you go."

"Mother, please relax! I don't see any no-parking signs here. It's a beautiful day and we are here to have a good time and to support Flavia."

The crowd by the main gate was so thick that Carmela had to hold on to the back of her daughter's shirttail to keep from being separated as Teresa wound her way toward the front. At times they looked like a two-person conga line; at other times they were packed so thickly in the crowd that Carmela felt that if she lifted her feet she would be carried along by the wave of strangers pressing in at her on all sides. The music hurt her ears. The pressing anonymity frightened her. She called Teresa's name to beg to be taken away from here, but her voice was lost. Towards the main stage, the crowd was less thick where those dancing had elbowed little circles of space around their twirling bodies.

"Teresa! Teresa!" she shouted, pulling on the back of her daughter's shirt. She was surprised by her daughter's face as she turned around to answer her. Teresa was smiling. Teresa was laughing and clapping her hands out in front of her. The little shuffling steps which Carmela had mistaken as the only way to move in the crowd were dance steps. Teresa threw her hands into the air and spun.

"Isn't this wonderful, Mama? It's so good to get out. Have

you ever seen such a beautiful crowd? And the music!"

"Teresa, when do you think Flavia is going to come on? Do you think there's a place I could sit down and meet you later when Flavia comes on?"

"Mama, please! Mama, have a good time. When are you going to give him up?"

"I have given him up," Carmela shouted with a jolt of realization. "I like my life the way it is." But her words were lost under a blast of trumpets issued from the stage.

"What?" Teresa shouted back. "This is great. Can you hear?"

Carmela couldn't hear anything so loud. She wanted to go home and tear the bars off her windows and kick her brother out the door. Her first thought when she saw him dancing with the large woman in the blue polka-dot dress was, I know that man. For a few moments she watched him pressed against the woman's hips. He kissed the woman's neck. And then in a quick panic she thought, Of course I know him! It was the man in the parrot shirt, except now he was wearing a suit.

"Did you see him?" Carmela shouted at Teresa. "Maybe it's a coincidence."

"I can hardly hear you. What are you talking about?" Teresa shouted back, still watching the stage and clapping her hands. "Are you having a good time?"

Juan Raúl Pérez removed his head from where he had wedged it kissing Dottie's neck. He caught Carmela's eye and held it as if it wasn't an accident that he was there. Still holding Dottie's hand, he moved towards her too quickly, too deliberately.

Dear God, Angel was right, Carmela screamed in her head, I need to protect myself and my daughter. She pulled the pearl-handled gun from her shoulder bag with all the cheap confidence an expensive gun gives. She took her stance against the moving target of the intruder.

CHAPTER 62

The man Carmela kept her gun pointed at remained a stranger until he moved quite close to her. Close enough that she could hear him and recognize his voice somewhere beneath the salsa frenzy.

"Papa," he yelled, "don't fire!"

She turned to see the old man in camouflage with a pistol aimed at her heart. She heard two shots. She lowered her gun.

But the shots that she heard weren't from her gun. The PI had shot Papa twice in the chest. Esteban Santiesteban knocked the gun from Carmela's lowered hand and started running. Life was too short with Dottie's family.

"What happened?" someone yelled only a few feet away.

"Fireworks," another called.

"No, it was the music," someone else shouted.

The music never stopped. And two hours later when Flavia called for Mr. and Mrs. Juan Pérez to be reunited on the dance floor after twenty years of separation, two people she had never seen before ran into each other's arms. The crowd went wild.

CHAPTER 63

Do you want to talk with him now?" Pirelli asked Carmela at police headquarters.

"Do I have to?"

"No, you don't. Your daughter has already spoken with him, at her request. She and Angel are waiting for you in Inspector Kemble's office, and you can go home right now if you want. There are no charges against you except for carrying a concealed weapon without a permit. And I think I may be able to get that dropped."

"And you're sure I didn't shoot that old man? I never wanted to shoot anyone. I never even wanted a gun."

"You didn't shoot him. He is dead but you didn't kill him."

"I know you keep telling me that, but when I heard those shots . . ."

"I know. But the shots didn't come from your gun, and you didn't shoot him."

"But I don't understand why he would have shot me."

"We can only go on supposition and what they have told us about him. They didn't know him before two weeks ago, and he was very protective of your husband. For all we'll ever know he could have been one of the ones Castro sent over from prison or an insane asylum, or he could simply have been an old soldier with a new loyalty."

They were sitting in the office Pirelli had been using as his base in Miami. The inspector whose office it was was on leave of absence. "You don't have to talk with him now."

"He was a good husband to me. I want you to know that." Yes, he had been a good husband for six years of her life many many years ago. But she didn't want him back. And not just because he was a stranger who was kissing another woman and had a friend he called Papa who was about to shoot her. In the six years she had been with him, she had never seen the kind of passion in his eyes that he had for the woman she saw him kiss. He had always been reserved, a little formal. He worried all the time. It would take her a long time to forget him dancing with another woman after she had waited alone for twenty years.

But she didn't want him back because he was an intruder from another time and another place. She hadn't just been waiting all this time, she had been working to build a life, and she had done a good job. She liked her life the way it was.

"Yes. I will speak with him now." She hoped he wouldn't ask her to take him back, because she would. He had been a good husband and he had been in jail for twenty years.

"I'll have to stay in the room with you, you understand that. It's a regulation—if anything happened and you were left without an officer or a guard. I don't speak Spanish, so your conversation will be private, but I can get someone else if you prefer."

"No, let's just do it. When will he come?"

There was mascara smeared below her eyes and her face had the events of the day stamped across it.

Pirelli called on the intercom, and they waited in silence. He moved an empty chair by hers. He turned to look out the window and didn't move from there when Juan Raúl Pérez was ushered into the room.

Juan Raúl Pérez turned the chair to face her and reached for her hand. She let it stay there. He was smiling. His sad eyes were eager.

"Why didn't you shoot me, my Love?" he asked.

"What?"

"I could have died peacefully in your arms and been happy for it."

"I don't want anyone dying in my arms. Besides, I didn't know it was you."

"I guess we are strangers. Do you know, I imagined you as a matronly old woman who could barely get along." He put his hand to her face. "You are very beautiful. I have loved you for many years."

"I loved you for many years also," she said.

"Do you know I will do anything you ask?"

She closed her eyes. He felt her features gently with his hand. The eyes. The cheekbones that disappeared when she smiled. The mouth that he had loved. She put her hand on his. The fingers he had counted.

"Do you know that I won't ask," she said.

"That's why I wish that you had shot me."

"Endings are never that simple, my Love."

"I'll come the moment you need, even to rise from my grave."

She smiled sadly. How many times can a man rise from the grave?

He took his hand from her face and walked from the room.

CHAPTER 64

San Lázaro was tired. His crippled legs ached from dancing and his arms ached from his crutches. It was after eight in the evening when he turned back up on Coral Way in his Plexiglas trailer behind the '64 Impala with the dogs barking at his feet. If his load hadn't been so heavy that day and his body so tired he would have looked up to see the sunset. Ribbons of rose and violet wove their way through the blue. Soft clouds gently combed the sudden strands of sunlight.

But loads were always heavy after a festival, and this Sunday was no exception. Aside from all the prayers and the pennies, there were fourteen gold coins in his Plexiglas trailer stamped with the portrait of José Martí above the words "Patria Libertad," and they weighed heavily on his mind. He knew he should not have taken them from the old woman dressed in white dancing with her nephew. They were not the small change the old woman thought they were and would net close to four thousand dollars, he estimated—offerings fit for a pope and not a simple man like himself. But he felt he deserved them; he had been working hard to sort out so many Pérezes and there was still so much to do. It would take him almost a year to finally get Carmela to believe Pirelli loved her. They'd be a good match, he decided—Pirelli spent so much time on the road, and Carmela knew how to wait for a man. Mortals were so foolish about how they wanted their lives arranged, he thought. John Wayne is dead, Dottie. And he could have never kissed away your tears like Juan Raúl Pérez.